BREATHLESS

Center Point
Large Print

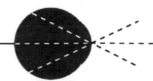

**This Large Print Book carries the
Seal of Approval of N.A.V.H.**

BREATHLESS

Beverly Jenkins

CENTER POINT LARGE PRINT
THORNDIKE, MAINE

This Center Point Large Print edition
is published in the year 2017 by arrangement with
Avon Books, an imprint of HarperCollins Publishers.

The text of this Large Print edition is unabridged.
In other aspects, this book may vary
from the original edition.
Printed in the United States of America
on permanent paper.
Set in 16-point Times New Roman type.

ISBN: 978-1-68324-430-1

Library of Congress Cataloging-in-Publication Data

Names: Jenkins, Beverly, 1951– author.
Title: Breathless / Beverly Jenkins.
Description: Center Point Large Print edition. | Thorndike, Maine : Center Point Large Print, 2017.
Identifiers: LCCN 2017013864 | ISBN 9781683244301
    (hardcover : alk. paper)
Subjects: LCSH: African Americans—Fiction. | Large type books.
Classification: LCC PS3560.E4795 B74 2017 | DDC 813/.54—dc23
LC record available at https://lccn.loc.gov/2017013864

BREATHLESS

PROLOGUE

Virginia City, Nevada
Autumn 1870

"Portia! Wake up!"

Twelve-year-old Portia Carmichael slowly awakened to her Aunt Eddy roughly shaking her shoulder. "I need you to get dressed! Quickly!"

Portia sat up and through groggy eyes saw that it was still dark. Aunt Eddy was now waking Portia's ten-year-old sister, Regan.

"Come on, girls! We have to leave the house!"

Portia heard what sounded like shouting off in the distance outside. "What's happening?"

"I'll explain later. Put your shoes on!"

There was a fear in her aunt's voice she'd never heard before and that alone made Portia throw off her nightgown and pull on the shirt and denims she'd left on the chair before going to bed.

Uncle Rhine rushed in. The moonlight streaming in through the windows showed the tense set of his ivory face and the rifle in his hand. "They're almost here!"

The shouting sounded closer, echoing like rumbling thunder.

Eddy was still helping the half-asleep Regan into her clothes. Once that was accomplished,

Eddy took Portia and Regan by the hand. "We have to run!"

They flew down the stairs behind Uncle Rhine and out into the night. A wagon with two horses waited. Jim Dade, Uncle Rhine's business partner, held the reins. Mounted on horseback beside it was Kent Randolph, Uncle Rhine's eighteen-year-old bartender.

"Eddy, you and the girls get in and lie down!" Rhine ordered. "Kent, get to a safe place!"

Kent rode away, and Portia and Regan scrambled into the bed of the wagon. Aunt Eddy followed and gathered them tightly to her side. Rhine tossed a tarp over them. Portia felt the wagon dip as he took the seat beside his friend. "Go, Jim!"

The wagon took flight and because she wanted to know what this all meant, Portia rose up and looked back. A crowd of men carrying torches surrounded the house. Windows were broken and the interior began glowing.

A male voice yelled. "They're getting away!"

Bullets hit the wagon and Eddy snatched Portia down. Only when the horses had put ample distance between themselves and the scene did Eddy raise the tarp. Portia and Regan watched the scene with wide eyes. Their home was fully engulfed. Flames shot out of the roof. Stunned, Portia asked, "Why did they do this?"

It took Eddy so long to answer, Portia didn't

think she would respond. "They're angry because Uncle Rhine pretended to be White."

Icy fear grabbed her. "Will they follow us? Will they lynch Uncle Rhine?" Portia read the newspapers. Men of the race were being lynched daily.

"We're far enough away that I don't think they'll follow us."

"Are we ever going to go back?" Regan asked.

Eddy replied grimly, "No, we're going forward."

Portia wanted to ask if she was sure the mob wouldn't come after them, and where the wagon was going, but her aunt said, "Lie down. Try to sleep. We've a long journey ahead."

Still afraid, Portia settled in next to her little sister and tried to be as brave as she knew Aunt Eddy needed them to be, but every time she closed her eyes, she saw the house afire, heard the roar of the angry mob, and thought about Uncle Rhine hanging from the end of a rope.

CHAPTER ONE

Santa Catalina Mountains,
Arizona Territory
Spring 1885

"I wonder how it feels to be that much in love."

In response to the question, Portia Carmichael glanced up from the ledger she was working on to look over at her sister, Regan, standing at the window. "I've no idea," she replied as she refocused on the column of numbers she was adding. Regan was gazing cow-eyed out at what Portia assumed were their aunt Eddy and uncle Rhine Fontaine. The sisters were in the business office of the Fontaine Hotel and although the twenty-five-year-old Regan longed for love and children, Portia, two years older, wanted neither. Being the manager of the family's successful hotel was more than enough to make Portia's life complete.

"To have someone look at you that way and know you are their entire world—oh my."

"Please don't swoon, or at least do it elsewhere," Portia teased. She didn't have to look up to know Regan responded with a shake of her head that held equal parts amusement and pity.

"Numbers won't keep you warm at night, sister mine."

"That's what quilts are for."

"One of these days, Cupid's going to hit you with an arrow right between the eyes. I just hope I'm around to see it."

Smiling, Portia ignored the prediction only to hear Regan gush, "Oh my, they're sharing a kiss."

Portia sighed audibly. "Why don't you step away from the window and let them have their privacy."

"They're having a picnic by the gazebo. If they wanted privacy they'd be in their suite behind closed doors."

She supposed Regan was right. The couple's love was legendary and they didn't keep their mutual affection a secret. At any moment of the day one could round a corner and find them stealing a kiss, holding hands as if still courting, or drowning in each other's eyes. Not that Portia found their affection unseemly; she was glad they were in love and that it extended to their nieces.

Regan vowed, "When I find someone to marry I want that type of love."

Their mother, Corinne, had been in love, and when her intended demanded she cast her daughters aside because they weren't his progeny, Corinne put the then twelve-year-old Portia and ten-year-old Regan on a train to their aunt Eddy in Virginia City and never looked back. In the fifteen years since, they'd not heard a word.

Portia wanted no part of something that could cause such irreparable harm. She planned to remain unmarried and immerse herself in work. Work didn't break hearts.

"Don't you want to marry, Portia?"

"Not particularly, but if I do, he'll have to be an exceptional fellow who loves me for my intelligence and business acumen, not for how I perform on my knees. I'm not Mama."

Regan turned from the window, her voice thoughtful. "Do you ever wonder where she is?"

"Sometimes." Portia would never admit how much her heart still ached from being abandoned so callously or how often she thought about her.

"Do you think she wonders about us?"

"I don't know."

Corinne had been a whore, and the hardship of their life with her still held a pain they rarely discussed. Thanks to Aunt Eddy and Uncle Rhine they'd survived though and were still together.

Regan's attention returned to the scene outside the window. "I would love to be as happy as they are."

"I added this column wrong," Portia muttered, and began searching for her mistake. She blamed the error on being distracted by her sister's chatter.

"Thoughts of being in love can do that."

"No, your going on and on about love can do that," she replied, humor in her voice.

"Don't you want a man you can sneak off into a corner with and who will kiss you so passionately you don't care if the whole territory is watching?"

Portia shook her head with amusement. Regan changed beaus as frequently as some women changed their gloves but never stayed with any of them very long. "You're so shameless."

"I know, but somewhere there's a man who'll appreciate that part of me. I have no intentions of relying on quilts to keep me warm at night and neither should you, sister."

"Don't you have mail to deliver or something?" In addition to his vast business holdings, their uncle Rhine owned the government mail contract, and the unconventional Regan had talked him into letting her take charge of delivery. Twice a week she and her mule, Josephine, drove the five miles to Tucson to see to its distribution. As far as Portia knew there'd been no complaints about Regan's race or gender; folks just wanted their mail.

"Not until the day after tomorrow, which you'd remember if you weren't so focused on your duties."

"I take my position very seriously."

"I know."

The tone made Portia look up.

Regan said sincerely, "I don't claim to know a lot about life but there has to be more to it than work. When was the last time you spent the day sitting in the meadow listening to bird songs or riding out to the canyon to take in the waterfalls?"

"I don't have time for that, Regan. A lot goes into keeping this hotel running. There's staff to manage and menus to approve, guests to oversee . . ."

"Which is why you have a staff. This place won't fall to pieces if you left your desk every now and again."

"You sound like Aunt Eddy."

"Good. She loves you, too, and we worry about you."

"No need. I'm fine."

Regan showed her exasperation and moved away from the window. "Am I to assume you don't need my help for the anniversary dinner this evening?"

"You're correct. Everything is in order." They'd be celebrating their aunt and uncle's fifteen years of marriage in the hotel's main ballroom.

"Okay. Then I'm going over to Old Man Blanchard's. He has a package for me to take to his daughter in Tucson."

"Okay." Mr. Blanchard lived on a ranch a short distance west of the hotel. "Make sure he's coming tonight. Aunt Eddy will be disappointed if he chooses to stay home and play checkers with Farley and Buck." Farley and Buck were his ranch hands.

"Will do," Regan promised, and she left the office.

Sitting alone, Portia knew her sister's gentle chastisement about the long hours she put in at her desk came from her heart, but there were those who thought the Fontaines mad for placing their niece in charge of their hotel— thoughts that never would have risen had Portia been a *nephew*. She wanted to prove she was as capable of the job as any man and so kept her nose to the grindstone. They were now living in the Arizona Territory in a beautiful, temperate area at the base of the Catalina Mountains a few miles north and east of the town of Tucson. Rhine and Eddy built the hotel from the ground up in '73 upon a large open swath of land originally owned by a mine president. When the mine went dry, his funds did, too, and her uncle Rhine and aunt Eddy were able to buy it and the hundreds of acres of open range surrounding it from the bank for a pittance. Over the years, the Fontaine Hotel became famous for its fine food and luxurious accommodations. Lately it also served as a magnet for well-to-do Europeans and Easterners wanting a taste of the Wild West; a new phenomenon Uncle Rhine called Dude Ranch Fever. Ranchers from the Rockies to the Mexican border were opening their doors to wealthy guests who wanted to hunt, fish, and ride the open ranges to take in the meadows, lakes, and canyon waterfalls. Some came strictly to view the myriad species of birds while others wanted to tour old silver mines or pretend to pan for gold. The Fontaine Hotel, in partnership with Mr. Blanchard's ranch, also offered guests the opportunity to watch cattle being branded, take roping lessons, and in the evening gather around a roaring campfire to eat and listen to Buck and Farley tell exaggerated stories of ghost towns, deadly outlaws, and dangerous Indians. The guests could then ride back to the hotel for the night or remain at the Blanchard place to sleep in tents or on bedrolls under the stars. It was a lucrative trade for both establishments, so much so that it was necessary for guests to make reservations a year in advance if they wanted to be accommodated. Coordinating all the details took a clear head and a steady hand, and with so much to do, there was no time for Portia to take leisurely trips to view waterfalls.

A soft knock on the open door broke her reverie and she looked up to see her aunt Eddy standing on the threshold. Like her nieces, Eddy Carmichael Fontaine was a dark-skinned, dark-eyed beauty and she wore her forty-plus years well.

Portia asked, "So are you ready for your grand affair?"

"I suppose. You know how much I dislike all this fuss. I would've been content to celebrate with a nice quiet supper, maybe a few musicians and a cake, but your uncle loves fanfare."

"So you tolerate it."

"Barely, but only because I love him so much."

"Regan was spying on you two in the gazebo. Says she wants the kind of love you and Uncle Rhine share."

"That's not a bad goal. Although it took me a while to see it."

Portia knew that when Aunt Eddy and Uncle Rhine first met, he'd still been passing as a White man. Eddy hadn't wanted to fall in love with him because of the societal dangers tied to such unions. "But you did."

"Yes, and sometimes, like with this anniversary business, I have to remind myself of that because only for him would I endure the torture of being fitted for a new gown."

Portia never failed to be amused by her aunt's aversion to dressmakers. "You have armoires stuffed with gowns yet you always say that."

"Because it's the truth. All the pin sticks, measurements, and having to stand still." She waved a hand dismissively. "A woman should be able to go into a dress shop, find something to her liking and leave with it."

"You can." Ready-to-wear gowns were becoming quite popular.

"But they all seem to be made for someone taller and they're never the right color. It's as maddening as the fittings." She sighed with exasperation and asked, "Is everything ready for the dinner tonight?"

"Yes, so no harassing the staff about what's being done or not being done." Her aunt and uncle had run the hotel as a team since its founding, but now Portia mostly held the reins. Although Eddy refused to relinquish control of the hotel's kitchen, Portia had relieved her of all duties related to the preparation of the anniversary dinner. She'd initially balked of course, then reluctantly agreed.

"Is Janie still baking the cake? Does she have enough eggs, flour?"

"Aunt Eddy," Portia chided. "Everything is being taken care of."

"But I feel so useless."

"I understand, but you aren't allowed to do anything except get gussied up and enjoy the party."

Eddy didn't like it and it showed on her face. She finally sighed audibly in surrender. "Okay, I suppose."

Portia almost felt sorry for her. Almost. Her aunt was the hardest-working woman she'd ever met and one of the reasons for the hotel's great success. Not being able to direct this event was threatening to send her around the bend. "If you want to do something, you can go over to the Wilson place and check on your centerpieces."

"I get to pick the flowers? Oh, be still my heart."

Portia laughed. "Or I could send Regan."

"Lord, no. She'd stick a bunch of saguaro on a plate and call it done. I'll go."

"Good."

There was silence for a moment as they viewed each other, and then Eddy asked, "Have I told you how proud I am of all you've grown up to be?"

Emotion filled Portia's throat. "Numerous times."

"I'm glad Corinne sent you and Regan to me."

"As are we." Had she not, both Portia and Regan would've had their virginity sold for a pittance and grown to adulthood with little knowledge of the world beyond the walls of their mother's shack. They most certainly wouldn't have attended Oberlin to complete their education, nor would Portia have been given the opportunity to hone her bookkeeping skills at the San Francisco bank owned by Uncle Rhine's half-brother, Andrew. Portia was grateful every day for being given a home by Eddy and Rhine.

"I'll ride over and check on the flowers in a bit," her aunt said.

"Okay, and no worrying allowed."

With a roll of her eyes, Aunt Eddy departed.

By late afternoon, Portia was done with her ledgers. Realizing she'd missed lunch, she pushed her chair back from the desk and left the office for the kitchen. The hotel was spread out over five, white adobe, one-story buildings with red tiled roofs. One housed staff and the business offices. The others held guest rooms, the family quarters, dining spaces, and kitchens. All the buildings were connected by covered breezeways. As she stepped out into the sunshine to walk to the kitchen she was brought up short by the unexpected sight of a brown-skinned cowboy seated on the broad back of a beautiful blue roan stallion. She couldn't make out the man's features beneath the black felt hat, so shading her eyes against the bright sunlight, she asked, "May I help you?"

He pushed back the hat. "Is this the Fontaine place?"

"It is."

For a moment he didn't say anything else, simply stared down at her from his perch before fluidly dismounting to stand facing her. "Hello, Duchess."

Portia froze. She scanned the unshaven features, trying to place him. *Duchess?* Only one person had ever called her that. Suddenly recognition solved the mystery. "Kent Randolph?"

He nodded and a glint of amusement lit his eyes. "How've you been?"

She found herself slightly mesmerized by his handsome face and teasing gaze. "I've been well. You?"

"Can't complain. Good seeing you again."

"Same here." When she first came to live with Rhine and Eddy in Virginia City, she'd been twelve years old. He had been six years older and the bartender at Rhine's saloon. She hadn't paid him much attention, except when he called her Duchess, which annoyed her to no end. The passage of fifteen years had turned him into a man taller than she by at least a foot and with shoulders wide enough to block the sun. Her eyes strayed over the worn gun belt strapped around his waist and the butt of the Colt it held. Snug denims on muscular legs were covered with trail dust as were his boots, single-breasted gray shirt, and black leather vest. She heard he'd gone back East to medical school. With such rugged good looks, he certainly didn't resemble any doctor she'd ever met.

"You've grown up." His soft tone grabbed her attention and touched her in a way that made her feel warm, female.

She blinked. "Um, yes."

"Is your uncle here?"

Realizing she was staring, she shook herself free of whatever his eyes were doing to befuddle her so totally. "Yes. He's inside. This way, please."

She waited while he tied the roan to the post and reached for his saddlebag. Tossing it easily over his shoulder, they set out, his heeled boots echoing against the wooden walk. She got the feeling that he was eyeing the sway of her blue skirt, but she was so overwhelmed by the air of maleness he exuded, she kept walking and tried to ignore his effects on her usually unflappable self.

Her uncle's office was in the same building that housed her own, so she led Kent back to the breezeway and past the giant oaks and flowers enhancing the landscaping.

"Nice place you have here," he remarked as he looked around.

"Thank you. We like it."

"When the man in Tucson gave me directions to the hotel, I expected something more like the hotels back East or in Virginia City, not a spread like this. Looks more like a ranch."

They approached the door. He reached around her to open it. His arm gently grazed her shoulder and Portia jumped nervously.

"Sorry. Not trying to scare you," he said apologetically. "Just wanted to get the door for you."

"Thank you," she said, looking up into his face. She wondered if he remembered how uneasy and fearful she'd been around men when she and her sister first came to Virginia City. Because of Corinne's way of life, Portia had imagined herself fair game to any man in a pair of trousers, and as a result she'd been as afraid as a tiny mouse in a world filled with large feral cats.

He held the door aside. "After you."

She inclined her head and entered.

The coolness of the interior's air always offered relief from the blazing Arizona heat. "My uncle's office is this way."

She led him past the large sitting room filled with elegant dark wood furniture. The white adobe walls were adorned with framed brightly hued paintings and plants stood in large colorful floor pots.

"Feels like Mexico," he said.

"We're not that far from the border." She stopped at her uncle's closed door and knocked.

He called, "Come on in."

Kent entered behind her and when Rhine, who was seated behind a big fancy desk, saw him, his jaw dropped and he slowly got to his feet. "Where in the hell did you find him?" There was a smile of wonder on his face.

"Outside on a horse," she said with a grin. "I'll leave you two to your visit."

Kent turned to her and said in the same soft tone he'd used earlier, "Thanks, Duchess."

"You're welcome." Forcing herself to break his captivating gaze, she turned and exited.

CHAPTER TWO

"Fifteen years is a long time."

Seated in one of the leather chairs in Rhine's office with a tumbler of fine scotch in his hand, Kent thought about all he'd seen and done since they'd parted ways in Virginia City. "Yes it is."

"Do you want to tell me about it?"

He smiled ruefully and sighed. "The long and short of it is, I bedded the wrong man's wife and spent three years in a Mexican prison for it."

Rhine showed his shock.

Kent explained. "He was a don. Pretty powerful, too. After he caught me in his bed, he convinced the local police I was responsible for a series of robberies in the area. Even supplied witnesses who swore they'd seen me at the scene. I was young, stupid, and full of myself. Not anymore." He slowly swirled the liquor in his glass. Memories rose of the hell he'd lived through and he turned his mind away.

"Does Doc know?"

He thought about his father, Oliver. "He was so upset about my not finishing medical school, I didn't have the heart to write while I was in prison, not that I had access to stationery, but once I was released, I did send him a letter detailing my sins. We've corresponded on and off since and in one of his letters he mentioned you and Eddy were here in Arizona Territory."

"What have you been doing since your release?"

"Went to San Francisco first and signed on with a merchant shipping company and sailed the world. Afterwards, went to work at a ranch up near Sacramento. Learned everything I needed to know about horse wrangling. Saved my money. Would like to start my own operation someday." And since then he'd drifted from California to Wyoming and places in between, hiring himself out as a ranch hand, riding herd on cattle drives, and taking any other work he could find.

"And now?"

"Hoping you can give me a job."

"How long do you plan on being around?"

"As long as you'll have me." He met Rhine's eyes and added truthfully, "Looking to settle down."

"We already have a bartender but we can find something for you, I'm sure."

"Whatever you have will be fine."

Rhine raised his glass. "Then welcome back."

"Thanks."

Fifteen years ago, after the mob destroyed Rhine's saloon and Eddy Fontaine's newly built diner, a younger and cockier version of Kent enrolled in Howard Medical School. Being a doctor was the last thing he wanted—all he ever

25

wanted to do was be a rancher—but he and his physician father had locked horns for years over his future, so to get Oliver off his back, Kent moved to Washington. He'd hated everything about it from the weather to the classes to the sneering condescending attitudes of the East Coast scions of the representative class. He'd enjoyed the young women though and spent an inordinate amount of time studying female anatomy, but in the end, not even that had been enough, so he'd left, much to his father's fury.

In response to a soft knock on the closed door, Rhine called, "Come in."

His wife, Eddy, entered. "Kenton! Portia said you were here." She threw her arms wide and a smiling Kent hugged her tight.

"So good to see you!" she gushed. "My goodness! Where have you been all these years? Did you fall off the face of the earth?"

"In a way. Rhine can explain."

She studied him, studied her husband's poker face, and said, "Okay. Are you staying?"

"I am if Rhine can find me a job."

Her joyful expression filled Kent's heart. He'd missed having them in his world. Rhine had been the older brother he'd always wanted and Eddy, the sister.

"Good. You could use a bath."

He chuckled. She'd always been frank.

Rhine asked her, "Should I put him in our wing?"

She nodded and said sincerely, "Yes, of course. It's wonderful having you here, Kent. Rhine will get you settled in and I'll see you at dinner— which is a party to celebrate our fifteenth anniversary."

He paused. "I don't own any fancy clothes."

"None needed."

He looked to Rhine for verification before asking, "Are you sure?"

"I am."

"Okay. Thanks, Eddy."

She left them and Kent said to Rhine, "Need to get my horse settled in first."

"Okay, stables are out back. Come on, I'll show you."

So Kent followed Rhine outside. On the way back to where he'd left his mount tied, they chatted about old times and old friends. "Is Jim Dade here, too?" Kent asked.

Rhine shook his head. "No. Jim's in upstate New York now. Opened a restaurant there. Eddy and I visited him last summer. He and his place are doing well."

James Dade had been in charge of the kitchen at Rhine's place in Virginia City and Rhine had looked upon him as an older brother, too. He'd hoped to find Jim still with Rhine and now the prospect of maybe never seeing him again was saddening.

When they reached his mount, Rhine assessed

the big stallion. "You don't see many blue roans much anymore."

Kent untied the reins and gave the strong neck an affectionate pat. "No. Have had him for a while now. Descended from Indian stock. Found him in a herd up in Montana. Broke him myself. Seems content to let me ride him, but I get the feeling that one day I'm going to wake up and find he's lit out for Montana again." The horse eyed him with the superior stare Kent had grown accustomed to as if acknowledging the accuracy of his assessment.

"Does he have a name?"

Kent smiled, "Blue, of course."

Rhine chuckled and they headed to the stable.

After getting Blue settled into the fenced-in paddock and stowing the saddle in the tack room, Rhine told Kent, "Our head groom is an old cowboy named Cal Grissom. He's off visiting his sister but will be back in a few days. You'll like him."

Kent saw Blue eyeing a beautiful Appaloosa mare. "That's a good-looking paint."

"Her name's Arizona. She belongs to Portia."

Kent watched Blue walking around the mare.

Rhine said, "I think Blue might be interested."

"I think you might be right."

Leaving the horses to get further acquainted, the two old friends resumed their walk to a breezeway that led to an adobe building with a red tiled roof that was set off by itself at the back of the sprawling property.

"Did you recognize Portia all grown-up?" Rhine asked as they entered.

"Took me a second or two, but I did." He didn't remember seeing a ring on Portia's finger. "Beaus coming out of her ears, I imagine."

Rhine chuckled, "Yes, but they may as well be fence posts for all the attention she gives them. She keeps saying she isn't interested in getting married. Her sister is just the opposite, though. Left to her own devices, Regan would have men dueling in the streets for her affections."

Kent found the information about Portia interesting. As a young girl she'd been stiff-backed and distant, and he'd given her the name Duchess just to tease her. But why didn't she want to marry? Did she think herself too good for the average male, or was she one of those so called modern women who thought men were as useful as a one-legged stool? Regan on the other hand had been quite the pistol at age ten—open and gregarious. In fact, both girls had been handfuls at first: sassing the teacher, fighting at school, being suspended at school. No one knew how the other children learned their mother was a whore but the girls were berated and teased mercilessly—thus the fighting. And when some of the more sanctimonious parents decided they didn't want the girls around their children, Eddy

29

had taken them out of school and hired a tutor to teach them at home.

And now, they were all grown-up. Although he had yet to see Regan, he assumed she was as much an ebony beauty as her sister and aunt. Kent followed Rhine past a nicely furnished sitting room. "This is the family's quarters. The kitchen and dining room are through that alcove. Eddy does the cooking. She says the staff have enough to do without waiting on us, too."

Rhine led him into a hallway and stopped in front of a closed door. "We'll put you in here. The girls' rooms are through that door down there, and Eddy and I are in the suite behind that one." The doors he referenced were at opposite ends of the hallway. "These three rooms in between are reserved for family guests, and since you are family . . ."

Rhine turned the knob and led him into a space that was large and airy. The bed looked big enough for his six-foot-three-inch frame to sleep in comfortably. There were thin drapes fluttering in the soft breeze from the open windows and a set of French doors that opened to the outside.

"I have to be frank," Rhine stated, his voice bringing his attention back. "Even with the prison sentence I'm assuming you're still no monk."

He hid his grin.

"If you think to add my girls to the notches on your bedpost, think again. I will geld you, Kent."

The hidden grin died. "Understood."

"Wanted to make that clear."

And then as if he hadn't just threatened to turn him into a eunuch, Rhine said, "Bath is through that door and there's inside plumbing. Feel free to walk around the place to get your bearings if you have a mind to before dinner. And if you need anything, press that button on the wall. It rings in the housekeeping office."

Kent glanced over at the small gold button and nodded. The place was even more modern than he'd first thought.

"Are you hungry?"

"As a bear."

"Okay. I'll have one of the staff bring you a tray."

"Thanks, Rhine."

Rhine moved to the door. "Welcome back, Kent. Glad to have you with us again."

Kent's heart swelled with deeply felt emotion. "Good being with you again, old man."

Rhine grinned. "I'll see you later."

After his departure, Kent glanced around. He hadn't had a room to himself since leaving Virginia City. It felt odd, but good, too. There were no dirt floors littered with sleeping bodies to maneuver around in order to find a spot to lie down for the night as in the prison, and no bunkhouse filled with belching snoring men like on the ranches he'd worked. He set his saddlebag

31

at his feet and stepped into the washroom. He eyed the big claw-foot tub and smiled his delight. All this luxury was going to take some time getting used to again but he was up to the challenge.

After his bath he dressed in the only clean clothes he had, a simple shirt and a pair of trousers, and walked outside to sit on the bench he'd seen there earlier. It was still desert hot but he hoped the temperature would drop and cool the air a bit now that it was past midday. Yesterday at this time he and Blue had been slowly making their way west from their last job on a spread in Colorado. The ride held no tub filled with hot water to soak away the weariness, no big bed to look forward to sleeping in. Just a bedroll on the ground beneath the stars. There'd certainly been no pretty girl to get reacquainted with. Which brought his thoughts to Portia. When she initially approached him outside, once he got a good look at her, he knew who she was right away, and her stunning beauty hit him like the kick of a mule. He thought he might have been struck dumb for a few moments because all he could do was stare at her gorgeous ebony face, the alluring, black feline eyes and the full sultry mouth. She was definitely all grown-up. With her hair pulled back and wearing a high necked blouse, she'd looked very prim and proper, even if the sway of her skirt belied that. However, the way she'd jumped when he accidentally brushed her arm gave him pause and brought back memories of how wary and fearful she'd been of men when she and her sister first came to live with Rhine and Eddy in Virginia City. He'd had no idea what she'd seen or experienced with her mother that made her so leery but she would visibly tense whenever a man came near, wouldn't hold lengthy conversations with him, Rhine, or Jim, and if any of them were in a room with her, she'd either abruptly leave or stand with a chair or sofa in front of her as if having a barrier made her feel more secure. Granted he hadn't given her problem more than a cursory thought back then, after all she'd been a youngster in his eyes and he was more intent on serving drinks and finding a willing woman to bed. He did notice that as time went by, she seemed to become more comfortable. So, could remnants of that fear be why she'd been so skittish when he brushed her arm and why she didn't want to marry? The realization that that might be the answer made him ashamed of his earlier judgmental conclusions. If Rhine was able to find him a job at the hotel, he'd be spending more time with Portia, so he needed to be the perfect gentleman and not give her a reason to feel threatened in any way.

Portia searched through her armoire for a suitable gown to wear to the evening's anniversary celebration. There'd be a large buffet, music, and drinks, and she'd be expected to wear something more stylish than her usual serviceable skirt and blouse. She took down the emerald green dress she'd gotten in San Francisco last year but thought the neckline might be too bold. Growing up in Denver her clothing had been hand-me-downs from churches and local benevolent societies and they'd always been threadbare, too large, or too small. That she would one day own more dresses than her arms could hold and shoes to match hadn't even been a dream in those days because it would have been too far-fetched. She paused, remembering the summer they'd received no donations and she and Regan were forced to wear the stitched together flour sacks their mother, Corinne, had somehow managed to obtain. They'd been barefoot that entire summer as well. Wondering if she'd ever rid herself of those tragic years, she pushed aside the haunting memories and refocused her attention on the emerald gown.

"You should wear that," Regan said behind her.

"No, I don't think so." She hung it back up in the armoire.

"Why not?" she asked, coming in and closing the door that connected their rooms. "You'd look beautiful."

"It's more suitable for the opera, not a dinner."

"How about that rose-colored one?"

Portia took it down and considered it. It was a lovely gown. The neckline was modest, the bodice fitted, and there were small satin roses of a darker hue along the hem of the flowing skirt. The short wispy cap sleeves would leave most of her arms bare but that wouldn't be bothersome.

"Have you heard that Kent Randolph is here?" Regan asked, pausing to check her lip paint and hair in the mirror of Portia's vanity table. "One of the maids brought him a tray earlier and said he's incredibly handsome."

"I was with him earlier," she replied, doing her best not to remember her reaction to his warm voice. "He was in need of a shave."

"Did he say what he'd been doing all this time?"

"No." And she told herself she wasn't interested, even though a small part of her was curious.

"Did he mention how long he'd be staying?"

"No, but you can quiz him as much as you care to when you see him." It never occurred to her that he might be staying. If he did, she hoped it would only be for a short time. She didn't want to have to spend her days battling her reactions to those male eyes of his, but then again, maybe she'd build up an immunity to them, the way children built up an immunity to the pox.

"He's in one of the guest rooms down the hall."

Portia almost dropped the gown. *That close!*

Recovering, she replied as disinterestedly as she could manage, "I had no idea."

Regan shrugged and took one last primping look in the mirror. "I suppose because he's family of sorts. Are you choosing that gown or not?"

"No." She put it back and took down one that was dove gray and had a high neck trimmed in lace. Something inside her deemed the gown safer.

"That one's lovely, too, but not as nice as the other."

"One of Uncle Rhine's associates may have a business question and I want their eyes on my face, not my neckline."

"You really aren't any fun, sister," Regan replied, smiling.

"You have enough fun for the both of us."

"I wish that were true."

Portia chuckled. "We need to find you a husband. Maybe you should answer one of those mail-order-bride advertisements in the newspapers."

"That's not a bad idea."

Portia was appalled that her sister appeared to be mulling it over. "I was just pulling your leg, Regan. I wasn't serious."

"But just think, somewhere there might be a man who needs a wife to help him work his homestead and have his children. He'd be strapping, strong, and handsome. We'd fall madly in love. It would be an adventure and you know how much I crave adventure."

Portia walked over and placed her palm against Regan's forehead. "I think you're coming down with something. You may need to see Doc Finney."

Regan laughed and moved the hand away. "That would be something, wouldn't it?"

"What, your coming down with a brain fever?"

"No, silly. My becoming a mail-order bride."

"As I said, it was a joke. Don't even consider doing something so harebrained."

"Women become mail-order brides all the time and besides, everyone thought my wanting to deliver the mail was harebrained, too."

"Some of us still do." Portia sat on the vanity's purple tufted bench and pulled on her stockings then anchored them with the frilly green garters Regan had talked her into buying last fall.

"Delivering the mail is another form of adventure. I enjoy getting to see new places and people."

The sisters were very different in that respect. Portia was content to sit at her desk, poring over ledgers and contracts while Regan always wanted to see what was over the next hill. "I don't like the idea of your being robbed or losing a wheel or being attacked by a puma or a bear, or Apaches. You're a pest sometimes but you're my pest and I love you."

"I appreciate your concern and I love you, too, but I can shoot just as well as you, and besides, everyone knows I only deliver letters and packages. Uncle Rhine won't let me carry gold or payrolls and neither will the mine owners."

"And that's a good thing."

"I know. I may be unconventional but I'm not irrational. Carrying gold dust can be extremely dangerous."

A few months ago, there'd been a gang preying on mail carriers. They were finally apprehended and jailed but not before they'd shot a man to death for the mine payroll he'd had on his wagon. Portia brushed out her hair and pinned it low on her neck. After removing her lightweight wrapper, she stepped into her gown and pulled it up over her flowered corset and shift. Once Regan helped fasten the line of small buttons on the back, Portia slipped silver hoops in her ear lobes and assessed herself in the mirror. "I'll do, I suppose."

"You'll more than do, sister mine. We Carmichael women are beauties, and when I find my mail-order husband, I'll ask if he has a brother."

Laughing, Portia playfully pushed her towards the door. "Let's go you silly goose."

They were still laughing when they stepped into the hallway, but then fell silent when Kent Randolph stepped out of his door at the same time.

"Ladies," he said.

Regan, never shy, walked up and said, "Hello. I'm Regan Carmichael. Are you Kent?"

"I am. Pleased to see you again, Regan. It's been a long time."

"It has indeed."

Portia's eyes gave a tiny roll and when they were horizontal again, they were caught by his.

"Duchess."

"Kent."

He was wearing a blue, long sleeved, double-breasted shirt that showed his muscular lines with a pair of dark trousers. Both had seen better days but were clean and pressed. His string tie was anchored by a lovely green agate. There was a thin silver bracelet around his wrist and his black leather boots were shined. He'd shaved but enough of a shadow remained to give him the look of a handsome and probably dangerous outlaw.

The silence grew as they assessed each other. Regan raised an eyebrow but Portia ignored it.

Still focused on Portia, he said, "I was hoping somebody would come along and show me the way to dinner."

"And here we are, right on time," Regan quipped.

"Much appreciated." He extended his arm. "Shall we?"

A smiling Regan obliged.

Portia knew instinctively that touching him, no

matter how innocently, would not be a good idea. Even though he stood a slight distance away his heady presence was already playing havoc with her self-control. For some reason all she wanted to do was stare at him. *Maybe I need to see Doc Finney, too.* "We should go. We don't want to keep the others waiting."

As if aware he'd rattled her, a slight smile played at the corners of his lips. She ignored that, too, and led the way.

When they entered the ballroom it was filled with the sounds of the musicians and a large number of guests conversing and milling about holding drinks and small china plates piled with food from the large sumptuous buffet. Tonight's invitation had been extended to just about everyone the Fontaines knew. Portia spotted her aunt and uncle across the room speaking with three people she didn't know. Most of the other faces were familiar, however: neighbors like Old Man Blanchard and his ranch hands Farley and Buck, some of the local businessmen and their wives. She and Regan nodded greetings to those they knew and made their way with Kent over to Eddy and Rhine.

Upon reaching them and before Portia could apologize for their tardy arrival, Kent said, "Sorry we're late. The ladies were waiting on me."

When he flashed Portia a quick conspiratorial wink, she hid her grin. *And he's charming.*

Their uncle waved off the apology. "You're fine." The strangers were introduced as Albert and Hattie Salt, and their adult son, Edward.

Hattie, a tall skinny woman with thinning, dyed-red hair said, "My, aren't you girls lovely."

"Thank you," they murmured, passing a look between them and waiting to make a graceful exit. Aunt Eddy, dressed in a lovely cream-colored gown, was viewing the Salts with a plastered-on smile. Portia got the impression the Salts had done or said something she'd found displeasing.

Over the musicians and noisy crowd, Rhine added, "Kent Randolph used to work for me when we lived in Virginia City."

Albert, whose large girth seemed ready to burst the buttons on the black vest beneath his suit coat, asked, "And what do you do now, Randolph?"

"This and that. Ranch work mostly."

Portia saw the son, Edward, sneer. Ranches couldn't survive without workers and there was nothing wrong with a man making his livelihood that way. Although she'd just been introduced to Edward Salt, she didn't care for him. The cold look in her aunt's eyes seemed to mirror her assessment.

"And what do you do, Edward?" Regan asked pointedly. Apparently she'd seen the sneer, too.

"I'm a teacher," he replied, his attention moving between the sisters. "Howard educated.

41

I'm thinking of starting a school here."

If invoking Howard was meant to impress her, it didn't. Neither did his heavily pomaded hair and soft-looking hands, which appeared to have never done a hard day's work. She wondered if he rode or preferred travel by carriage. She'd put her money on the latter. "It was nice meeting you," she lied, and then she and Regan and Kent drifted away. Regan waved at a friend across the ballroom and said to Portia, "I'm going over to speak to Damaris. I'll see you two later."

After her departure, Kent asked, "Are the Salts family friends?"

Portia smiled at an acquaintance and shook her head. "Never seen them before."

"You think he rides or drives?"

She stopped. Unable to mask her amusement, she said, "You're not supposed to be able to read my mind, Kent Randolph."

"Sorry, Duchess. I'll try and remember that for the future."

The eyes were so potent she swore he had some kind of mystical power. Finally shaking herself free, she smiled. "You do that."

With her aunt and uncle still occupied with the Salts, she knew it would be rude to leave Kent alone in a gathering of strangers, so she'd have to play hostess. "Do you want to get something to eat?"

"That would be fine."

42

On the way to the buffet table she stopped and introduced him to a group of ranchers and then to two of the mine owners. No one sneered when he described himself as a ranch hand. In fact, rancher Howard Lane said if Kent needed work to stop by.

"Nice man," Kent said as they continued on their way.

"Most people here aren't like the Salts. I saw the way their son sneered."

"I did, too. But a man like that doesn't matter to me, unless he has a gun in his hand."

"How are you, Miss Portia?"

Startled, she turned to the smiling face of the spectacles-wearing James Cordell. He was the son of the local reverend and a bookkeeper for one of the mines in the area. "I'm doing well, James. You?"

"Just fine." He was tall and so thin he always looked as if he was wearing his father's suits.

She saw him assessing Kent so she did the introductions. "I'd like you to meet a friend of the family. Kent Randolph. James Cordell."

Kent stuck out a hand and they shared a shake.

"How long have you known the Fontaines?" James asked, eyeing him suspiciously.

"I worked for Rhine fifteen years ago in Virginia City."

"I see. Miss Portia, I came to ask if you'd like to go riding with me tomorrow."

43

She pasted on a smile. "I'm sorry, James. I'm going to be busy." He was really a nice fellow and she felt bad about turning down his offer, but he was hell-bent on courting her even after being gently told a few years ago that they didn't suit. He'd make some young woman a very nice husband, so she dearly wished he'd set his sights on someone else. "And next week I'll have guests to tend to, so . . ."

"I—I understand."

"Thank you, James."

He didn't move, seemingly content to stare at her.

"Um, I have to introduce Kent around. Thanks for coming to the party."

"You're welcome."

They moved off and Kent said, "He's sweet on you, I take it."

She sighed. "Yes. He's very nice and I have gone riding with him on a few occasions, hoping that would be enough."

"But it wasn't."

She shook her head. "He's painfully shy and never says more than a few words the entire time." She couldn't understand why he and a few others who kept coming around refused to take her refusals seriously. She supposed they assumed because she was female she didn't know her own mind.

"From some of the looks I've been getting,

44

there are a number of men unhappy to see me with you."

"They can all shear sheep."

He laughed.

A smile teased her lips.

They finally made it to the buffet table. Among the many people there was Old Man Blanchard speaking with haberdashery owner, Darian Day, another of Portia's frustrated suitors. But unlike James, she took great pleasure in refusing his company because he was such a condescending ass.

Before she could introduce Kent to Mr. Blanchard, Day said, "You're looking lovely, Portia."

"Thank you, Mr. Day." As always, he was overdressed for the occasion, this time in a black long-tailed coat, white bow tie, and white wing-tipped shirt. Instead of the boots men like Mr. Blanchard and Kent were wearing, Day had on narrow-toed black shoes.

"And who's this?" he asked, staring Kent up and down.

"Darian Day. Kent Randolph. Kent was an employee of my uncle's when we lived in Virginia City."

"Welcome to Arizona Territory. I own a haberdashery in Tucson. When you get the extra funds, stop by and we can see about finding you something to wear that's a bit more suitable for a gathering like this."

Kent gave him a wintry smile. "I'll keep that in mind."

Day added, "And as the menfolk here will probably tell you, I've had my eye on this little filly for some time, but she's being real prickly about accepting my saddle."

Portia tossed back, "Probably because I abhor being referred to as a 'little filly.'"

Old Man Blanchard barked a laugh. "You tell him, Portia."

She loved the old man. "I need to check on things in the kitchen, Mr. Blanchard. May I leave Kent in your capable hands? My aunt and uncle are occupied." They were still across the room with the Salts.

He smiled. "Sure can. Grab a plate, Randolph, and let's get acquainted."

She gave Kent a departing nod, shot Day a glare, and walked away.

The kitchen was a beehive of activity. The head cook, a young Englishwoman named Sarah, was adding more sliced beef to a depleted tray while the other kitchen workers carried in empty platters needing to be refilled. Setting aside her irritation with Day, she asked, "How're things in here, Sarah?"

"Hectic but under control. We had to shoo your aunt out earlier, though."

"Why? What did she want?"

"To make sure the pie slices were evenly cut.

I told her she taught me everything I know and I would sic you on her if she didn't go back out and enjoy herself. She pouted and left."

Portia shook her head in amazement and amusement. "Whatever are we going to do with her?"

"You tell me, miss. She's your aunt."

Smiling, Portia scanned the organized chaos. Satisfied her help wasn't needed, she said, "If Aunt Eddy comes back, send someone for me. She's a guest of honor. Not the caterer."

"Yes, ma'am."

By the time the cake, ablaze with fifteen sparklers, was wheeled out, Portia was glad the evening was about to come to an end. Her feet were tired of being encased in the fancy heeled shoes, the corset beneath her dress pained her as it always did when propriety dictated she wear one, and she could feel a headache coming on from all the noise and the press of so many bodies. To escape the heat, some of the guests were enjoying their cake and ice cream outside at the trestle table. As she walked the area to make sure everyone was having a good time, she spied Regan seated with her beau du jour, a young army sergeant she'd met a week ago. Beside them sat Old Man Blanchard, apparently playing duenna, and Portia smiled at the unhappy look on her sister's face. There'd be no sneaking off for stolen kisses with Mr. Blanchard around.

A laughing Eddy was seated on Rhine's lap, however, and he was feeding her cake from a fork. The amused Portia hoped she wouldn't have to send them to their suite to keep their ardor from getting out of hand.

"Brought you some cake, Duchess."

Surprised, she turned and the closeness of Kent's presence wafted dizzily over her again.

"You do eat cake, don't you?"

She extricated herself from his silent spell and sputtered, "I do. Yes. Thank you." Admittedly moved by his thoughtfulness, she took the plate from his hand.

"Shall we find a seat?" he asked. "Or are you still on duty?"

"I am but I would like to sit for a moment." Usually her needs were secondary because of all that needed doing like making innumerable visits to the kitchen, saying "Thank you for coming" to the departing guests, and keeping an eye on the remaining amounts of food and drink.

"Good cake," he said.

"Glad you like it."

"You don't seem to be enjoying yourself very much."

She paused and wondered how he knew. She shrugged. "Managing a party of this size doesn't leave much time for enjoyment."

"I suppose you're right. Do you ever get to have fun?"

She thought about the conversation she'd had with Regan yesterday. "I have a lot to do."

"Not judging, Duchess. Just asking."

The sincerity in his manner and tone made his words believable. She wondered what kind of man he was. Their interactions in Virginia City had been minimal due to the difference in their ages and the fact that he worked in the saloon, a place she and her sister weren't allowed to enter when it was open to clients. What would she learn about him now that their ages and his employment weren't a factor?

Edward Salt walked up. "Ah, Miss Carmichael. I finally find you seated. May I speak with you?"

"Of course."

"Privately," he added.

Kent rose to leave them alone, but Portia said, "No, Kent. Please stay. I'm sure whatever Mr. Salt has to say will be all right for you to overhear. Finish your cake." She had no intentions of being spoken to privately by him.

Salt didn't appear happy.

She didn't care.

He cleared his throat. "I'd like to call on you tomorrow if I might. Being new to the area, I'd be honored to have you show me around."

"Unfortunately I'm going to be busy. The hotel has guests arriving in a few days and there are a hundred things I have to oversee to get ready.

I'm sure someone else can show you the sights better than I."

He didn't like that either.

She didn't care.

"Some other time then."

She didn't commit.

He walked away.

She blew out a breath.

Kent quipped, "Snappy dresser though."

"If you like that sort of thing."

Salt's black suit and gold-trimmed vest looked quite expensive, as did his shoes. She eyed Kent's plainer and more honest attire and must have scrutinized him longer than was polite because he said, "Fanciest set of duds I own, Duchess. Sorry."

"No. I was—just thinking how much more I liked your attire than his." Embarrassed by her admission and doing her best to ignore the heat searing her cheeks, she dragged her eyes to his and found a quietness waiting there that spoke to her wordlessly. "Please, I wasn't judging you."

"Are you always this sincere?"

Portia felt as if they were alone in an empty room. "When I need to be, yes."

"Good to know," he said softly.

The three words left her heart pounding.

Regan walked up. She looked to Portia first and then Kent. Waving her hand in the space that separated them she said, "Hey, you two. Aunt

Eddy and Uncle Rhine are saying their good-byes. Everyone is going home."

Portia stood. Whatever was unfolding inside herself wasn't something she'd ever experienced before, so she had no name for it nor any idea how to go about handling it. But she did know that this cowboy and his compelling gaze was the source. "I—I have to go."

He nodded, and as she and her sister walked away, she didn't see his smile as he finished his cake.

CHAPTER THREE

Kent had no idea what time breakfast was served or how it was handled but as was his custom, he got up before dawn and went in search of food. The hallway anchored by the girls' bedrooms at one end and Rhine and Eddy's at the other was quiet. If they were still sleeping, he didn't want to disturb them so he left the hallway as quietly as he could. Retracing the route from yesterday, he walked down another short, tiled hallway that led to the family sitting area. Hearing voices, he followed the sound into the dining room. Eddy and Portia were seated at the table. There were plates in front of them and cups of coffee.

Eddy greeted him with a smile. "Good morning, Kent. Join us please. Did you sleep well?"

"I did. Been a while since I slept in a real bed." For a man more accustomed to sleeping on a bedroll on the ground or the hard slats in a bunkhouse, it had been wonderful. He gave Portia a nod. "Morning."

She glanced away from her newspaper. "Good morning." Her attention immediately returned to the paper but not before letting her eyes stray his way one more time.

"Do you want eggs with your breakfast?" Eddy asked.

"Yes, but I can cook them myself. Just show me where things are in the kitchen." He noticed Portia's look of mild surprise.

Eddy shook her head. "No. I haven't been allowed to cook in days, so humor me."

He was accustomed to taking care of his own needs, including his meals, but he knew a losing battle when he was in one, so he offered a compromise. "Okay, but I cook them tomorrow."

"That's agreeable. Now, how do you like them?"

"Scrambled."

"I'll be back in a moment."

She went into the kitchen and left him alone with Portia. He didn't want to disturb her reading while he waited for Eddy to return so he walked to the windows that faced the well-manicured grounds. The sun was just coming up.

"How long are you planning on staying with us?" she asked.

"Rhine's offered me a job, so it depends on what it's going to be." He turned to gauge her reaction. Her face showed nothing. She'd be a good poker player. "Do you and your sister help out around here?"

"Yes. I manage the hotel, the guests, and the books."

He raised an eyebrow. He didn't know what he'd been expecting her to say but it certainly hadn't been that, but then again he remembered all she'd done last night at the party. "Lots of responsibility."

"Yes and responsibilities some people believe I shouldn't have."

That confused him. "Why?"

"Because I'm female."

"Ah." That now made sense, so he added, "Not all women are flighty. Just as all men aren't jackasses like Day."

Her mask dropped and there was interest in her eyes again. He decided he liked surprising her. He got the impression that the men who did were few and far between. "Remember, I lived in Virginia City with Eddy and Sylvie as examples of female know-how." Sylvia "Sylvie" Stewart, married to his father, had owned quite a bit of property in town. Her business acumen was as well-known and respected as Eddy's had been.

"You have no idea how many men think otherwise."

"I can only imagine."

Eddy returned with a bowl of steaming eggs. He took a seat and filled his plate. There was a platter holding warm biscuits—hidden beneath a tea towel to keep in the heat—fresh butter, slabs of crisp bacon, and orange marmalade. After pouring himself a cup of coffee he started in. The eggs were wonderful, far more expertly done than he could have managed but he was determined to cook tomorrow. The spoiled boy he'd once been had died in the Mexican prison and he didn't like being waited on—not even by friends. "Where's Rhine this morning?" he asked Eddy.

She smiled over her raised cup of coffee. "Still sleeping of course. He's never shaken the habit of owning a saloon and staying awake until dawn. Personally, I don't think he's ever made a serious effort to change. He enjoys lazing about until midday."

The younger version of Kent had enjoyed that as well, but when you hire on with a ranching outfit, foremen didn't pay you for lying in bed. There were horses to feed, fences to mend, cows to herd, and broncs to break. He looked to Portia. "Is your sister still sleeping?"

She spoke as gracefully as she could around the biscuit she'd just bitten into. "No. She's having breakfast with Old Man Blanchard. She eats with him a couple of mornings a week. His wife died about ten years ago and he likes Regan's company. He has a married daughter in Tucson but she doesn't visit him very much."

"Which is a shame," Eddy opined. "Because he's a nice man and he's lonely. He looks on Regan as an adopted granddaughter."

Portia added, "And she has a big heart so she keeps an eye on him."

He heard the affection for her sister in her voice. When he'd known them in Nevada, the two had been very close. He was glad time hadn't eroded their love for each other. Being an only child, he envied that sibling bond. "Eggs are real good, Eddy. Thank you."

"My pleasure. Did you enjoy the party last night?"

"I did."

As he and Eddy chatted about the party and the people he'd been introduced to, Portia found herself further intrigued by him. Where most men were content to sit back and be waited upon, including her uncle whom she adored, Kent had seemed genuinely sincere about wanting to make his own eggs. Having grown up as the daughter of a prostitute, Portia learned at an early age that men could be vile, controlling, and prone to using their fists. Until she and Regan became Eddy's wards, she never knew a man could be as tender and loving as Rhine was to their aunt. She'd been so wary of men it had taken her years to fully comprehend that Rhine and his former partner Jim Dade had no designs on her physically and would stand between her and a barreling train if necessary to keep her safe. Once she was able to come to grips with that, those parts of herself that were constantly on alert and fearful faded somewhat. She still tended to believe the world held more men like her mother's customers and haberdashery owner Darian Day than the good and decent type like her uncle.

"Portia?" Eddy's voice cut into her thoughts.

"I'm sorry. Wool gathering. Did I miss something?" She glanced over and saw Kent watching her with an unreadable expression. She moved her attention to her aunt.

"I said, I doubt we'll be entertaining the Salts in the future. If I never see them again, it will be too soon."

"How long have they been in Tucson?" Kent asked.

"Just a few weeks. Rhine met the husband at the barbershop and invited them to the party because he thought it would be a nice way for them to meet some folks. Who knew that as soon as they arrived, he'd pester Rhine for a loan?"

"A loan for what?" Portia asked.

"A grocery store, I believe."

"And his collateral?" She saw Kent pause and view her as if she was the most interesting thing he'd seen in some time. Something inside her buzzed with an odd sense of pleasure.

"Rhine asked the same question. Salt said they could discuss it later."

"I don't want to be rude, Aunt Eddy, but I wouldn't lend them rusty nails."

"Agreed."

"I thought you looked a bit put out when we walked up," Portia said.

"I was. When the wife asked me what kind of hoodoo I used to snare such a handsome light-skinned man like your uncle, I almost punched her."

"Glad I missed that," Portia said, hiding her smile.

Eddy looked put out over the encounter all over again. "And we won't even discuss the way that son of theirs sneered at Kent."

"I ignored it," he told her.

"I didn't. When you and the girls left I told him if he sneered at any of my guests again, I'd have him thrown out."

Kent said, "That wasn't necessary, Eddy."

"In my mind it was. It is my home after all."

Portia saw him incline his head as if acquiescing.

"And, on top of all the other rude behavior, he had questions about you and Regan."

Portia was instantly wary. "Such as?"

"Were you two married? Did you have beaus? Were you due to inherit Rhine's estate? I told him your affairs were none of his business."

Portia added, "He asked if he could call on me today so I could show him the sights. I turned him down."

Edward Salt with his sneers and baby-soft hands had not made a good first impression. She found herself studying Kent's hands as he wielded his fork. They were clean and the calluses and shadows of healed cuts and abrasions on his long fingers were the result of hard work. Catching herself wondering how it might feel to touch them, she quickly turned away, but not before seeing his amusement as if he'd peeked inside her head and knew what she'd been thinking.

Regan entered and her eyes were red and swollen.

"What's wrong?" Portia asked with alarm.

"Old Man Blanchard died sometime during the night. I sent Farley for the doc and . . ." She paused to wipe the tears. "He's gone," she whispered.

Portia went to her and held her close. "Oh, honey. I'm so sorry."

Eddy got up from the table. "Let me go get Rhine." After placing a solemn kiss on Regan's cheek she hastily left the room.

Kent wasn't sure what he was supposed to do but watching Portia console her sister made him feel like an intruder. Since he was done with his breakfast, he stood and picked up his plate and carried it into the kitchen. When he came back out, the room was empty. He figured everyone would probably be gone for at least a little while. The table still held their dishes and what was left of the food, so he cleared the settings.

When Portia reappeared thirty minutes later, he was washing up the dishes. She stopped and stared.

"How's Regan?" he asked.

"Doing okay. She rode back over to Old Man

Blanchard's place with Uncle Rhine and Aunt Eddy."

He nodded and set a clean cup in the dish drain.

In a voice filled with wonder, she asked, "What are you doing?"

Guessing he'd surprised her again, he smiled inwardly. "Washing the dishes."

"But why?"

"You and your family have a death to deal with. Thought I'd help out. Men around here don't do dishes?"

"You've met some of the men around here. What do you think?"

He chuckled. "You always so blunt?"

"It's my Carmichael blood."

He faced her. "Last night after you cut Day to the quick and went into the kitchen, he said you needed a man to rid you of what he called your uppity mouth."

"Really?" she replied in a tone that let him know she wasn't pleased.

"Mr. Blanchard came to your defense, though." He set another plate in the drain. "How long has Day been trying to court you?"

"About a year and a half."

He looked her way. "Personally, I like your uppity mouth."

She swayed for a split second. He liked that, too.

She stammered, "I—I was coming back to

clean up, but you seem to have everything in hand."

"For the most part, but I've no idea where some of these things go."

"You can just leave them in the drain. I'll—put them away later."

It didn't make a whole lot of sense for her to come back later when all she had to do was direct him now, but he didn't push. She seemed slightly rattled and he was enjoying that as well. "Okay. So since you hold the reins here, do you know what my job will be?"

"No. Uncle Rhine will handle that."

"Anything you need done in the interim?"

She hastily shook her head.

"Fine. I'll go say good morning to Blue, maybe go for a ride, and wait for Rhine to return."

"Blue?"

"My horse."

"Oh yes. Of course."

He watched her watch him. In truth he wouldn't mind looking at her all day and she seemed torn between staying and fleeing. She finally muttered "I have to go" before beating a hasty retreat. Chuckling to himself, he went back to the dishes. He was enjoying Miss Portia Carmichael, probably more than Rhine would like so he needed to pull back on the reins a bit. If he could.

Kent saddled Blue a short while later, and rode off to do some exploring. Mountains both far and near were everywhere he looked, as were valleys, clear running streams, and stands of thick forest. One of the reasons he'd hated being at Howard was that there'd been no peace or silence. All the noise and commotion from the streetcars and crowds was so overwhelming it didn't allow a man to think. The wide open spaces that made up the West were far better. He waded Blue into a standing pool so the stallion could drink. Savoring the surrounding beauty, Kent thought he would enjoy living here. For some reason he felt more settled and content than he had in a long time. Even though he'd only been back with Rhine and Eddy a day, it was as if all the years of drifting like a windblown tumbleweed had finally led him back to them in a way that felt as if he'd come home. He sensed he could put down roots here, build a home of his own and maybe find a wife and raise some children, which surprised him because he'd always been too restless to contemplate the possibility of marriage and a family. But in truth, he was tired of drifting, tired of being alone with no set place to come home to at the end of the day and having nothing to call his own but his horse, saddle, and the clothes on his back. He looked up at the cloudless blue sky, felt the gentle breeze on his face, and wondered what it was about this place that seemed to ease his loner's soul. He had no answer but was willing to stick around long enough to find out. With that in mind, he reined Blue around and headed back to the hotel.

Entering the hotel, he wondered how the family was faring with the death of their friend Blanchard, and if Rhine had returned. Thoughts of Portia's whereabouts arose as well, but he set them aside for the moment. When he reached Rhine's office the door was open and Kent saw him inside at his desk.

"Come on in," Rhine said to him.

Kent took a seat. "Wanted to convey my condolences."

"Thanks. Blanchard was good man and we cared about him very much. Especially the girls. When they were growing up he taught them everything from how to ride bareback to building a smokeless fire. We'll miss him." He paused and asked, "Are you settling in?"

"I am. That bed is going to spoil me for the rest of my life, though."

Rhine smiled knowingly. "Only the best at the Fontaine Hotel. You told me you'd been a foreman?"

"On a couple of outfits."

"Are you up to doing it again?"

"Sure. Where?"

"The Blanchard place. His daughter's decided she doesn't want the property so I made her an offer that I'm hoping she'll accept. Portia has been keeping his books and his son-in-law wants them reviewed before going forward."

"Did he have a foreman?"

"Yes, but he wants to move on. Says the place won't be the same without the old man."

Kent understood. When a long-time owner sells, or as in this case dies, a new regime often brings change to the old employees along with a level of uncertainty as to how the place will be run. "Is it cattle or horses?"

"Horses mostly but he has a small herd of longhorns."

"What about the other hands? How many are there?"

"Small outfit so only five counting the foreman. Blanchard used to break wild horses to supply the army but demand's faded. He now buys from an outfit up near Prescott and sells to individuals. He also maintains the mounts our guests ride."

"So no riding up to Montana or Wyoming for wild mustangs."

"No. Is that a problem?"

"Not really. Spent almost a decade chasing and breaking stallions and mares. After busting my collarbone twice, my wrists too many times to count, and my leg in two places a few years back, being a gentleman foreman may be just what I need at my age." The leg break had been so severe that, though healed, it still pained him in damp weather.

Rhine cracked, "You are getting fairly long in the tooth."

"Yours will always be longer." The shared grin reminded Kent just how much he'd missed having him in his life.

They spent the next few minutes talking about salary. Kent thought the figure Rhine offered to be fair.

"As I said, Portia's been handling Blanchard's books and payroll, and I don't see that changing once I'm the new owner. She'll also take care of ordering of any supplies you can't get in Tucson."

Kent wondered how she'd feel about his taking over as foreman. He found himself looking forward to interacting with her on a regular basis.

"You'll need to sit down with her and go over how the dude ranch visits are handled, too, since she's the one who coordinates it all. Any questions on anything we've talked about so far?"

"No. I would like to ride over and take a hard look at the buildings and the stables, but out of respect for his passing, I'll wait until after the funeral."

"The wake will be at his place, so you'll be able to see some of it, if you want to go."

"I only met him at the party last night but I liked him, so I would like to pay my respects if that's okay."

"That would be fine."

"Are the other hands staying on?"

"They said they'd let me know after the funeral."

"Did you tell them you were bringing in a new foreman?"

"I told them there was a good possibility."

"Were any of them hoping to move up to foreman?"

Rhine considered that for a moment. "I don't know that either. I probably should have considered that."

"Yes, but then I wouldn't have a job, so we'll wait and see what happens. If they all decide to move on, we'll hire new men. It may take some time but the work will get done." Kent was accustomed to putting in a full day's work so if he had to run the place shorthanded for a while he would. "Anything you want me to do in the meantime? All this sitting around is wearing on me."

"As a matter of fact, I do. How are you at chopping wood?"

Kent shrugged. "I've chopped a few piles in my life."

"Good. The kitchen always needs wood and Eddy says they're running low. The man who usually does it hasn't shown up for the past week or so. Not sure if he's quit on us or what, but there are enough logs out by the barn to keep you busy for a few days."

"Okay. You spoke of the wake. When's the funeral?"

"In a few days, I suppose. His daughter is his

only family so there's no one else she has to wait for to arrive."

Kent wondered who'd mourn him when his time came. He assumed his father would see the Pearly Gates first but afterwards? There were no other Randolphs either—at least as far as he knew. Burying the maudlin thoughts, he asked Rhine, "I assume you'll want me living there as opposed to here?"

Rhine nodded. "He has a nice-sized place so you may as well move into the house."

"Where'd the old foreman stay?"

"Bunkhouse."

Kent mulled that over for a moment, too. If the other men stayed, he wondered how they'd feel about him being in the old man's house, or if they'd care. It could pave the way for some resentment and he didn't want to start off that way. He supposed he'd have to wait and see. No sense in worrying over something that might come into play. "How about I decide after I talk with the hands, if they stay."

"How about you simply move into the house. I don't want it sitting empty."

He nodded. "Whatever you say."

"Good. Anything else for now?"

"No. I'll get started on Eddy's wood. Where is it?"

"I'll show you."

CHAPTER FOUR

Carrying the Blanchard ledgers and receipts Rhine wanted her to review, Portia decided to check on Regan before heading to her office. She knocked on the connecting door to her sister's room and when Regan answered, stepped inside. Unlike her own neat-as-a-pin living quarters, Regan's always resembled the aftermath of a storm. All the gowns she must have considered wearing last night were lying across the bed and over the backs of chairs, the shoe choices covered the floor, and her vanity table was a chaos of face paints, hair brushes, and combs. Accustomed to the sight, Portia ignored it and concentrated on the sadness in her sister's eyes. "How are you feeling?"

Dressed in a shirt and denims, Regan, standing in front of the open French doors, shrugged. "I'll be better eventually, I suppose."

"We'll all miss him."

"He's the first person to die that I truly loved."

"I know." Portia couldn't imagine a world without the crusty old horse wrangler who'd been such an important part of their life. Fifteen years ago when they moved to the Territory, he'd given them their first mares. Because of his lessons, she and Regan could ride hell-bent for leather and clear fences without fear. She could still hear his voice in her mind. *Horses don't care if you're girls. They just want to know you can ride!* "No one will fault you if you want to spend the day in your room."

"No, I have a few deliveries to make. He wouldn't want me in here moping."

Portia agreed. Because of the strength he'd instilled in them, coupled with the fearlessness they'd learned from Eddy and Rhine, she and her sister felt capable of weathering any storm, and they'd weather this one, too. "If you need me, I'll be in my office."

Regan nodded and Portia closed the door softly.

Seated in her office with the doors that led outdoors open to the warmth and breeze of the afternoon, Portia pored over Mr. Blanchard's books, looking for anything that might prove problematic to Rhine's purchase of his ranch. She knew there wasn't, but according to her uncle, Blanchard's son-in-law, Charlie Landry, had hired someone to review the books, and Portia didn't want anything found that required an explanation. With that in mind, she double-checked payroll records, bank deposits, supply orders, and everything else, and when done, she was satisfied that the ledgers would pass muster. She stood and stretched to get the kink out of her spine. Hearing the ringing of an axe, she assumed Bailey Durham the wood chopper had finally shown up to do his job. He wasn't the most reliable worker and where he'd been for the past week was anyone's guess. Unlocking the small strongbox she kept in the bottom drawer of her desk, she counted out what he was owed for his services and left her office to pay him.

But it wasn't Durham. It was Kent attired in denims and the shirt portion of a gray union suit. The sleeves were pushed up past his elbows and he was swinging the axe with accurate authority. Over by the breezeway she spotted Gabriella Salinas and Rosalie Cork, two of the young women from the kitchen, spying on him with girlish adoration. Portia couldn't fault them. He was gloriously made, an attribute Portia rarely commented on even inwardly. The girls met her eyes, grinned, and quickly ducked back inside.

He worked the axe free and was preparing to swing again when he finally noticed her. Pausing, he took a moment to wipe the sweat from his brow with his sleeve. "Duchess."

She also didn't want to admit the way her senses fluttered when he addressed her thus, a completely different reaction from when she was twelve. "I heard the axe. I thought it was Bailey Durham."

"He the guy who usually does this?"

She nodded. "I came to pay him."

"Ah." He raised the axe and lowered it again. Tossed the split wood onto the pile and began again. "How's your sister?"

"She's doing okay. Mr. Blanchard wouldn't want her holed up in her room being sad so she's going to take care of some deliveries."

"Only met him last night, but I liked him because of the way he stood up for you when Day complained about your uppity mouth."

His eyes were on her mouth and she swallowed with a suddenly dry throat.

He went back to chopping. "Blanchard told him you'd marry a man who appreciated your mouth and if Day didn't, he should take himself out of the running. And I agree."

Her senses leapt like flames. Did that mean he was considering a run for her, too? For a woman determined to remain unmarried, her reactions to him were slowly tearing down the walls she'd encased herself in and she wasn't sure what to do with that.

His next words threw her further off balance. "Rhine asked me to be foreman once he buys Blanchard's place. You and I will need to get together so I can learn how you run the dude ranch."

"Of course. Whenever you're ready we can discuss it." She could hardly keep her walls intact if circumstances kept plotting to throw them together.

He brought the axe down again and she fed her eyes on the way his strong hands gripped the handle and the play of the muscles in his arms.

Gabriella walked up carrying a jug of water. "Mr. Randolph, Mrs. Fontaine thought you might need this," she said. "Rather warm today."

"Thanks." He took the offering and the smile he turned on young woman seemed to melt her where she stood.

"You're welcome."

Seeing Portia watching her, she said, "I should get back to work."

"Wait," he called to her. "What's your name?"

"Gabriella Salinas."

"Thanks again, Gabriella. Tell Mrs. Fontaine thanks, too."

"I will," she tittered as she hurried away.

He raised the jug and took a long drink. A trickle of the water slid down the corner of his mouth and Portia, struck by the urge to lap it up, unconsciously ran her tongue over her lips.

"Do you want some, Duchess?"

His voice was as soft and filled with intent as she imagined a lover's invitation might be. Startled, she shook her head. "No. I—I have to get back to my office."

As she fled from him for the second time that day, she didn't see his knowing smile when he hefted the axe and returned to work.

At dinner that evening, Portia sat across from him at the table, still thinking about her reaction to him and the water jug. She hazarded a look his way and he smiled. Whatever she was coming down with must be serious for her to imagine licking him like a tamed cat. *Or a lover,* quipped an inner voice she'd never heard before. That caught her so off guard, she dropped her fork and it clattered onto her plate.

"Something wrong, Portia?" Eddy asked from her seat at the table.

"No. Just clumsiness on my part. Sorry." Embarrassed, she kept her eyes from Kent's but his presence continued to plague her and she was at a loss as to how to make it stop.

Regan's voice distracted her from her inner turmoil. "I told everyone on my route today about Mr. Blanchard's wake. If all the people who said they'd be stopping by to pay their respects actually come, there won't be enough room in his parlor."

"He was well loved," Rhine said.

"He was," Regan replied somberly. "But you know each time I thought about him today, it was about something that made me smile." She looked over at Portia. "Remember when we were chased by those hornets and had to jump in the pond to escape them?"

She laughed, "I do. Why he didn't wait to smoke them out at night like Tana told him I'll never know."

Regan supplied the answer. "Stubborn."

Portia nodded.

"Who was Tana?" Kent asked.

"An Apache who worked for him," Portia said. "The nest was a good size and it was right under the lip of the porch, so Mr. Blanchard got a ladder—"

"Which Portia and I were holding," Regan added.

Portia grinned. "He lit a torch, climbed the ladder, and tried to set the nest on fire."

Regan laughed, "Those hornets came tearing out of that nest and we dropped the ladder at the same time that he jumped down. They chased us all the way to the pond."

Eddy took up the tale, "The girls came home soaking wet from their braids to their boots."

Regan said, "Tana laughed so hard he fell on the ground."

Kent asked, "Does he still work at the ranch?"

Rhine replied solemnly, "No. He joined Geronimo when he escaped from San Carlos back in '81. Blanchard said he was killed in Mexico during a gun battle with the 6th Cavalry."

Portia remembered how saddened he'd been by the news. She and Regan had been as well. The old Apache taught them many things about life in their new home, and because he refused to speak English, they even spoke a bit of the Apache language.

Kent asked, "So what's the situation with Geronimo now? I think every newspaper in the country covered his surrender last year."

"Tenuous at best," Rhine said. "There are rumors that he's ready to bolt again. Can't blame him. His people are penned up like animals, dying from disease and starvation—soldiers torturing them for sport. I wonder what we Americans would do if somebody with bigger guns invaded us and started stealing our land and killing our kin. We'd go on the warpath, too, I'd bet."

Portia agreed. For the past thirty years the Apache had been doing their best to retake the land their people had lived on for as long as they could remember. Portia couldn't condone the killing and raiding they'd been doing in retaliation, but because the government had broken treaty after treaty, the old chiefs like Geronimo and Cochise felt they had no other choice.

"Have you finished reviewing Blanchard's ledgers?" her uncle asked, interrupting her thoughts and changing the subject.

"I have and everything is in order."

"Good. I'll turn them over to the Landrys' bookkeeper in the morning. Once the sale is finalized Kent will be our foreman."

"He mentioned it earlier." She gave him a quick glance.

"The sooner the two of you can discuss how the place is run, the better."

"How about after we're done here, Portia?" Kent asked.

Portia froze. Lord knew she wanted to come up

with an excuse to delay it. Her reaction to him by the woodpile had left her scandalized enough to last a lifetime, but she knew she had no legitimate reason to weasel out of it. "That would be fine. We can use my office."

"Okay."

Again, she caught herself staring at his lips, the slope of his beard-brushed jaw, his eyes. She quickly dropped her gaze but not before noticing Eddy's slightly raised eyebrow and the silent look she and Rhine passed between themselves. Pretending there was nothing amiss, Portia took a sip of her wine, set the goblet down with a slightly shaky hand, and returned to her meal.

After dinner, she and Regan were in the kitchen cleaning up. Portia was doing her best to ignore the amused look her sister had been wearing since entering, but unable to bear it any longer, she said, "Okay. Out with it. You obviously have something to say."

Hands in the soapy water as she washed the dishes, Regan replied, "Who me?"

"Yes, you. Tell me before I bash you over the head with this last chicken leg."

They shared a smile and Regan mused aloud, "I wonder how long you'd be sentenced by a judge for such a *fowl* deed."

"Lord, save me," Portia groaned in response to the terrible pun, and she shook the leg at Regan. "Tell me!"

"I was just watching you and Kent."

"And?"

Regan mimed pulling back the string on a bow and letting an invisible arrow fly. "Right between the eyes."

Portia shook her head. "So now you're a mime?"

"No, I'm Cupid and don't pretend you've no idea what I mean. You were looking at the man like he was a piece of chocolate cake."

Portia put the last of the leftover chicken in a bowl, covered it with a plate and placed it in the cold box. "I was not."

"Yes, you were. Aunt Eddy and Uncle Rhine saw it, too. It's nothing to be ashamed of. Kent's terribly handsome."

Portia picked up a kitchen towel and busied herself drying the wet dishes Regan had set in the drain.

"So you aren't going to admit he's handsome either?" Regan asked.

"I don't have to admit anything to you, Regan Marie." They were playfully bantering the way they'd been doing their entire lives.

"Just wait until he pulls you into a corner and kisses you until your garters catch fire."

"You're always so scandalous."

"You're going to be scandalous, too, when he cracks your highly prized control like a dropped hen's egg."

"That will not happen."

Regan studied her and said earnestly, "You need a nice man in your life, sister mine."

"My life is fine just the way it is."

"Okay," Regan said softly. "I just want you to be happy, Portia. You've earned it. We both have."

"I've been happy since the day Aunt Eddy and Uncle Rhine saved us. I don't need anything more."

Regan nodded and went back to washing. Her solemnity pulled at Portia's heart but they finished the rest of the task in silence.

Seated in her office while waiting for Kent to join her, Portia thought back on her sister's words and on the incident at the woodpile. *What's wrong with me?* She was twenty-seven years old, far past the age of being rendered mindless by a man, yet here she sat. Granted Kent was more handsome than a man had a right to be, but what she sensed about him beneath the surface was attractive as well. He was funny, treated her respectfully, and unlike some of the other men she knew, he didn't think her odd or less than a woman for managing the hotel. In fact, he seemed quite impressed by her business sense, and during the party, he'd even brought her a piece of cake. A small thing yes, but it had been a kind gesture nonetheless. However, she had life planned out with the goal of forming her own bookkeeping business at some point in the near future, and a man wouldn't be penciled into the ledger, no matter how tempting she thought him to be. Having always prided herself on approaching difficult situations head-on she spent a few moments mulling over her options. It occurred to her that her thoughts about children building up an immunity to the pox might be a solution. Maybe if she asked him to kiss her, it would feed her attraction enough to bring about a cure for what ailed her. Lord knew she needed one because she'd never wanted to lick a man's mouth before in her life. Her mind slid back to the image of the water trailing sinuously down corners of his lips and when her senses rose again, she hastily forced the image away. Yes, she needed a cure because the sooner she did away with this distracting attraction the better off she'd be.

Kent assumed that when he and Portia met to talk about the dude ranch, she would sit behind her desk, tell him what he needed to know, and send him on his merry way, but he wanted to spend some time with her, preferably away from her office. Even though he was supposed to be keeping his distance, he wanted to know her better. He was intrigued by both her beauty and the intense smarts underneath. She was no meek wallflower waiting to be picked and he liked that, too. He wondered if she'd be agreeable to talking outside. There were still a few hours of daylight left and they could conduct their business at one of the tables. That way he could enjoy her along with the view of the mountains and the cooling breeze. He might even be able to make her smile. He got the impression she didn't share her smile much outside of family, so when he stuck his head in her office, he asked, "How about we talk outdoors? It's too nice an evening to be cooped up inside." He saw her hesitate.

She finally responded. "Sure, okay."

Outside, they sat at the table opposite each other. As he savored the sight of her and the sounds of the breeze playing against the leaves, he said, "This is much better than being inside, don't you think?"

"I do."

"So, tell me what I need to know."

Rhine had already given him a brief explanation of how the dude ranch worked, but Portia's was more detailed. In truth though, only part of him was listening because the others were wondering how she'd react if he kissed her, what scent she wore hidden beneath the high collared blouses she favored, and how he might go about achieving answers to those questions.

"Kent? Are you listening?"

"Sorry. Got distracted there for a moment. Did you ask me something?"

"Yes. Do you know any stories about outlaws,

ghosts, or lost gold? It's something the guests look forward to around the campfire during supper."

"I do."

The look on her face said she didn't believe him.

"Do you know the 'Legend of La Llorana'?"

"No."

He deepened his voice and slowed the cadence. "A woman in white drags helpless children to a screaming watery death."

She looked so startled he almost smiled. "Or, I could tell the story of the hell dogs of Eldorado where large ferocious ghost dogs haunt the abandoned mines in Nevada. You can hear them dragging their chains, but you never see them."

He continued. "El Muerte, the headless horseman. He rides the plains of Texas with his severed head hanging from his saddle." He grabbed her arm and she jumped.

"Stop that," she demanded with a laugh. She studied him for a long moment. "How many stories like that do you know?"

He enjoyed surprising her again. "A fair amount. I worked on a spread in Montana and there was an old cook who had more tales than a porcupine has spines. He kept us entertained on the long winter nights. Impressed?"

"Yes. That's just the type of story the guests will want. Thank you."

"You're welcome. I like impressing you. Only

because it seems most men don't. Impress you I mean."

"I want you to kiss me."

Caught off guard, he froze. "I'm sorry. I must've misheard you. Say that again."

She looked irritated. "I want you to kiss me."

"May I ask why?"

"I need to cure myself of whatever these feelings are I'm starting to have for you, and don't ask me what feelings. You know what I mean."

"I do," he said as he studied her gorgeous ebony face. She looked so put out he wanted to smile but kept his features bland. "Have you ever been kissed before?"

"No."

"Then I should warn you that this probably won't cure you, Duchess. In fact, it might make matters worse."

"I don't think it will."

He sat back and folded his arms. "And you think this because . . ."

"Once I know what it feels like I should be able to manage it from now on."

"Like you manage a ledger or the hotel?"

"Maybe not quite the same thing, but in a way, yes."

"Woman, you are going to be in so much trouble."

She refused to meet his eyes and he couldn't

help the soft chuckle that slipped out. "So much trouble." As the silence lengthened he asked, "Are you sure about this?"

"I am."

Kent pondered the proposal for a second or two, weighed the pros and cons and, because he couldn't come up with any of the latter, said, "Okay. Get your horse. Let's go for a ride. If Rhine sees us kissing, he'll geld me." Maybe one con. "And, Duchess, this isn't going to be a Sunday school peck on the cheek. Do you still want to do this?"

"Yes."

Portia left him and went inside and found Rhine and Eddy in the sitting room. "I'm going to show Kent the waterfall. We'll be back shortly."

Interest filled their eyes, but before they could react further, she went to her room to change into a riding skirt. With that accomplished, she quickly headed to the stables to saddle her mare, Arizona. *This is going to be a real kiss from a real man.* Second thoughts about her plan began to rise. What if he was right about a kiss only making matters worse? A part of her wanted to turn tail and run but she had never run from anything and was not about to start now. She could handle this.

When she rode up he was on his stallion waiting beneath the big wooden arch that held the sign with the hotel's name.

As she neared, his roan reared in challenge,

but Kent kept his seat easily. "Stop showing off," he said to the stallion, but it reared again, eyes on the mare, and Arizona backed away.

Kent told Portia, "He's just letting your mare know he's interested. How old is she?"

"Four."

"She ever been mounted?"

The question had Portia's second thoughts flooding her mind, but she managed to answer, "No. Can we go now?"

He touched his hat. "After you."

She turned Arizona and they rode at a slow pace away from the hotel. Her mare had never been mounted and neither had she. As the daughter of a prostitute, Portia had witnessed her mother coupling with men on more than a few occasions. Because their one-bedroom shack had been so small, it was nearly impossible to avoid. She remembered her mother's dispassionate face as the grunting men rutted over her with their pants pulled down and their behinds bared. It was an activity she'd vowed to avoid because it hadn't looked pleasurable or pleasant. In fact, her mother didn't seem to feel anything at all, leaving the then young Portia with the impression that it was an emotionless exercise. But being around Eddy and Rhine showed her how wrong her impressions had been. Her aunt and uncle loved and cared for each other in a way she would probably never know. Their connection was so passionate it was almost embarrassing to be around them sometimes. But Portia didn't want passion from Kent, just a kiss so she'd know what it felt like, and once that was accomplished, her inner curiosity would be satisfied and she'd be fine.

When they reached the spot she'd picked out, she pulled back on Arizona's reins. The gray rock canyon was one of her favorite places because it held the waterfall she and her sister had named Carmichael Falls. She dismounted. Leaving Arizona to graze on the sparse grass she walked towards the falls.

He dismounted and came up beside her, "Nice spot."

"We bring the guests here. Many have never seen a waterfall and they're always awed by the sight."

"Can you get closer to the water?"

"Only on foot. Regan and I used to come here when we were younger and swim in the pool below. It's quite a hike to thread your way through the canyons but well worth it."

"Never pegged you for a swimmer."

"Why not?"

He shrugged. "You seem too serious for something as carefree as swimming."

"I have my moments."

"Sorry. Didn't mean to offend you."

Portia was terribly nervous and she didn't like

it. She was a lot more confident when in control of herself and the situation. "Let's get this over with. I told Eddy and Rhine we'd be back shortly." When he shook his head and smiled, she asked, "What?"

"This isn't something you rush into if you want to do it right. I assume you do want to do it right."

Portia didn't know what she wanted but, grabbing hold of her nerves, she replied with a firmness she didn't feel. "Yes."

"Okay, come walk with me." He held out his hand.

She glanced down at it and then back up into his eyes. Reminding herself that she'd asked for this, she placed her hand in his and the sweet warmth that slid into her blood made her tremble both inside and out. He upped the ante by gently threading his fingers through hers and it felt so natural it was almost terrifying to a woman who'd spent her entire life certain she'd never be moved by any man. When he raised her hand and placed a soft kiss on her fingertips, her emotions swelled with such force her legs wobbled and her eyes closed for a long second. When they opened again, his were waiting but he didn't speak. Still holding her hand, he started for the canyon.

There were a few trees lining the canyon's lip and he stopped them there. Usually the sight of the water cascading down was enough to steal her breath, but because of his presence and what was about to come, the vista barely registered.

"So," he said softly. "Let's give you this kiss . . ."

He released her hand and when he slowly traced a finger down her cheek, the resulting spark was so startling, she jumped.

Amusement shone in his eyes. "I can see you're going to manage this real well, Duchess."

She came to her own defense. "You—you surprised me. I thought you were going to kiss me not touch me."

"Touching's important sometimes. You don't want a man to just grab you and plant his lips on yours. There's no passion in that."

"I don't want pass . . ." The word died as his finger boldly traced her bottom lip. All thought fled.

"I don't think this uppity mouth knows what it wants," he husked out, and when he kissed her what little control Portia still possessed tumbled away like wind-blown autumn leaves.

"Make your lips soft, baby."

Mindless, she complied and was swept away. He taught her thoroughly and completely just what a kiss entailed, and no, she'd had no idea. The heat in it, the fire in it made her moan in response. She didn't know when he eased her in against his body but it felt so right she wanted his strength closer. She wrapped her arms around him and hoped the large hand moving slowly and possessively up and down the back of her blouse wouldn't stop. Her lips parted of their own accord giving his searing tongue access to hers, and it cajoled, seduced, and tutored until she was mimicking the lesson willingly. Breathless, she wanted to be kissed by him forever, only to have him gently turn her loose and step away.

It took a few moments for Portia's mind to climb up from wherever the kiss had sent it and for her eyes to open. When they did, he was there.

"Now you've been kissed . . . with passion."

She couldn't deny it but told herself she didn't have to like it, even though she had. Very much.

"Still think you can manage what you felt like a ledger or the hotel?"

"I'm ready to go back."

"Made things worse, didn't it? Told you so. I can give you another if you think it might help."

"I'm leaving." If she didn't, she'd be begging for more and she was already appalled enough by her uninhibited response.

"Okay, but I did enjoy kissing your uppity mouth. You're a very passionate woman, Duchess."

She turned and stalked back the way they'd come.

As they rode home in silence Kent decided he

was going to have a real difficult time staying away from her after this. She had no idea how tempting she'd looked with her eyes closed and her mouth swollen from his kisses. He'd had to turn her loose to stop them from slipping into territory not ready to be explored. She was far more passionate than she knew and her uncle notwithstanding, he wanted to be the man to gently coax that passion to the surface. He wasn't sure how to accomplish that and not be turned into a eunuch but he was thoroughly captivated by the force of nature known as Miss Portia Carmichael, so he'd figure it out. He glanced over. Outwardly, she was tight-lipped but looked none the worse for wear. He wondered what might be going on inside, though. Was the kiss still resonating within her as it was for him? Would she continue to fight the passion she'd allowed herself to enjoy, and what might it be like when she surrendered to it fully? Of course, there was no guarantee she would, but he had a feeling that she'd dug a hole for herself that she was going to have a lot of trouble climbing out of.

Later, alone in her room, Portia paced. No matter how hard she tried, she couldn't rid herself of the memory of her first kiss. He'd made her so breathless, it was a wonder she'd been able to mount Arizona and ride home. And Lord help her, she wanted more. A hundred times more. More of his palm moving over her spine, more of his hard body against her soft one, more of his seeking tongue. She hated to admit it, but he'd been right about it only exacerbating the problem. She felt as if she'd lost her mind.

A soft knock on the connecting door interrupted her inner tirade. "Come in," she all but snarled.

Regan entered, took one look at Portia's face and asked, "What's wrong? Aunt Eddy said you and Kent went riding. Did you two argue?"

"No," she replied tersely.

Regan studied her silently for a long moment and then asked with a grin. "Did he kiss you, sister mine?"

The snap in Portia's eyes was her reply.

Regan stilled. "Without your consent."

"No of course not."

"Then, knowing you, I'm assuming you're mad because you didn't believe it would be so wonderful."

"Let's just say I had trouble remembering my name afterwards."

Regan laughed. "I think I'm jealous."

Portia blew out a breath. "What a naïve ninny I am."

"Portia, you can look at that cowboy and know he can kiss."

Portia threw her a quelling look.

"Sorry," her sister offered contritely, but amusement continued to play at the corners of her lips.

"I asked him to kiss me, thinking I'd be able to control my reaction."

"You asked him?"

"I did."

"Some things can't be controlled."

"I understand that now, which means no kissing Kent Randolph."

"If you couldn't remember your name, I'm thinking you're not going to have much control over the future either, but I wish you luck."

Seeing the humor in that, Portia sighed, "I'm doomed aren't I?"

"I believe so."

"You're supposed to offer me hope."

"I'm your sister, I'm supposed to offer you the truth, so when should I begin looking for a gown to wear to the wedding?"

Portia's eyes widened and she laughed. "Wash your mouth out with soap, you horrid girl."

The grinning Regan walked over and gave Portia a peck on the cheek. "Good night, Portia. I used to practice my kissing on the back of my hair brush. You might want to try it."

Portia firmed her lips to keep from laughing. "Good night, Regan."

Regan exited.

Alone, Portia wondered what she'd do without her silly little sister. Her eyes strayed to her hair brush lying on the vanity table. Chuckling, she turned away and prepared for bed.

Later, lying there in the dark, she once again weighed her options. She decided she wasn't doomed. All she had to do was not ask for anymore of his kisses and she'd be fine. Problem solved. A voice inside laughed, but she ignored it and burrowed down to sleep.

CHAPTER FIVE

Portia and Regan entered the dining room for breakfast just as Kent was bringing a steaming bowl of scrambled eggs out of the kitchen. Seeing him brought back memories of their smoldering encounter at the canyon and Portia was torn between looking at him and not. He seemed to have no such problem.

"Morning, ladies. Help yourself to the eggs if you like."

Regan picked up a plate. "There's something special about a man who knows his way around a skillet. Don't you think so, Portia?"

"I suppose" was all she allowed herself to say. A quick glance showed him watching her. She returned his gaze steadily, her way of showing she was again in control, but as if he knew his kiss had been her first conscious thought upon awakening, his eyes sparkled with teasing amusement.

Eddy followed him out with a platter of biscuits and set it down by the eggs. "Thanks for your help with breakfast, Kent. You're going to make some woman very happy one day."

Mentally shaking her head, Portia picked up a plate and helped herself to the offerings. When she was done she took a seat across from Regan, whose knowing grin she promptly ignored. Kent set his plate down beside Regan and everyone started in on their meal.

"What time are we leaving for Mr. Blanchard's wake this evening?" Portia asked her aunt.

"Around six or so. Kent, would you care to go with us? I know you didn't know him."

"I talked with Rhine about it and I'd like to pay my respects."

"Then you're welcome. Buggy only sits four so you'll have to ride."

"I prefer horseback so that's not a problem."

Portia wondered when he'd take over as fore-man of the Blanchard ranch. Once he stepped into the role, he'd be living over there, which would give her the distance from him that she needed. Granted, because of the dude ranch partnership, she wouldn't be able to avoid him totally, but with him not living at the hotel maybe she could focus on something beside the way she'd felt in his arms, the sensual play of his tongue on hers, and the way he whispered, *Make your lips soft, baby*. Shaking herself free from the torrid memory, she looked up as Rhine entered the room.

"Well, look who's joining us this morning," the smiling Eddy called out.

He grinned, gave his wife a quick kiss on the cheek, and whispered something to her that only she could hear. She smacked him playfully on the arm, and as he moved away to grab a plate, Portia saw the passion in her aunt's eyes. What must it be like to fully embrace such feelings, she wondered, especially knowing it was returned in equal measure? A few days ago, Regan had asked a similar question and Portia had been so dismissive she was now ashamed of her response.

Rhine took the chair beside Eddy, saying, "The only reason I'm up at this ungodly hour is to ride into Tucson to pick up a bank draft and stop in at the Landrys to hand over Blanchard's ledgers." He looked to Kent and asked, "Would you like to ride with me?"

"Sure. It'll give me a chance to get a look at the town."

"We'll leave once we're done eating." Rhine then turned his attention to Portia. "Which falls did you take Kent to see?"

She drew in a deep breath and said nonchalantly, "Carmichael Falls. I told him how much the guests enjoyed the view."

"I assume he was a gentleman?"

While living with her mother, Corinne, Portia learned at a young age how to keep her emotions masked. "Yes, he was." She met her uncle's gaze steadily and didn't allow her eyes to stray to Kent.

Kent weighed in. "I'll always be on my best behavior with her, Fontaine, so quit your worrying." He saluted Rhine with his coffee cup.

Portia didn't know Kent well enough to tell if Rhine's question had offended him but everyone went back to eating and making small talk so she relaxed and shot him a covert glance. He responded with a secretive smile.

After breakfast, while Rhine and Kent went to take care of the business in Tucson, Portia, Regan, and Eddy headed to the kitchen to see about the food the hotel would be contributing to the wake. They were greeted by the fragrant smell of chicken frying, Gabriella and Rosalie making potato salad and dumplings, and Sarah rolling out dough for the apple pies, Mr. Blanchard's favorite. As Eddy and Regan took down aprons, Portia, not the best of cooks, asked, "Anything I can help with?"

"No!" all five said in unison, and then they laughed. Portia did as well. She could balance a ledger with her eyes closed and standing on her head, but she couldn't boil water. Watching Regan begin peeling apples and Eddy take her rolling pin to the dough, Portia asked, "How many pies do you think you've made for Mr. Blanchard since we moved here?"

"Hundreds probably. He did enjoy them. I think he'll be pleased that Rhine's buying his place."

Portia agreed. The two men had gotten along well. The old man had been instrumental in recruiting the army of workers and artisans the Fontaines needed to build the hotel.

Eddy fit the rolled-out dough into a pie tin. "Everything ready for our new dude ranch guests?"

"Yes." They'd be arriving in a few days. "Mr. Blanchard's death may complicate things but as long as Farley and Buck stay around until the visit ends, it should go well."

"How many people are in the party?"

"Only four. Two are doctors. One's bringing his mother and another his sister. They're from San Francisco but are stopping here on their way home from a medical convention back East."

Eddy looked up. "Kent's father, Oliver, wanted him to be a doctor."

"I know."

She rolled out another circle of dough. "He didn't finish medical school though. The only thing Kent ever wanted to be was a rancher, but he attended to appease Oliver. That he's grown into such a fine man is a bit surprising."

"Why?"

"He was quite the cat house king back in Virginia City. A lot spoiled and very full of himself where the ladies were concerned."

"Really?" Portia didn't know anything about his comings and goings. She'd been too busy adjusting to her new life with Eddy and Rhine.

Eddy smiled. "Yes he was. The young Kent I knew back then would never have cooked his

97

own breakfast. Ever. Like I said this morning, he'll make some woman very happy one day if he's as mature as he appears to be."

Eddy glanced up and eyed Portia speculatively.

"Yes?" Portia hoped her aunt had no prying questions about what took place at the falls. Eddy had always been perceptive.

"Nothing. Let me get back to these pies. Regan, hand me that jar of cinnamon."

Grabbing an unpeeled apple from a bowl, Portia left the kitchen and headed outside to say good morning to Arizona. Her mare along with Eddy's mare, Denver, and Regan's Catalina were out in the paddock enjoying the sunshine. Cal Grissom, the old gray-haired cowboy who'd ridden the Chisolm Trail was the hotel's head groom. He was seated on the top rung of the fence, keeping an eye on his charges.

"Morning, Miss Portia."

"Good morning, Mr. Grissom. Did you enjoy the visit with your sister?" He'd returned last night from visiting his recently widowed sister in Phoenix.

He nodded. "I did and she's doing well considering."

"I'm sure she was pleased to see you."

"Yes, she was."

"Have you met Uncle Rhine's friend Kent Randolph yet?"

"I have. I met him before he and Mr. Fontaine rode off. He seems like a nice enough man. His stallion's sweet on your Arizona. Saw them courting earlier this morning. You might want to start thinking about names for a foal."

Portia went still.

He laughed. "Don't look so shocked. She was bound to find her a fella sooner or later."

Portia knew he was right, but . . . She shook herself free of the thought. "I brought her a treat."

"You go ahead. I'll be in the tack room if you need me."

He walked away with the slow easy stride that all cowboys seemed to have and she whistled between her fingers for her mare. The Appaloosa came galloping to the fence and Portia hugged her neck affectionately. "Brought you something."

The mare took a bite out of the apple Portia held. "I hear you're being courted. Are you sure you're ready for motherhood?"

There was no answer of course. Portia couldn't imagine her lovely mare heavy with a foal but knew nature would run its course. Her thoughts slid to Kent and wondered what nature had in store for her. Hastily backing away from that, she watched Arizona for a few moments longer then left her to play while she went to her office to look over the duty roster tied to the hotel's soon-to-arrive guests.

• • •

As Kent and Rhine rode across the desert, Kent asked, "So tell me about Tucson. What's it like here?"

"Much sleepier than Virginia City," Rhine replied. "It's growing though, now that the Southern Pacific has come to town. Politically, lots of shenanigans."

"You involved?"

"Behind the scenes."

"Because of what happened in Virginia City."

"Yes. I'm not putting Eddy and the girls in harm's way ever again. Portia had nightmares for months about that mob."

Kent had been with them that night. He'd helped Rhine and Jim Dade hastily pack the family's essentials into the wagon they'd escaped in only a few minutes before the mob arrived. On horseback, he'd fled, too, but only far enough to watch from a safe distance as the men of Virginia City set fire to the Fontaine home, Rhine's saloon, and Eddy's new diner. That Portia had experienced nightmares from the cowardly deed added to the lingering embers of rage he still carried inside. Escaping with little more than his life and the women he loved had to have made Rhine seek a new direction. For those in Virginia City's Colored community the atmosphere after the fires had been tense. Because Rhine was beyond reach, threats were made against those who'd remained behind. Men like Kent's father were confronted and roughed up, but when Rhine and his banker half brother, Andrew, began taking financial revenge, the bigots suddenly found themselves too busy scrambling to keep their homes and business out of foreclosure to further exhibit their hate and disdain. "How are you and the family treated here?"

Rhine shrugged. "Not bad. Everyone is too busy looking over their shoulders for the Apaches still up in the mountains to worry too much about race. Many Mexicans live here of course and Chinese, too, because of the railroads."

They entered the town proper a short while later. As they slowly rode down the main street, they passed myriad shops and saloons and, yes, it was much smaller than Virginia City. They rode past the large Cathedral of St. Augustine with its adjacent convent, and Rhine related that some of the streets like Pennington and Jackson were named after men who'd been killed in Apache attacks. There were quite a few people of various races on the wooden walks and a decent number of riders and wagons in the street. Kent was surprised to see a river on the edge of town and the stand of orchards fronting it.

"Apples," Rhine explained.

Kent was still pondering the oddness of apples in the desert as Rhine reined his mount to a halt in front of a small adobe home. "This is where the Landrys live."

They tied up their mounts, walked to the door, and knocked. Once inside, Kent was introduced to Old Man Blanchard's daughter, Missy Landry, a short buxom woman with very large teeth. She nodded a greeting and introduced her accountant, a tall balding man named Alistair Gerber.

"Do you have the bank draft?" she asked Rhine. "I do."

Any grief her watery blue eyes may have held for her father was elbowed aside by a flash of eager greed.

"And the ledgers," Rhine added, handing them to her.

"And I have the deed," she said. "Shall we get down to business?"

Gerber looked startled. "Mrs. Landry, my advice is to let me take a day or two to look over the books to make sure everything is sound. After all, that's why you hired me."

She waved him off. "Only reason I hired you was to appease my husband, Charlie, but since he had to leave for St. Louis yesterday to see about his sainted mother, I've decided I don't need your advice. Portia's been the only person handling the books, Mr. Fontaine?"

Rhine nodded.

The accountant stared. "Portia? Is she a woman?"

Rhine replied coolly, "Yes."

Missy said, "She went to Oberlin. Smart as a whip and more honest than the sun in the sky. Here's the deed, Rhine."

Rhine took the papers, read through them slowly, and said, "This looks fine, Missy."

"Good."

Once signatures were attached in the appropriate places, Rhine folded the document and placed it in his inner coat pocket. He handed her the bank draft.

"Thanks," she said. "Nice doing business with you."

"Same here."

"Now, wait just a minute," Gerber protested. "What about my fee?"

"Send me a bill if you want," she said, "but do it quickly. I'll be leaving town the day after the funeral."

"Are you going to join your husband in St. Louis?" Rhine asked.

"No, but you can tell him that's where I was headed when he comes back and finds me gone."

Kent's jaw dropped.

Rhine stared.

She smiled coldly. "Been trying to get away from him and this place for years. Now"—she waved the draft—"I can. I'll see you tonight at the wake, gentlemen."

A stunned Kent followed Rhine back outside to where their tethered mounts waited.

"Interesting woman," Kent quipped.

"That's one way of describing her," Rhine responded.

"Will the deed hold up?"

"I've never known her to be dishonest."

"Can it be challenged because of your race?"

Rhine shrugged. "Anything is possible, I suppose, but she has no other kin, and the land will be rolled into the company my brother, Drew, and I founded, which is based in San Francisco. My interests are hidden."

They mounted and headed back to the main part of town.

Kent asked, "Do you know a place where I can buy a couple of shirts, but not have to put any money in the coffers of that ass Day?"

Rhine laughed. "Sure do."

The store owned by a short German immigrant named Krause had just what Kent needed. After purchasing the shirts, he spied a dark gray Stetson on display that seemed to call his name. The price was dear but it was a hat he'd be able to wear to fancy occasions for years to come as long as he took good care of it, so he counted out the money for it, too, and he and Rhine left the store.

On the ride back, Kent asked, "Did you question Blanchard's hands about their plans?"

"I spoke with the two older men. He left them

a fair amount of money in his will and they'll be leaving to enjoy it elsewhere. The other two weren't around."

"So, I may have to hire all new depending on whether the others stay?"

"Looks that way."

Kent wasn't sure whether he was disappointed or not, but at least the men he hired would be his men and there'd be no divided loyalties.

CHAPTER SIX

Upstairs in what had been Blanchard's bedroom, Kent eyed the sorry cards in his hands and fought to keep his disgust from showing. Across the table, Rhine smiled. Kent sighed. He hated playing poker with Rhine mainly because that smile meant he either had the best cards in the house or a handful of nothing like Kent, but there was no way of telling which. The other two players, rancher Howard Lane and Cal Grissom, the hotel's horse wrangler, had already tossed in their hands. That left Kent and Rhine. Kent assessed Rhine, hoping to find any flaw in the ivory face that might give away what he actually held, but it was the same elusive flaw Kent had been searching for unsuccessfully since he began playing poker with Rhine at the age of fifteen back in Virginia City. Cursing inwardly, Kent threw his hand in, too. Grinning, Rhine showed his humble pair of threes and slid the large stack of chips over to the small mountain already in place in front of him.

"I hate you, old man," Kent groused, chuckling.

"*Rich* old man, to you," Rhine countered, and the other men in the smoke-filled room laughed.

Kent pushed back his chair. "I'm leaving before you take my new Stetson."

"Smart man." Rhine then called out, "Next!"

Hoping the new pigeons fared better than he had, Rhine left the room to get some food.

Kent had been to a host of wakes in his time. Many were solemn and others so raucous the only thing missing were *nymphes du pavé*. Blanchard's was somewhere in between. There was plenty of good food, lots of drink, and a houseful of men and women talking, laughing, and raising glasses to the man inside the wooden coffin resting on sawhorses by the window in the front parlor.

The noise grew louder as he descended the stairs. There seemed to be even more people squeezed into the house than when they arrived if that was possible. He was searching the crowd for Portia when Regan appeared at his side.

"If you're looking for my sister, she's outside with Eddy and the other married hens."

"How'd you know I was looking for Portia?"

"Who else would it be?"

He studied her amidst the press of bodies, the buzz of voices, and the occasional loud cackle of laughter.

"Just be patient with her," Regan advised. "Being raised the way we were has left her somewhat mixed-up inside."

"And what about you?" he asked gently.

"I'm mixed up, too, but I'm not afraid of myself the way Portia is sometimes."

Her honesty made him go still. "Thank you for the advice."

She shrugged. "You're welcome. I told her you're going to make her garters catch fire. She's choosing not to believe me."

Kent threw back his head and laughed. Regan was destined to give some man a run for his money in the future, too. He hoped to be around to watch.

"See you later," she said before disappearing into the crowd.

Kent made his way to the buffet and thought about what Regan had revealed. He didn't really understand what she'd meant about Portia being afraid of herself sometimes. He knew about their mother and that she'd mailed her young daughters to Eddy in Virginia City unaccompanied. Admittedly he and his father had locked horns while he was growing up. Having lost his mother during his birth, Kent spent a lot of time being resentful because Oliver's profession kept him away from home more than he wanted, but he'd never treated Kent as less than his son—nor had he ever sent him away. That Portia's mother had must have been painful. Was Portia's cast-iron demeanor something she used to protect her still-fragile feelings? Had she and her sister heard from their mother? Kent found this all very interesting and it further stoked his need to learn more about her. With his plate now filled, he made his way through the pandemonium and headed for the door so he could get some fresh air and find Portia.

Portia was glad to be outside with Eddy and her friends and not in the madness going on inside Mr. Blanchard's ranch house. Like some of the other people attending they were seated on blankets spread out on the ground beneath a small stand of pondcrosa pincs. Portia cnjoycd her aunt Eddy's friends because they were all forward-thinking women and did what they could to uplift the race with their volunteer work in the community and their support of women's suffrage. At the moment they were discussing a women's convention being held in San Francisco in a few weeks and the prospect of them all attending.

"So are we decided?" Eddy asked.

Everyone nodded except Mamie Cordell, the wife of the African Methodist Episcopal pastor and the mother of Portia's suitor James. "I'll have to see if my Bertram will let me go," she confessed. "You know he's not a forward-thinking man sometimes."

Eunice Forth, Mamie's sister, groaned, "Oh my goodness, Mamie, I told you twenty years ago not to marry that man."

Julia Lane, said, "So did I."

"I thought he'd change."

"Into who, Fred Douglass?" her sister asked. "Even with all his personal scandals, Fred the Great supports women's suffrage."

Suffrage for women continued to be one of the most widely discussed topics on the nation's agenda. More and more women of the race were jumping on the bandwagon even as some White women were doing their best to keep their darker sisters away from their conventions. In response, the Colored women were sponsoring their own conferences and the gathering being held in San Francisco would be one.

Apparently knowing she was losing her battle, Mamie said, "I'm changing the subject. Portia, when are you going to give my son, James, the time of day?"

Portia sighed. Before she could explain to Mrs. Cordell for the two hundredth time why she had no plans to marry, her son or anyone else, Eddy came to her rescue. "Mamie, you know he and Portia would never suit. James is much too shy. He hardly says a word when he's near her."

"But marriage may change that."

Julia laughed. "The same way you marrying Bertram changed him? Leave our Portia alone. As much as I love my husband, Howard, had times then been like they are now, I may have chosen not to marry either."

Eunice added, "Stick to your guns, Portia. If you don't wish to marry, don't. You young women have opportunities we old hens never even imagined having. You're doctors and teachers. You're working in banks and writing for newspapers. All we were expected to do was marry and birth children."

Portia loved them all. They'd been a supportive group of mother hens since she was young. When she and Regan went to Oberlin, the ladies took turns writing to them and occasionally sent little gifts like ear bobs, combs for their hair, and writing tablets and pens to let them know they were thought of and loved.

With the issue of her courting stance tabled, the conversation moved back to the convention and speculation as to who the sponsors might bring in as the main speaker. Portia hoped it would be Frances Watkins Harper the former abolitionist she'd always wanted to hear speak. Portia was about to say that when a harried-looking Missy Landry came over to where they were sitting and asked, "Ladies, can you give me a hand in the kitchen? The girls I hired have to go home and I need to fry more chicken."

Portia couldn't believe all the chicken Eddy and her friends supplied was gone but the crowd was a large one. Since it was well-known that she'd be of little assistance, the ladies gathered up their blankets and followed Missy, leaving Portia alone. Before she could get to her feet and make her way back to the house to find Regan,

James Cordell walked up and said shyly, "Hello, Miss Portia. How are you?"

She looked up. "Hello, James." Given the way he kept glancing from her to the blanket, she assumed he was waiting for an invitation to join her. She got to her feet instead, just as Darian Day walked up. Wondering what she'd done to deserve such a boon, the situation went from bad to worse when Edward Salt suddenly appeared. Why he was at the wake was beyond her since she was pretty sure he didn't even know Mr. Blanchard. The men all began talking at once, but James, apparently intimidated by the blustering Day stood silently while Salt did his best to lord it over Day with pompous boasting about his Howard education and the school he planned to open. Portia felt a headache coming on.

When Kent walked up, the posturing and bluster petered out into silence and she wanted to shout with joy.

"Gentlemen," he said. "How are you this evening?" His eyes brushed Portia's and as if he'd read her silent plea, he handed her his plate. "Brought you a plate," he said as if they were alone. Salt and Day both bristled. Cordell's thin lips tightened.

"Thank you." She sat down again and placed the plate on the blanket beside her. Day, dressed in a brown and gray window pane suit, sneered, "New shirt, Randolph?"

Kent studied him for a silent moment. His hands moved to his gun belt and the three wide eyed men took a quick step back. Watching them with a smile that didn't reach his eyes, he slowly untied the strings of the belt, removed it and the Colt it held, then sat at her side—bold as day. Finally, in reply to Day's question, he said, "Yes. Bought it from Mr. Krause. Nice man." He didn't add more.

As the silence lengthened, Cordell waked away without a word. Day and Edward Salt seemed to want to challenge his presence but apparently thought better of it because they stayed just long enough to glare their displeasure before moving off.

Watching them go, he asked her, "How in the world did you get trapped out here with them?"

Portia saw the curiosity on the faces of some of the other people seated nearby and wondered if sitting with Kent would cause gossip, but she went ahead and told him about Eddy and the other ladies leaving her to help in the kitchen.

"You didn't want to help?"

She smiled ruefully. "Let's just say I'm better with numbers than I am with pots."

"Can't cook, huh?"

"No."

"Then you'll need a man who can."

"Are you volunteering?"

He shrugged. "If it'll keep you from starving

to death, I suppose I can make myself available, if called upon."

She wondered if he had this effect on all women.

"How's the managing of that passion going?" he asked.

Her heart thumped. "Fine." His eyes were so piercing, she trembled in response.

"You're fibbing of course, but that's okay."

"I am not."

"Uh-huh."

She leaned closer so they wouldn't be overheard. "I am not. One kiss was all I needed and now I'm fine, just as I said I would be."

"Duchess, your uppity mouth's been wanting another taste all day."

Heat sent her senses galloping. "It has not, and stop calling it that."

"Okay. Your *sweet* mouth has been wanting another taste all day."

She almost keeled over.

"I do like those high-collared blouses you wear."

She looked down at herself.

"Makes me want to undo all the little buttons and see how you manage with my kisses against your bare throat. Curious about what scent you place there, too."

Her eyes widened.

He smiled. "No?"

"No."

"Okay. Just something for you to think about later. Do you want the legs or the wings?"

Her mind was stuck like it had stepped in tar. How in the world was she going to remain unmoved by his teasing ways without wanting to box his ears or wonder how his kisses would feel against bare throat? "I'll take the wings."

"We have only one set of flatware. Shall I feed you or do you want to feed me?"

Scandalized by the suggestion, she forced herself not to glance around to see how closely they were being observed. "Neither," she said. "I'll have the wing. You can eat the rest."

"Thought I'd ask."

They ate in silence, sharing the occasional glance. Him smiling. Her not.

Regan walked up. "How are you two?"

He replied, "We're fine. At least I am. Your sister's managing, I believe."

Portia wanted to punch him in the nose.

Regan said, "I told him about your garters catching fire, Portia."

Portia choked on a bite of chicken and before she could punch her sister in the nose, the smiling Regan walked back towards the house.

"I like her," he said.

"Then maybe you should direct your attention her way."

"I prefer the challenge of you."

In response, her body bloomed like a rose opening to the sun.

As if oblivious to his effects on her, he added, "So, now we have two items on your management list: me kissing your throat and your garters catching fire. Are you writing all this down?"

She firmed her lips to keep her smile hidden. "No. I think I can remember."

"You sure?"

They were so close to each other she could feel the kiss about to come. "If you kiss me in front of all these people, I will hit you so hard you'll wake up in Florida."

He laughed with such gusto he fell back on the blanket. Her humor died upon seeing Rhine watching them from a few feet away. "Here comes Uncle Rhine."

He sat up and was still smiling when Rhine arrived.

Hoping to distract her uncle, she asked, "Why is Edward Salt here? Kent saved me from having to endure his company."

"And from that ass of a dandy Day," Kent added.

"I wish someone would save me from Salt," Rhine said. "He wants me to help fund his school in addition to his father's grocery." Although his words were about the Salts, his green eyes were focused on Portia and Kent. She knew him well enough to know he was trying to determine

116

what was really going on between them. She also knew he'd be speaking to Eddy about it, and in turn Eddy would find a way to speak to her. To keep him off balance, she asked, "Are we going home soon?"

"In a while. Have you seen your sister?"

"She was here a few minutes ago but I believe she was on her way back inside. Is something wrong?"

"No. Just trying to keep up with the ladies Carmichael. Where's Eddy?"

"In the kitchen."

"Okay. I'll let you know when we're ready to head home. Kent, you're the official unwanted-suitor sheriff for the rest of the evening."

Kent saluted.

Rhine chuckled and left.

Kent looked her way. "I now have an official title. Can I shoot them if they get too close?"

"Are you planning on shooting yourself?"

"I'm not unwanted."

"Yes, you are."

"That's not what your garters are going to say."

She said quietly but with emphasis, "You aren't going to get close enough to my garters to hear them say anything."

"Remember you said that."

"As long as you remember what I said."

"Don't worry. I'll be writing it down just so I can make you read it once we put the fire out."

She rolled her eyes even as she wondered how fiery garters might feel.

"Be grateful for all these people, though. Otherwise . . ."

He didn't need to say more. The timbre of his voice and the look in his eyes were enough to put a shimmering in her blood.

"I'll never put you in a position to be gossiped about. Okay?"

She nodded and her opinion of him rose higher. "Where did you work before coming here?"

"Spread up in Colorado."

"Cattle or horses?"

"Both, plus the owners ran a sawmill so we cut lumber on the side."

"What made you leave?"

He shrugged. "Restless, I guess. I never like staying in a place for very long."

"And before Colorado?"

"Montana and Wyoming. And before that Canada."

"My. And how long will you be here?"

"Not sure. I'm getting kind of tired of pulling up stakes and starting over. So who knows, I may stick around for a while. That okay with you?"

Portia wanted to say it didn't matter but found herself nodding instead.

"Good," he replied with a smile. He'd finished his food. "I'm going to take this plate back inside. Thanks for the company, Duchess."

She watched him get to his feet, and as he walked away, she wanted to call him back. She'd enjoyed conversing with him and learning just a bit more about him. She also enjoyed their bantering. He was right about not many men being able to make her smile and yet she did with him. That he hadn't wanted her to be the subject of gossip pleased her. Her mother had had no reputation to speak of. Those who knew her called her Corinne the Whore, as if it was the name she'd been born with. One of Portia's most painful memories was being with her mother one day on the streets of Denver. She couldn't have been more than nine or ten, but old enough to know how her mother made her living. She didn't remember where they were going or why, but watching her mother be verbally confronted by another woman was as vivid as if it had happened yesterday. The woman screamed at her mother for entertaining her husband and said Corinne was going straight to hell. She then leaned down to Portia and snapped, "And you're going to be a nasty little whore, too!" Portia remembered her terror and trying to shrink into herself so the raging woman would leave her be. Corinne finally snatched Portia by the hand and stalked away. Tears running down her face, Portia had hurried to keep up, all the while vowing never to be a whore or anything else that would allow anyone to make her feel so small and dirty again.

"Portia?"

She snapped back to the present. "Yes?"

It was Regan. "Are you okay?"

"Just wool gathering. Did Uncle Rhine find you?"

"Yes. Mrs. Landry just announced the funeral will be this evening, so we'll be going to the cemetery first and then home."

"What?" The funeral was supposed to be tomorrow at dusk.

"Reverend Cordell is as surprised as everyone else. Mrs. Landry said she forgot to tell him, but apparently the grave is ready and waiting." Regan continued to study her as if hoping to discover why Portia had been lost in thought. "Are you sure nothing's wrong?"

Portia offered a small smile. "I'm sure. When are we leaving for the cemetery?"

"In a few minutes. We're to meet at the buggy."

Portia picked up Eddy's blanket and folded it so it could be carried. "All right. Let's go."

After returning from the funeral, Portia took off her hat and walked outside onto the small porch attached to her bedroom. Taking a seat on the padded bench, she drew in a deep breath of the cool night air and looked up at the star-filled sky. She would miss Mr. Blanchard. He'd lived a long full life and she hoped he would rest in peace. As she savored the silence, the tension of the day melted away. Off in the distance came the familiar high pitched call of a coyote. She loved the night but it had taken moving to Virginia City to do so. Nights in Denver with Corinne had been filled with constant footfalls and the sounds of the old front door opening and closing as her mother plied her trade. Portia and Regan slept on a rag-filled pallet on the back stoop, which also doubled as her mother's waiting area, so it was not unusual for them to be startled awake by a strange man standing nearby. But in Virginia City there'd been no rag-filled pallets or strange men, just the velvet night and the low-voiced hum of the mining machines. Jim Dade taught them the names of the stars and Rhine let them use his spyglass to take a closer look. She and Regan often sat out at night giggling and talking. Eddy hadn't minded as long as their school work was done and they were up fresh and ready for lessons with their tutor the following morning. After the mob that burned their house made it impossible for them to remain in Nevada, she'd been afraid of the darkness and had nightmares for weeks, but eventually they passed and her connection to the night reestablished itself and again brought her peace.

Now however it was the disturbance of her daytime peace that worried her. Everything about Kent Randolph left her unsettled. Everything from his intense dark eyes to his beard-shrouded jaw was making her second-guess all she thought she knew about men and women, and she wasn't sure how to proceed. On the one hand, it was best to nip this growing flirtation in the bud, but on the other hand, a seemingly uncontrollable curiosity about where it might lead was gaining strength. She hated to admit it but she was no match for him in this. Eddy called him a cat house king, which of course meant he had much more experience with women than she would ever have with men. And as the daughter of a prostitute, she wasn't sure how she should feel knowing he'd patronized such establishments. That he was unmarried certainly made her feel better. Whenever her mother's married customers encountered Corinne on the streets or in shops, they went out of their way to avoid eye contact while the well-dressed women on their arms acted as if they'd catch the plague having to breathe the same air. Looking back, it had been an awful life but she was an adult now, her circumstances were radically different, and she had no business judging anything or anyone. The issue with Kent would eventually resolve itself, so putting him and the conundrum he created out of her mind for the moment, she left the bench and went inside to prepare for bed.

CHAPTER SEVEN

With so much going on during the wake last night, Kent hadn't been able to get a sense of the Blanchard place. Riding over with Rhine the next day, he looked forward to seeing it devoid of people and commotion.

Upon arrival, he took in the small herd of longhorns milling off in the distance and the horses running free in the large fenced paddock. Men he assumed to be the hands stopped what they were doing to view their approach and he wondered what kind of reception he'd be given.

Rhine made the introductions and Kent saw the four men sizing him up while he did the same. The elderly Farley Wells, with his white mutton chops, sun-weathered skin, and keen brown eyes, immediately extended his hand. "Pleased to meet ya."

Kent felt strength in the shake. "Thanks. Same here."

Buck Green, short, dark-skinned, and as aged as Wells, also shook his hand. "Welcome."

Blond haired Matt Iler was the youngest. Kent estimated him to be no more than eighteen. There was a shyness in his blue eyes when he shook Kent's hand. "Nice meeting you." The last man was brown-skinned Ty Parnell. Kent's age maybe. Thin, wolflike, unshaven face. He wore a weathered black vest with silver buckles and his jaw bulged with a wad of tobacco. He offered a terse nod but nothing more.

"Kent's going to be the new foreman," Rhine told them.

"The old man gave me the job the day before he died," Parnell stated.

"I appreciate your pointing that out," Rhine replied. "But I'm the new owner and Kent's foreman now. Stay on or head out. Your choice."

Parnell registered his displeasure by spitting a stream of tobacco juice just inches from Rhine's boots only to find himself slammed bodily into the side of the buckboard behind him and pinned there by the force of Kent's forearm across his throat. The suddenness caused him to half swallow his chaw, and with it stuck in his windpipe, he clawed at Kent's arm to free himself in order to breathe. Glaring, Kent held him until his eyes looked ready to pop from distress then finally let him go. Gagging and vomiting, Parnell slid to the ground.

Kent met Rhine's eyes and received a grim nod of thanks. Wells and Green were grinning but the blond-haired Iler stared at Kent as if he were a two-headed elephant.

Kent told Parnell quietly, "Get up and clear out your bunk."

Parnell fumbled for his gun but Kent's big Colt

was already drawn. "Do you really want to die here?"

Everyone waited.

"Get up."

The furious Parnell moved his hand away from his holster and slowly staggered to his feet. Because Kent didn't trust him out of his sight, he escorted the man to the bunkhouse, watched him pack his gear, and waited while he mounted his horse. Seeing Parnell about to speak, Kent shook his head. "Whatever you're going to say, keep it to yourself so I won't have shoot on sight next time I see you. Now get off Fontaine land."

And he did.

For the next hour, Kent, Rhine, and the remaining hands walked the property and talked about stock, work schedules, and feed. Having been told by Rhine that the two older men would be leaving in a few days, he wanted to get as much information from them as he could before they departed. He wasn't sure what Iler's plans were but decided he would ask him later.

A tour of the brick icehouse showed it in need of some repair as were the paddock fences. There were portions of the bunkhouse roof open to the sky. Buckets were set out in various places on the packed earth floor to catch the rainfall.

Rhine viewed the holes and said, "This needs to be fixed immediately."

Kent agreed. "Can we get shingles in Tucson?"

Buck Green asked Farley, "Don't we have shingles around here someplace?"

Farley seemed to think on that for a moment. "I remember Miss Portia ordering them and Bailey Durham delivering them. We never got around to using them though. They're probably in one of the barns."

Kent asked, "Why didn't you use them?"

Farley shrugged. "We planned to but the old man was more concerned with fishing and playing poker than keeping the place up towards the end and we just plum forgot. I remember the delivery, too, but Buck and I are too old to be on the roof and Parnell was only good for bossing folks around. The kid here can't even shoe a horse so no sense in him trying to fix a roof."

Matt's face turned beet red. He shot Farley an angry look to which the older man asked challengingly, "Am I lying?"

The younger man's lips tightened.

Kent found the interplay interesting and wondered how long Matt had been working there. He figured he'd find out soon enough. "How about you and Buck see if you can find those shingles so we can get the roof repaired. I'll have Matt show me anything else I need to see."

Buck and Farley walked off.

"Let's go see the house," Rhine said.

Kent knew it was a two story but the interior

126

looked much smaller now than it had during the wake. There was a front parlor, a dining room, and the outdoor kitchen. Remembering all the food from the wake, he opened the cold box but found it empty. He asked Matt, "Who cooks your grub?"

"Mrs. Salinas comes in every Sunday. She also cooks for Miss Portia's dude visitors, but the rest of the time we had to make do with whatever the old man burned."

Kent turned to Rhine. "Is she related to Gabriella over at your place?"

"Yes. Her mother."

He wondered if she was available to cook full-time. With all the work needing to be done, the hands deserved a good meal at the end of the day, but he'd ask Rhine about that once he'd taken a full measure of the place. Exploring further, he surveyed the small bedroom off the kitchen. It came with its own washroom, but it didn't look as if it had been used in years. The tub's interior was coated with dirt and cobwebs and had a hole in the bottom rivaling the ones in the bunkhouse roof. He and Rhine exchanged a silent look and headed upstairs. The second floor was in better shape. The bedroom where they'd played poker was arguably the best kept room the house had to offer, but its washroom had water-warped wooden floors and no running water.

"Pipe busted a year or so ago," Matt said by

way of explanation. "We've been washing down at the pond."

Kent took one last look around, blew out a breath and said to Rhine, "Lots to do around here, old man."

"I agree. The value is in the land though. Houses and washrooms can be repaired. Make a list of what you want to work on first, besides the roof, and we'll discuss it and the costs later."

"Okay."

"I need to get back to the hotel," Rhine said.

Kent nodded. "I'll ride over later to pick up my gear. I'll sleep here tonight. I don't want Parnell coming back and taking out his hurt feelings on the place."

He saw Matt watching him and wondered what he might be thinking.

Rhine said, "Good plan but bring the men over for dinner. I'm owner now. They shouldn't have to scrounge like hens for a meal."

Kent nodded.

That evening, with Regan off on her overnight mail run, Portia and Eddy were the only women at the dinner table. Portia had known Buck and Farley most of her life so their presence was a pleasure. She didn't mind that Parnell wasn't with them because she'd never liked him. There was always an ugly intent in his eyes that made her never want to be alone with him. Young

Matt Iler usually had very little to say and that evening was no exception. She assumed there was a story tied to Parnell's absence and planned to ask her uncle about it later. Kent seemed more subdued than usual as well. He'd given her a nod of greeting when he and the men entered the house, but there'd been no hint of flirtation or amusement in his manner.

"Portia, were you aware of the sad state of Blanchard's bunkhouse?" her uncle asked.

"If you mean the holes in the roof, yes. I ordered new shingles and he kept promising to get to it but never did. I think he was more concerned with beating Buck and Farley at poker and checkers."

The two men smiled in reply.

Kent said to her, "We found the shingles in one of the barns. Matt and I will start work first thing tomorrow morning."

Rhine said, "I'd offer to help but I'm heading to San Francisco in the morning for business."

"Do you want my help?" Portia asked, and she saw Kent pause. Confusion etched his face.

Farley said, "She and Miss Regan helped us roof the bunkhouse and the main house the last time we did them. They were just little ladies back then."

Buck saluted her with his glass of sangria. "But they put in a full day's work just like we did. Didn't you, missy?"

The praise made her smile. "We had fun. We weren't old enough to know girls weren't supposed to do that sort of thing."

Kent was eyeing her the way he had when she told him she handled the books and ran the hotel. She supposed he wasn't sure what to make of her or her offer, and she found she enjoyed throwing him off balance. She added, "I can help most of the day. If Regan were here, we could get it done faster, but she's not."

Kent finally said okay and shook his head with what appeared to be wonder. "Join us as early as you can."

"I will." She saw Eddy and Rhine share a speaking look. Her aunt then met Portia's eyes and smiled.

Instead of the usual high-collared blouse and flowing skirt, Portia showed up at the ranch the next morning striding to the bunkhouse in a pair of snug-fitting denims. Kent almost fell off the roof. Taking in the bewitching sight, he whispered appreciatively, "Damn." So mesmerized was he watching her walk, he only belatedly noted her black flat-crowned hat, red flannel man's shirt, and the red bandana tied around her throat.

Matt, working beside him on the roof, glanced up to see what had grabbed his attention. He eyed Portia, took a look up at Kent, shook his head, and went back to nailing shingles.

Kent ignored him.

"Good morning," he called down to her.

The unconventional picture she presented made him want to drag her behind the barn, but she'd come to help, so he had to put thoughts of slowly unbuttoning her shirt and placing kisses against the vee of her throat out of mind. At least for the time being. "Come on up," he invited.

She climbed the ladder and joined them. "Morning, Matt."

He nodded. "Morning, ma'am."

Up close she looked even more delicious and Kent wondered how in the hell he was supposed to keep the distance Rhine wanted when she looked good enough to eat. "Are you ready to get to work?"

"I am."

For the next hour, she worked beside him and proved she not only knew what she was doing but knew far more about laying shingles than Matt, who Kent had to show more than a few times how to line them up and the best spot to place the nails. Portia worked quietly and efficiently. Kent found himself savoring the curve of her gorgeous behind in the denims and the vee of her throat bared by the two undone buttons of her shirt. She even graced him with a few of her rare smiles, which resulted in his hammering his thumb instead of a nail. He cursed, stuck the thumb into his mouth and cursed some more.

"Are you okay?" she asked, stopping to eye him.

"No." He'd sent Matt after more nails, so the two of them were on the roof alone. "I'm being distracted by a duchess in denims."

"I can't very well work up here in a skirt." She drove in a couple more nails and moved to the next shingle. "Do you need a bandage?"

The thumb throbbed. "No. It'll be bruised for a few days but I'll live."

"You should pay attention to what you're doing."

"There isn't a man alive who can pay attention with your lovely little behind waving before his eyes like that."

"It's not waving."

"Maybe not but it is lovely and very distracting. Makes me want to set your garters on fire."

"Is that all men think about?" She positioned another shingle and expertly placed the nails.

"I can only speak for myself, but when it's you—yes."

She looked his way. "This roof will never get done if you can't concentrate. Shall I leave?"

"And deprive me of the fantasies playing in my head? Not on your life."

She chuckled softly. "I'm not going to ask."

"That's probably for the best but hopefully sometime soon I'll get to show you."

Her eyes met his and he wondered if she knew

he could see the heat they held. "Interested, I see."

"No. I'm not."

"You're fibbing again, Duchess."

"And you're supposed to be nailing shingles."

He wanted to nail something all right—real slow and real thorough like, but decided to keep that to himself. "Yes, ma'am."

As the first hour melted into the second, Portia became more and more aware of his nearby presence and her growing inner heat. She wanted to blame it on the sun but knew it stemmed from the outrageous bearded cowboy working a few feet away. They made a good team, even if Matt was more of hindrance than a help, and they'd gotten a good portion of the roof done. Society frowned on women doing such work but she enjoyed the physical exercise and how strong she felt both inside and out. Kent however made her feel female by the way he looked at her, the way he smiled, and it added to the simmer in her blood. She wondered what kind of fantasies he had on his mind and, yes, she was fibbing saying she didn't want to know. Setting another shingle in place, she decided she really needed to put his distracting presence out of her mind, but so far hadn't found a way to do so. *Because you don't want to.* She shushed the inner voice and continued working.

The sun was climbing to its zenith and the

temperature soaring when Eddy drove up in a wagon. She'd brought lunch, and a tired starving Portia was glad to climb down from the roof. After using the water in the kitchen to rinse away the sheen of perspiration on her face and neck and to wash her hands, she joined Kent, Matt, Farley, and Buck on the porch to eat the sandwiches along with the salted and fried thinly sliced potatoes Rhine's partner Jim Dade had made so popular at the saloon in Virginia City. There was also cake and jugs of lemonade to wash it all down.

Kent popped one of the salted potato slices in his mouth and sighed with pleasure. "These are so good. Haven't had any since Virginia City. Thanks, Eddy."

"You're welcome. And I may have found you a cook. Luz Salinas has helped out here in the past and her daughter, Gabriella, says she's willing to hire on full-time as housekeeper, too, but she wants to live in so she doesn't have to travel back and forth. Rhine will pay her salary of course."

Kent liked the idea. "We could fix up that bedroom off the kitchen for her, but the plumbing isn't working."

Farley said, "Buck and I can get on that right away. Place will need a new tub and sink though, Mrs. Fontaine."

"I can see about purchasing those, Eddy,"

Portia said. "Shouldn't be a problem. There's bedroom furniture in storage at our place that we can use for her room, too."

"When can I meet her?" Kent asked Eddy.

"I'll see if she can drop by this evening."

"That's fine. When do the dudes arrive, Portia?"

"Day after tomorrow."

"Okay," Kent said. "If Mrs. Salinas agrees to hire on, she can use Blanchard's bedroom for now. I'll sleep in the bunkhouse."

Eddy said, "And feel free to take your meals with us until she gets settled in." With that settled, she stood. "I need to get back. I'll see you all at dinner. Portia, are you coming back with me or later on?"

"Later. I want to take a look at Mrs. Salinas's room and figure out what else needs purchasing. We'll need paint for sure."

"Okay. Sun's too high to be up on that roof."

Feeling like a reprimanded twelve-year-old she replied, "I know, Auntie. I'll finish lunch, make my list, and head home when I'm done."

Eddy nodded and departed.

After lunch, because the back of the house was relatively shaded, Farley, Buck, and Matt began digging to unearth the broken water pipe while Portia and Kent took stock of the run-down interior of the bedroom off the kitchen that would eventually be used by Mrs. Salinas.

Portia asked, "I'm not much of a carpenter but

135

how long do you think it might take to make the room usable again?"

Kent shrugged. "I'm not sure. Floor needs replacing. Walls need patching and paint. The biggest job will be repairing the washroom."

She glanced down at the warped wooden floor. "I haven't been in here in years. Had no idea he'd let the place go this way." When she looked over he was watching her. Time stretched. Her eyes strayed to his mouth and lingered. When she raised them to his again, the air seemed to thicken.

He said, "When you look at me that way it makes me want to do all manner of things, Duchess, and keeping my hands to myself is not one of them."

His voice was barely above a whisper but it echoed within her like distant rolling thunder. She knew she should probably leave the room to avoid the inevitable, but when he put actions to words and ran a slow possessive finger over her lips, passion rooted her where she stood and she couldn't move, nor did she wish to. Instead, her untutored senses drank in his touch like the desert did rain. The kiss that followed, so sweetly powerful made her hungry for more. He drew her closer, fitting her against him until they melted into one and she didn't care that they might be discovered as long as he continued to feed the longing he'd aroused. His mouth was experienced, masterful, dizzying. Her lips parted. Their tongues mated, danced, and she groaned with the rising pleasure.

"I want to strip you bare and kiss you here . . ." he rasped as his hand moved to her breast beneath the thin fabric of her shirt and toyed with the nipple until it bloomed and hardened. As the words shook her, he lowered his head and bit her gently through her shirt before taking the nipple into his mouth. She responded with a hushed harsh cry.

"Like that, do you?" he asked with wicked amusement.

And Lord help her, she did. She also liked the way he slowly treated the other breast to the same bold claiming. Breathing was difficult as was maintaining her footing. Her entire being roiled like a pot of simmering water, and it boiled over when he undid her shirt's buttons to reveal the gray silk shift she had on beneath. Hot eyes holding hers, he traced a finger down her trembling throat and over the rise of her breasts before placing his lips against the bared vee of her throat. He flicked the tip of his tongue against her flesh. When he tugged the front of her shift down, she drew in a shuddering breath and thrilled to the feel of his hands sliding over the length of black silk she'd bound herself with in lieu of wearing a corset.

"You could kill a man wearing this."

And before she could react, he moved the silk aside and feasted. A strangled cry slid from her lips. No man had ever touched her let alone used his mouth to do so, and the glorious sensations overrode how scandalous she knew she must be to allow such liberties. Yet she allowed him to suck and tongue and tug with his teeth until her eyes slid shut and the moans stacked up in her throat. Small shards of lightning settled between her thighs. Her hips began to move in a subtle rhythm only her body could hear and he answered with the hard thick part of himself that made him male. It was shameless, illicit, and so decadent she felt like someone else entirely, and that woman was breathless and greedy for more.

He finally lifted his head and the flame in his eyes increased her need. "You should button yourself up and get out of here before I tug those denims down and kiss you in places you never imagined. Or maybe you have."

Portia had no idea what he was referencing. All she knew was that he'd left her mindless and befuddled and that parts of her would rather walk through the desert naked than leave now. But she knew he was right. Where another man might have taken advantage of her in ways she would most certainly regret, he was attempting to do the honorable thing and she had to admire him for it, so while a part of her wailed in regret, she righted her shift and did up her buttons. He stood there with those burning eyes and watched and waited.

"You might want to try again."

She looked down and saw that the shirt was sideways because the buttons weren't lined up properly. Her fingers fumbling, she did them up again—this time successfully.

"Portia?"

She looked up.

"Thanks for your help on the roof and for the kisses."

She drew in a calming breath. The memories of being in his arms poured back clear and true and her now covered nipples berried in response. Uncertain what to do with herself let alone her traitorous body, she nodded and hastened away.

Aching and hard from their play, Kent pulled himself together then walked out to the porch just in time to see her riding off. Her sister's words rang softly in his head. *Be gentle with her.* He planned to do just that.

Matt appeared beside him. "Um, we found the pipe. Buck and Farley are hauling out the busted section now."

"Okay. Good to know." Kent studied him for a moment. "Thanks for your help with the roof."

"You're welcome. Sorry I wasn't good at it."

"No apologies needed. Takes a time or two to

get the hang of it. You did fine. How long have you worked here?"

"About a year. Met the old man in Tucson."

"You from there?"

He shook his head. "No. Little one-shack town near Page called Quint."

"Family there?"

He looked out at the mountains. Seeing the hardness that settled over his features made Kent offer an apology of his own. "Sorry. Wasn't trying to pry."

The boy shrugged. "No. It's okay. Got a sister, but she left soon as she was old enough. I did, too. Got tired of the beatings."

Kent stilled.

"Both my ma and pa were drunks and when things didn't go right, they took it out on us." He quieted again as if thinking back. "Cissy's two years older. She must've been fourteen or so when she lit out. One morning I woke up and she was gone. Told my pa I didn't know where she went, but . . ."

"He didn't believe you."

"Nope. Blacked both my eyes. Knocked out my two front teeth, which is why I don't smile much."

"Are your parents still living?"

He shrugged. "Don't know. Don't much care."

Kent thought back on his own somewhat privileged childhood under a parent who'd only wanted the best for him and how he'd rebelled in response. They'd argued fiercely. He knew being a doctor was not what he wanted to do with his life, but looking back he could've been more respectful.

Matt asked Kent about his raising and upon hearing that his mother died in childbirth and that his father was a doctor, a surprised Matt looked him up and down. "A doctor? Why are you a ranch hand?"

"It's what I've always wanted to do."

"Your pa still living?"

"Yes."

Kent thought the short time spent talking with Matt had been worth it. He now knew more about him and that he'd spent his childhood dodging fists, which was why he didn't know much about ranching. "How'd you meet Blanchard?"

"Saw him coming out of a store in Tucson one day and asked him if he had any spare change. He told me I should've asked for a meal. Said he'd seen dying cattle with more meat on their bones." Matt smiled for the first time, showing his missing teeth. "Brought me here, fed me, and offered me a job. I had a real bed for the first time since leaving Quint."

Kent wondered how he'd managed to live on his own during the years in between, but felt he'd pried enough. "If you plan on staying, I'm going to make you assistant foreman."

His eyes widened. "Why?"

"Farley and Buck are leaving, so you're it. Plan to teach you all I know. That okay?"

He nodded hastily.

"Good. Let's go see about that pipe."

After dinner at the hotel, Farley, Buck, and Matt rode back to the ranch, leaving Kent, Eddy, and Luz Salinas to talk about the housekeeping job. Portia hadn't joined them for the meal. Kent's initial disappointment was overridden by concern when Eddy explained that Portia had a slight headache from being in the sun all day. Eddy assured him that after a good night's sleep, her niece would be right as rain, but he knew he'd continue to worry until he saw her for himself.

"What will my duties be, specifically?" Luz asked, breaking into his thoughts.

"Meals three time a day and the upkeep on the house. Your Saturdays and Sundays can be your own if you want."

She assessed him silently. To Kent she appeared to be about Eddy's age and was just as beautiful. There was a bit of gray in the long jet-black hair.

"We're going to fix up the bedroom off the kitchen for you, but until it and the washroom are ready, you can use Blanchard's room."

"Salary?" she asked Eddy.

Because the Fontaines would be paying her, Kent let Eddy ride point and simply listened. When the discussion ended, Luz said, "The salary sounds fine, but these are my conditions. My bedroom door has a lock. I will take Sundays off. If I need a Saturday instead I will give you plenty of notice."

He nodded.

"You will have no women in the house overnight and there'll be no walking around in your drawers."

He suppressed his smile.

"I want to plant a garden and get some hens for that old coop on the property. I will do your wash—"

"I'm accustomed to doing my own, so not necessary."

She looked surprised.

"He cooks, too, Luz, so you can decide whether you want him in your kitchen or not," Eddy cracked.

"He any good?" she asked, showing a small smile for the first time.

"He is."

"Good or not, they're paying me to cook, Mr. Randolph, so I expect you to let me do my job. If I ever need your help, I'll let you know."

"Understood."

"Also I don't like drunks."

He thought about Matt. "Neither do I."

143

She seemed satisfied by his answers. "When do you want me to start?"

"Tomorrow, or as soon as possible."

"How's tomorrow at noon sound? That will give me a chance to make arrangements with the landlord where I'm living now."

"That sounds good."

Riding back to the ranch under the light of the moon, Kent was glad to have settled things with Mrs. Salinas but his thoughts were still on Portia. He felt guilty about having her out in the sun to the point where she'd had to pass on coming for dinner. He thought maybe he should apologize next time they crossed paths, but he wouldn't apologize for their passionate interlude. He'd enjoyed it and she had, too.

CHAPTER EIGHT

So that the guests wouldn't be tossed around in the bed of a wagon on the unpaved roads to the Fontaine Hotel, Portia and Regan each drove a buggy to the train depot while Cal Grissom guided the buckboard that would transport their luggage. Kent was mounted on Blue and rode slowly beside Portia while Matt flanked Regan.

"How long are these people staying?" Kent asked her.

"Five days."

And she was looking forward to immersing herself in her duties so her mind wouldn't have time to dwell on the kisses from the man riding beside her. For the past two days, she'd done a good job of keeping herself focused on the last-minute preparations, but when her guard slipped the memories roared back of how shamelessly passion had made her behave. As if in agreement her nipples tightened. A glance his way showed a ghost of a smile playing at the edges of his beard-shrouded lips as if he knew where her thoughts had led.

"Penny for your thoughts," he said.

"Just thinking about the arrivals."

"Uh-huh," he replied knowingly.

"What else would I be thinking about?"

He leaned down and said, for her ears only, "Me. You. The band of silk I hope you're wearing beneath that schoolmarm blouse and what's going to happen if I catch you alone to see."

The reins went slack in her hands.

"No?" he asked innocently.

She didn't reply but she knew by that seductive smile of his that this was not over and the parts of herself that couldn't wait for him to catch her alone shouted with glee.

The train was just pulling into the depot when they arrived. As the four guests stepped out of the car, Portia was finally able to put faces to the names of the people she'd been corresponding with for the past few months. Dr. Phillip Pratt was tall with light skin. He greeted her with a smile.

"Welcome," Portia said.

"Thanks. This is my sister, Elvenna Gordon."

Elvenna nodded and Portia couldn't help admiring her fashionable sable-brown traveling ensemble and matching confection of a hat.

The brown-skinned Dr. Winston Jakes's startling gray eyes flashed surprise when Portia introduced herself. Standing with him was his short stocky mother, Ada, in an old-fashioned rumpled black ensemble and matching wide-brimmed hat.

Portia then introduced her sister and the men who'd accompanied them.

Elvenna immediately sidled up to Kent and said huskily, "My aren't you a handsome cowboy, Kent Randolph. May I ride with you? You do let widows ride, don't you?"

Her brother, Phillip, shook his head with apparent disgust. Portia hid her displeasure but knew right away the widow Gordon was going to be trouble.

Ada Jakes asked, in a voice Portia imagined a bullfrog would have, "Can you at least wait until we reach the ranch before you throw yourself at the man?"

Elvenna raised her chin. "That was very unladylike, Ada."

"And you're very unladylike so the shoe should fit."

Elvenna gasped.

Portia shared a speaking look with Regan before clearing her throat. "Mr. Grissom will take care of your trunks. This way please." She gestured them towards the waiting buggies.

"Mr. Pratt, you and Mrs. Gordon will ride with my sister, Regan." Elvenna glanced over at Kent mounting his horse and remained where she stood as if waiting for him to look back her way. When he didn't, her lips tightened and she let her brother hand her into Regan's buggy.

That left Portia with Mrs. Jakes and her son, who was still eyeing her with barely masked interest. Portia didn't encourage him. With his good looks and respectful smile, she thought he could be someone Regan might care to know better.

On the ride back to the Fontaines', Portia was peppered with questions about the hotel.

Ada Jakes asked, "Do you get many Colored guests?"

Portia shook her head. "No. Most are European or Whites from back East."

"Will there be any Europeans during our time here?"

"No. Mixing the races has caused problems in the past."

"What do you mean?" Mrs. Jakes asked.

"Some of the Europeans mistook our Colored guests for servants. It happened on enough occasions that we stopped having both races on the property at the same time."

The deciding incident took place two years ago when a German guest stopped the wife of a prominent New York City newspaper owner in the hallway and demanded she bring him fresh towels. She patiently explained that she, too, was a guest. He refused to believe her and grabbed her arm to force her to do his bidding. Her husband, viewing the assault, punched the German in the nose and a full-fledged fight ensued. The bloodied German wanted the husband arrested. The enraged newspaper owner demanded an apology, which was never given.

The next day both parties decamped in a huff. Neither ever returned.

Ada asked, "Is it always this warm here? My goodness I feel like I'm melting."

"It is Mrs. Jakes. Even though we're in a more temperate part of the territory this is still the desert. It will get much warmer as the day goes on, I'm afraid."

"How do you stand it?"

"You get accustomed to it after a while. There's a water jug in the crate by your feet."

"Thank you."

She drank a bit, then passed the jug to her son. It was a warm morning. Even with the buggy's canopy sheltering them, the sun's heat was stifling. She wondered how Regan's passengers were faring, but didn't worry overly much because their buggy had water, too, and Kent and Matt had canteens.

"I have to admit, the countryside does have its own beauty," Dr. Jakes said. "I don't think I've ever seen a bluer sky."

That he appreciated the slate gray mountains and the clear blue sky where some other guests saw only starkness added another feather in his cap.

He added, "I also admire a woman who can drive well. Many men don't believe your gender should drive at all."

"Or vote," his mother added tartly.

Portia smiled. "Do you believe women should have the vote, Mr. Jakes?"

"Call me Winston, and of course they should. Some of the most astute minds I've ever encountered are female."

"As you can hear, I raised him well," his mother said, chuckling.

To which Portia replied, "It's a pity the men in Congress weren't raised that way, too."

"True."

For the rest of the ride, she and Ada discussed the suffrage movement and the vote. Ada took issue with the way the great Sojourner Truth was being held up as ignorant and illiterate. "The manner in which her words are portrayed in some of the pamphlets irks me to no end. She speaks English and Dutch, which is one more language than any of those other women speak."

Fascinated, Portia admitted, "I didn't know that."

"She began life as a Dutch slave. English is not her first language, but to hear the movement's leaders tell it, she speaks like an unschooled Deep South slave. And why they refuse to allow Colored women in their ranks says a lot about who they are. Especially Elizabeth Cady Stanton. This phrase they're beginning to use—*intelligent suffrage*—is designed to leave women of our race on the side of the road. As if they're the only ones with enough smarts to read a ballot."

Portia had seen the phrase bandied about in the newspapers. Stanton and some of the other leaders were advancing the notion that a test of some sort be applied to ensure that only women of sound mind be given the vote, which of course everyone knew would be applied specifically to women of color. Stanton was still smarting from Colored men having been given the access to the voting booth ahead of them with the passage of the Fifteenth Amendment. In Portia's mind, if they were all so keen on an immediate solution they should be advocating a movement to Wyoming Territory where women were given the vote in 1869. All in all, she enjoyed her conversation with the fiery Ada Jakes and looked forward to further talks during their stay.

Arriving at the hotel, Regan escorted her charges inside and Portia was about to do the same when Winston Jakes said, "What will we be doing in the morning and at what time?"

Before Portia could reply, his mother said, "Winston, let me know what she says. I need to go inside and get out of this heat."

She hurried in behind Regan's group.

"We can go in, too," Portia said.

"No. If I might be so forward, I'd like to enjoy your company alone for just a bit longer."

Seeing no harm in granting him the small boon, she smiled. "Breakfast is at six, and we'll head to the stables around seven-thirty."

"So early?"

"Yes, it's best to get started before the heat of the day."

"I see."

They were interrupted by Kent riding up. "Excuse me, Miss Carmichael. Sorry for the interruption. I just wanted to let you know that the guests' trunks have been taken inside and the staff is placing them in their suites."

"Thank you, Mr. Randolph."

Jakes was eyeing Kent's horse. "Randolph, what breed of horse is that? I don't believe I've ever seen one quite that color before."

"He's a blue roan."

"Where did you buy it?"

"I didn't. I found him in a wild herd in Montana. Broke him to the saddle myself."

He looked startled. "My. That's impressive."

"All part of a cowboy's life." Kent then turned his eyes to Portia. "Do you need me for anything else today? If not, Matt and I are going back to the ranch."

"You aren't joining us for dinner?"

"No. I know we had some things to discuss this evening, but I'll let you get settled in with your guests. The other thing can wait."

Only they knew what he was really referencing. That he was able to relay it so blandly was impressive. "No, I won't need your help with anything else." The scandalous parts of herself that had looked forward to being caught alone were disappointed.

"Then I'll see you in the morning. Sorry again for the interruption." He touched his hat, turned his stallion, and rode off.

"So that's a real cowboy," Jakes said, eyes focused on the departing rider.

"As real as they come. Aren't there Colored ranch owners in California?"

"I'm sure there are but none are in my circle of friends or acquaintances."

"I see." From his tone, she couldn't tell if he was like Darian Day and Edward Salt and thought himself superior to men who worked cattle and busted broncs. "Let's go in and join the others."

That evening as the guests gathered in the dining room for dinner, Rhine, with Eddy by his side, welcomed them to the hotel. "Although my wife, Eddy, and I own the Fontaine, our niece Portia is responsible for putting together the activities you'll be enjoying so if you have any questions or concerns please let her know. Let's move to the table."

In keeping with the hotel's stellar reputation for quality and elegance, the white-clothed table was splendidly set with Eddy's imported Minton china, silverware polished to a high shine, and delicate crystal stemware.

As they took their seats, Ada seemed particularly taken by the blue, gilded Minton plates. "These are stunning."

"Only the best for our guests," Eddy replied.

Elvenna said, "I have a question." Her low-cut gray gown showed off the rise of her breasts. "Where is Mr. Randolph? Isn't he part of the activities?"

Portia took in the dress and saw Eddy eyeing it critically as well. "Mr. Randolph will join us tomorrow. Any other questions?"

There were none so the meal commenced. They made small talk at first and Portia learned that the two doctors shared a practice in San Francisco and were indeed on their way home from a medical convention in Atlanta.

"Rhine's brother lives in San Francisco," Eddy said. "We visit him quite often. In fact, Portia apprenticed at his bank for a time after she and Regan finished their schooling at Oberlin."

"I attended Oberlin as well," Mrs. Jakes said, sounding pleased. "What did you train for at the bank?"

"Bookkeeping."

Elvenna tossed back skeptically, "I've never seen any Colored women at any of the banks. Which one was this?"

"The Bank of California."

"Why that's one of the state's biggest and most

influential," Winston said, eyeing Portia with even greater interest.

"My brother's on the board of directors," Rhine explained.

"Is he married?"

"Elvenna!" her brother gasped.

Wineglass in hand, she waved him off, "I'm just making conversation, Phillip."

Portia shared a look with Eddy.

Rhine replied to her question, "He is, and very happily, I might add."

"Pity," she said. "My Saul's been dead three years. I'm very lonely without him. Have you ever been married, Portia?"

"No."

"Then you're probably lonely as well."

Portia responded politely. "Honestly, I'm not. My life is very full."

Elvenna chuckled knowingly, "Unmarried women always say that, but everyone knows the truth. Deep down inside every woman wants to be married. Society holds her in higher esteem if she is. It pities her if she's not."

Ada snapped, "That is narrow-minded rubbish."

"Maybe, but you have to admit it's true."

"Views change," Portia told her coolly. "Thirty years ago, society doubted the race would ever rise like it has. Now we have colleges, doctors both male and female, and our men have been in Congress. In '81, Colored washerwomen took on the city of Atlanta and forever changed how they are viewed. In the end what society thinks is never set in stone."

Winston raised his glass. "Well said, Miss Carmichael."

Portia met her aunt's and uncle's approving smiles and caught Regan's wink. Having put the now sour-looking widow Gordon in her place, Portia returned to her meal.

"That was a perfect set down," Ada said to Portia later as she walked the Jakeses to their rooms after dinner.

"It needed to be said." She disliked being underestimated.

Winston walked beside his mother and although he hadn't had much to say after toasting Portia with his glass, he'd spent the rest of the meal watching her with unmasked admiration. "Any man able to engage you in conversation on a daily basis would be lucky indeed, Portia."

"That's very kind of you to say."

"I plan to add you to that list of astute women I mentioned on the ride from the depot."

Portia was warmed by the praise. "I'm honored."

Ada seemed pleased as well. "Winston bemoans the fact that the women he meets leave a lot to be desired intellectually. But you give him hope."

"Mother!"

"I'm simply stating fact. She'd make an excellent daughter-in-law. You have the length of our five-day stay to make your case."

He shook his head with amusement. "As you probably sense, my mother's impossible to manage."

His usage of the word *manage* brought Kent to mind. She thought it probably ill-mannered to think of one man while conversing with another, so she put the cowboy out of her mind. "Even though I have no plans to marry, I appreciate a woman who speaks her mind. My aunt Eddy is that way."

"Then you're accustomed to unmanageable behavior," he said.

"I am." Memories of the unmanageable Kent rose to bedevil her again, making her wonder if she'd have to contend with them for the rest of her life.

Upon reaching the suite, Winston opened the door and Ada asked, "How long have your aunt and uncle been married?"

"They recently celebrated their fifteen-year anniversary."

"They look to be very happy."

"They are." Not wanting to say anything else that might encourage Ada's attempt at match-making, Portia said, "I hope you enjoy your stay with us."

"I'm looking forward to it," Winston Jakes replied.

Ada eyed them both. "Five days, Winston. Good night, Portia."

Amused, Portia said, "Good night."

Ada went inside. Winston lingered for a second longer. "Good night, Portia."

"Good night to you as well, Winston."

She turned and struck out for her return to the main house.

Later, Regan and Portia sat talking in Portia's room.

"The widow is going to be a bother," Regan said from her spot on Portia's bed.

Standing by her open doors and looking out at the night, Portia turned. "I agree."

"I enjoyed the look on her face when you were done with her, though."

"I don't like being challenged."

"I think she knows that now. She seems pretty anxious to make a run at Kent."

"Hopefully, he'll simply ignore her the way he did at the depot." She knew it wasn't her place to tell him not to fraternize with the guests but it was obvious that Elvenna wanted to make herself available and she did wonder how he would respond.

Regan interrupted her thoughts. "Wondering whether Kent's going to help himself to the widow's buffet?"

"No."

"Liar. He likes you, Portia. I doubt he'd be so disrespectful as to pursue another woman right under your nose."

"It doesn't matter to me who he pursues." That, too, was a lie.

"It does, so stop being a ninny."

Portia blew out a breath and changed the subject. "Winston Jakes is a doctor, unmarried, well-spoken, and very forward thinking where women are concerned. You might consider getting to know him better."

"The man spent the entire dinner looking at you. I could have been wearing my nightgown and he wouldn't have cared."

"His mother thinks I'd make a great daughter-in-law. She's given him the duration of their stay to win me over. I suppose were I in the market for a husband, he might fit the bill." And if she knew how long it would take for the memories of Kent's kisses to fade.

"He doesn't fit mine. I'm going to be a mail-order bride, remember?"

Portia laughed softly. "You're just not letting that go, are you?"

"No, and I'm still scouring the newspapers."

Portia didn't believe her for a second. "Go to bed, Miss Mail Order. Dawn comes early."

Regan gave her a kiss on the cheek, "Good night."

"I'll see you in the morning."

Alone, Portia changed into her night things and wondered how Kent might react to Winston Jakes's interest in her. Not that the cowboy had staked his claim on her. Or had he? She certainly felt as if she'd staked her claim on him, watching the widow Gordon throw herself at him like feed to a stallion. Turning her mind away from the startling realization that her reaction could be seen as jealousy, she thought back on her conversation with the Jakeses instead and wondered where Kent stood on issues like women and the vote. Western-raised men weren't the most progressive thinkers. Finding one who was was akin to hitting the mother lode, but Kent was different. The man cooked his own eggs for heaven's sake and as she'd noted before, didn't think her odd for running the hotel. She assumed he was a progressive thinker, too, but the only way to know for sure would be to question him.

At precisely seven-thirty the next morning, Portia escorted the small group of guests out to the stables. Cal Grissom would be pairing them up with mounts. Afterwards, they'd be led on a short trek to the nearby canyon. She had no idea if they were experienced riders but would find out. Ada was dressed in a black divided skirt. It and the matching jacket, like her traveling costume, had seen better days. On her gray head sat the brown felt western-style hat the hotel presented as gifts to all its guests. Portia thought she looked very dashing. Elvenna's blue silk riding togs appeared more fashionable than practical and Portia hoped she was prepared for how dusty her clothing might be by the end of the day. Her footgear looked brand-new, which gave Portia some concern. Breaking in new boots before arriving had been emphasized in the mailed instructions but the widow's looked like they'd gone straight from the store to her feet.

"Mrs. Gordon, did you follow the suggestion to wear your boots a bit before your arrival?" Portia asked as they approached the stable.

"No. I was too busy."

"I see." Portia hoped she was prepared for the blisters she was sure to have.

It turned out that none of the guests had ever ridden a horse before. This wasn't a surprise. Most of the people from back East and in large western cities like San Francisco used carriages and streetcars for transportation so Cal gave them mounts he was sure they could manage. Gentle mares for the ladies and two well-trained, docile geldings for the men.

Ada needed a stool to aid her mounting, but once seated, she smiled. "My goodness, I had no idea I'd be so far off the ground."

Both Winston and Phillip wore nervous smiles atop their geldings.

Cal walked over to help Elvenna mount the chestnut-colored Cassandra, but was met with "I prefer to ride in a carriage. I don't care for the animal's odor and I certainly don't want that stink in my clothing."

Astride Arizona, Portia shared a silent look with Cal and noted the irritation radiating from the widow's brother. His sister wasn't the first prickly female guest Portia had encountered and so offered a solution. "You're more than welcome to spend the day in your suite. We only provide carriage rides to guests who are aged or physically impaired in some way."

Her brother voiced less patience. "Oh for heaven's sake, Venna. Get on the horse. You knew we'd be riding."

Cal offered encouragement. "Come on, ma'am. It'll be fun. You'll see."

She appeared doubtful, but the disapproving glare of the others in her party must've carried some weight because she finally relented and huffed, "All right. Fine."

Cal linked his hands together and held them out for her to step into. "Put one foot in my hands and I'll lift you up."

Portia would have been more sympathetic had Elvenna admitted to a fear of riding, but not wanting to because of how the mare's scent would affect her clothing? Portia kept her features bland.

Up on Cassandra's back a disgruntled Elvenna held the reins.

Cal offered a false smile. "That isn't so bad, is it?"

"I suppose."

Ada snapped. "Oh my word, Venna. Are you going to play the put-out belle all day?"

Elvenna flashed around to respond, which made Cassandra take a step back and Elvenna's eyes widen in fear. "Be quiet, Ada, before you make me fall off and hurt myself."

"We should be so lucky."

Portia was enjoying the plainspoken Ada more and more. "Let's begin by learning how to use the reins."

For the next hour, she and Cal taught them proper reins management, drilled them gently on maneuvering and turns, and followed with instructions on the basics of using their boot heels to communicate commands. Elvenna had the most trouble of course. Horses are intelligent animals and her mare balked more than a few times because of what she sensed coming through Elvenna's reins. At one point, while they were riding slowly around the outside of the paddock, Cassandra simply stopped and refused to take another step. Cal urged Elvenna to relax but she was determined to lay the problem on the animal. "Get me another horse."

163

"She's the gentlest we have."

"I want a different one."

Cal looked to Portia who sighed inwardly. At that moment, Kent and Matt rode up. Portia's heart leapt and she couldn't help but admire everything about him, from the way he sat the big blue stallion to his all-black attire and gray hat to the way his eyes scanned her face and held there, making her body warm and her mind remember.

His arrival moved the widow, too. "Finally, you're here. Will you tell this man to get me a better horse and then show me how to ride properly, because those two"—she glared at Portia and Cal—"don't seem to know what they're doing."

Ada called out, "She doesn't like her mare's scent, so you'll need to make the new one smell like fine perfume, too."

The corners of Kent's mouth lifted and Portia dropped her head to hide her smile.

"Mrs. Gordon," he said. "I'm sure Cal has given you the best mount he has to offer and I know Miss Carmichael bends over backwards to accommodate her guests. Now if you'd like to stay behind and let Cal give you more lessons, that's fine with me. Once you're more comfortable, he can ride with you to the ranch so you can join us."

From the way she stiffened, it was obvious

she'd been expecting him to take her side, which Portia found illogical considering he'd spent so little time in her company, but she supposed Elvenna was accustomed to having men fall at her feet.

Kent asked, "Are we ready to ride, Miss Carmichael?"

"I believe we are." Pleased that he hadn't succumbed, she glanced over at Phillip and the Jakeses. Upon receiving their affirmative nods, she'd turned to the tight-faced widow. "Your decision, Mrs. Gordon? Are you staying behind for further lessons?"

"No." And showing a skill she'd not displayed an hour ago, she brought her mare into line and set out with their small party for the ride to the Blanchard place.

CHAPTER NINE

While Matt and Portia flanked the slow-moving riders, Kent brought up the rear. Although he was keeping a keen eye on the guests, he was also paying close attention to the lovely lady in charge and musing on what it might be like for the two of them to share a slow easy morning ride like this one alone. In his fantasy, they'd find a meadow and have breakfast; they'd eat, talk. He'd make her laugh and she'd make him wonder how soon she and her bear-trap mind planned to take over the world. As it stood though, they were escorting a bunch of greenhorns at a pace so slow even a caterpillar would've been mad about it. The widow had managed to fall back far enough to be riding beside him. Although she was minding her reins, he sensed her waiting for him to strike up a conversation. Before the visit was over he was going to have to deal with her but not in the manner she'd be expecting. He had no interest in sampling what she was so brazenly offering. The younger version of himself would have gladly accommodated her anytime and anyplace, but he was far more selective in his old age. His jail sentence played a small part in his current stance, but maturity played a larger one.

He no longer wanted to pursue women other men had ridden hard and put up wet.

"Were you born out west, Mr. Randolph?"

"Yes. Virginia City, Nevada." Even though Portia was his prime focus he had no problem making small talk.

"Have you ever married?"

"No."

"Do you plan to?"

"No idea."

"Suppose you do. What kind of woman will she be?"

"When I find her, I'll know."

"Would it be possible for us to have, say, dinner and you can explore what kind of woman I am?"

"I don't socialize with the guests."

"Not even on your own time?"

"No."

She blew out a breath. "You're no fun."

"No, I'm not."

"I could fix that given the chance."

"Not in need of fixing, Mrs. Gordon."

Riding ahead of them, her brother snarled, "Good Lord, Venna. The man isn't interested. Does he have to paint you a sign?"

Kent hid his amusement.

"Mind your own business, Phillip!"

Portia looked over. Kent didn't know if she'd overheard his conversation with the widow or not, but Phillip's voice had been loud enough

167

for everyone's ears. When she rolled her eyes, he laughed softly. If he was forced to choose between the duchess and the widow, Elvenna Gordon didn't stand a chance. Kent saw Winston Jakes looking back at him with cool eyes. After a long moment, the man faced forward again, leaving Kent to wonder what he'd missed.

With the granite gray mountains looming off in the distance and the sky overhead a brilliant cloudless blue, the riders rode single file up the narrow rocky pass. When they began the descent to the valley below, Portia, who was leading the column, turned in her saddle and screamed, "Kent! The ranch house is on fire!"

He quickly worked his horse around the others to get to her side and what he saw stole his breath. Both the ranch house and bunkhouse were fully engulfed. "Stay here. Cal, keep them safe! Matt, you're with me!"

As they barreled down the ridge. Kent couldn't imagine how both buildings came to be ablaze but arson came instantly to mind. "Keep your eyes open, Matt!"

"Yes, sir!"

Later, Kent would gauge his reaction to being called sir for the first time in his life, but at the moment, he was too worried about Mrs. Salinas, Farley, and Buck, who were nowhere in sight.

When he got off his horse he already had his Colt drawn. The air was thick with the smell of kerosene and smoke. "Check near the bunkhouse. See if you can find anyone!"

Matt rode off.

The flames had eaten through the ranch house roof and were licking at the sky. Kent got as close as to the structure as he dared. "Luz!" She was supposed to have been making lunch for them. He shouted her name again and ran around to the back. "Luz!" If she was inside, there was no way he could get to her without losing his own life.

Behind him a voice gasped softly, "*Gracia a Dios!*"

He spun. Luz Salinas stumbled out of the ramshackle chicken coop. Her clothes were covered with filth. He hurried to her side.

"I am so glad you are here," she gasped.

He looked her over. "Are you hurt?"

"No." She clung to his arm as he escorted her clear of the heat from the fire.

"What happened?"

"Masked riders. Farley saw them coming. He and Buck grabbed rifles and yelled for me to hide in the coop. As soon as I got inside I heard gunfire. The fire started almost immediately after. Are they all right?"

"I don't know. Bunkhouse is on fire, too. I sent Matt to look for them."

Matt rode up.

"Did you find them?"

He nodded solemnly. "Farley's dead. Shot in the back. Buck's still alive, but barely. You need to hurry."

Kent saw Portia and the others arriving. "Mrs. Salinas, can you make it to Portia on your own?"

"Yes. See to Buck. I'll be fine."

He ran to Blue and yelled at Portia, "I need the docs!" He rode off, hoping the men would arrive swiftly.

Buck was lying on the edge of the pond. Farley's silent body lay a few feet away. Blood covered them both. Kent quickly dismounted, knelt beside the dying man and lifted his head. He knew his limited medical education wouldn't be enough. "Hold on, Buck. Docs are right behind me."

He grimaced a grin and whispered, "Too late. Farley and the old man are already pulling out my chair for the poker game."

"Who did this?"

"Parnell. Had men with him. Made us run then shot us in the back."

Kent's anger boiled.

"Coward had his face hid, but couldn't hide his voice. Get him for us, would you?"

"Will do. I promise." A promise he'd keep.

By the time Jakes and Phillip Pratt arrived, they were too late. Kent gently lowered Buck's lifeless body back to the ground. Seeing Portia, he shook his head to let her know he was gone. Her jaw tightened and a sheen of angry tears filled her eyes. Kent hadn't known the two men long enough to call them friends but they'd impressed him as good people. They hadn't deserved such ignoble deaths. "Portia, take Mrs. Salinas and your guests back to the hotel. Let your uncle know what's happened. Have him tell the sheriff that Parnell was one of the killers. I'll come soon as the fire's out."

She nodded. The doctors mounted, Cal took Mrs. Salinas up behind him and he and Portia led the party back across the meadow.

The fires were subsiding, leaving behind charred smoky skeletons. That it hadn't been a windy day or the height of summer was a blessing. The wind would've spread the embers to the surrounding grasses, setting it afire, too. As it stood only a bit of the grass near the house had burned but both buildings would have to be replaced.

"Stock's gone."

Kent noticed the empty pens for the first time and swore softly. "Parnell must've run them off."

"Riders coming."

Kent looked up at Matt's warning and watched them approach. There were four of them. They weren't masked but he and Matt drew their guns and waited. As they neared Matt identified them. "Mr. Lane."

Kent remembered meeting the big burly

171

Howard Lane at the anniversary party. Lane and his men stopped to survey the charred house before continuing to where he and Matt stood by the pond.

"Saw the smoke. Sorry I didn't get here earlier. We rode as hard as we could." Only then did he see the bodies. He dismounted slowly and walked closer. "Damn," he whispered emotionally. "Who did this?"

"Buck said it was Ty Parnell and that he had men with him, but he didn't say how many. They made him and Farley run and shot them in the back."

Angry murmurs came from Lane's men.

Lane didn't hide his reaction. "In the old days we'd've hunted the bastards down and strung them up."

One of Lane's riders said, "Still might. Those two never hurt a fly."

"Does Rhine know?"

Kent answered the question. "Sent Portia to tell him, and to let the sheriff know."

Lane added, "One of my men is driving a wagon that should be here shortly. When we saw the smoke we weren't sure what Farley and Buck would need so we piled it up. We'll use it to take the bodies to the undertaker in Tucson."

"They have family?"

"Not that I know of."

"Then I'm sure Rhine will want to pay for the funeral."

"I'll contribute, too. Known them a long time. Should've died of old age in their beds like Blanchard. Not cut down with no dignity. What's Parnell's beef?"

Kent told him what he thought to be Parnell's motive. "When Rhine introduced me as the new foreman, Parnell said Mr. Blanchard had promised him the job. Rhine told him his mind was made up, so Parnell spit tobacco juice at Rhine's boots. I had to teach some manners, then made him pack up and leave."

"He always did think he was the biggest bull in the pen. Can't believe Blanchard made him any promises to be foreman. In fact, the old man was planning to let him go. Hadn't cared for his attitude or his bullying the others into doing his share of the work."

Kent turned to Matt and received a terse nod of agreement.

Lane continued, "If the sheriff needs men for a posse, he won't have any problem finding volunteers, myself included. Farley and Buck were well liked."

Kent would be volunteering as well. "Parnell wouldn't be stupid enough to still be around would he?"

"Maybe. Especially if he doesn't know Buck lived long enough to point a finger his way."

The wagon arrived a few minutes later. The bed was filled with tin buckets, shovels, and other items needed to put down the fire. Once it was unloaded, the bodies were carefully laid in and a tarp placed over them. As the wagon drove away, Lane said, "May they rest in peace. But I won't be at peace until Parnell and the others swing from the end of a rope."

Watching the wagon bump along the track and disappear from sight, Kent agreed.

Kent and Lane's men set up a line and used buckets of water from the pond to douse the last of the embers, then with bandanas tied over their noses and mouths to keep from breathing in the smoke, they used shovels, hoes, and pickaxes to turn over the debris to make sure no hot spots remained. Once they were finished he thanked Lane and his men.

"We'll keep an eye out for your cows," Lane promised as he and his men mounted up. "I'll pass the word on to the other ranches as well."

"Thanks."

Lane nodded. "And if Parnell and the other killers are still in the territory, we'll find them."

On the ride back to the hotel, Portia chafed under the slow pace. She wanted to kick Arizona into a full gallop for home so Rhine would know what had happened, but the inexperienced riders under her escort made that impossible. She'd considered taking Luz up with her and sending Cal on ahead but if their party ran into trouble she'd need his gun. The guests came to Arizona to experience the Wild West and had gotten more than anyone could have imagined. She glanced back. Both Ada and the widow looked shaken. Phillip was staring ahead as if still seeing the bodies. When she met Winston's eyes he asked solemnly, "You knew those men well?"

"Since I was young."

"My condolences on your loss."

"Thank you." In the past week, she'd lost three dear friends and her heart ached.

"I have to say, when you first yelled that the ranch house was on fire, I thought it was an act— something staged for our benefit. But then . . ." His words faded.

"No, it wasn't an act."

"What will happen next?"

"The sheriff in Tucson will form a posse to find the killers. They'll be brought back, tried, and a jury will decide their punishment."

"Will they be hung?"

"Possibly." She wondered if it was wrong for her to want Winston and the others to pack up and go home. She didn't have it in her to pretend that all was well and go on with her day. More than likely Rhine and Kent would be joining the posse, and with Blanchard's ranch house burned to the ground, she had no way to entertain them even if she wanted to. Granted, she'd been looking forward to knowing Ada better, and although her interactions with Winston had been minimal, she'd enjoyed his company as well. Maybe they'd return sometime in the future, but at the moment, she didn't care.

Portia put off the urge to run inside when they finally arrived at the hotel because her duties came first, and so she called on Luz Salinas. "Can you go in and tell my aunt and uncle what happened?"

Luz dismounted and hurried off. As a grim-faced Cal led the mounts back to the stables, Ada stepped up. "Thank you for your hospitality, Portia, but we'll be going home in the morning. This has been an awful experience. I doubt I'll ever get over the sight of those poor men."

"I understand."

"Come, Winston. I need to lie down." He offered Portia a stiff nod of farewell and escorted his mother away.

"We'll be expecting a refund."

Portia took in the widow's angry face. "I'm sure that can be arranged."

"Make sure it is. I'm going to have nightmares for the rest of my life." She stormed off.

Phillip watched his sister go and sighed. "We certainly got more than we bargained for. I'm sorry we arrived too late to help those men."

"So am I."

"I'd like to come back, maybe next spring, but I'll leave Venna at home. Thanks for your hospitality and for putting up with her tantrums."

Portia offered a small smile. "You're welcome. Let the others know that I'll have the maids bring lunch to their rooms."

"Will do."

Her duties done, Portia hurried inside.

Rhine looked up when Portia walked into his office, and she could tell by the anger and distress in his eyes that Luz had already passed along the story. He was in the process of putting on his gun belt. She assumed he was on his way to Tucson to notify the sheriff. Luz and Eddy were seated in chairs near his desk.

Eddy stood and scanned Portia anxiously. "Are you all right, dear?"

"A little shaken but I'm okay. Kent and Matt stayed behind to put the fires out."

One of the maids stuck her head in the door. "Mr. and Mrs. Fontaine, the sheriff's here."

Tucson sheriff Zeb O'Hara stepped inside. He was a redheaded, brown-eyed Irishman of average height, but much of the red had been replaced by gray. He'd been the sheriff for as long as the Fontaines had been in the territory.

Rhine said, "I was just on my way to see you."

"Then you've heard?" O'Hara asked.

"Yes. Portia just got back. My foreman is still there making sure the fires are out."

The sheriff's brow furrowed with confusion. "What fires?"

"The ones out at the Blanchard ranch," Portia replied.

"First I'm hearing of it."

Portia and Eddy exchanged a look of surprise as Rhine asked, "You don't know about Buck and Farley being murdered?"

His astonishment gave them their answer. "Okay. Start from the beginning."

Portia told him the story. When she finished, he swore, then hastily apologized to the ladies for his language. Eddy waved him off.

Rhine said, "I thought that was why you were here."

"No. Geronimo escaped the reservation last night. I'm riding around to alert everyone."

They stiffened with shock.

"The army says he left with about sixteen warriors, a hundred women, and nine or ten children. They figure he and his people won't get far, but the last time it took the army, what, almost three years to run him to ground. I'm not holding my breath that he'll be found soon."

Rhine voiced what Portia had been thinking. "He and his people could be anywhere by now."

"Yes, and the army wants all the local sheriffs in on the hunt. Which means I can't muster a posse to track down the men who killed Farley and Buck, at least not right away."

"Can you spare one of your deputies?"

"No, I can't." His voice was sincere as he continued. "If times were different, I could deputize you—but I can't. Some of the folks around here would have my head and my badge if I did."

Eddy's voice was cold. "So these murderers get off scot-free?"

O'Hara looked decidedly uncomfortable. "No. I'll send out a Wanted bulletin, and if you can find someone I can deputize, I will. Nothing says Rhine and the others can't join the posse, but the deputy has to be White."

Rhine's reply was terse. "Understood."

Portia knew the sheriff dealt with people of color as fairly as he was able but the restrictions were still bigoted and senseless.

"Sorry, Rhine."

"As you stated, these are the times. Thanks for stopping by."

After the sheriff's departure, there was winter in the green eyes that assessed Portia and Eddy, but they were well aware that there was nothing they could do.

Eddy looked to her husband. "Do you know anyone Zeb can deputize?"

Rhine blew out a sigh of frustration. "Not off hand, and with Geronimo on the loose, no one's going to want to leave their family to lead a posse."

Portia agreed. People in the area were terrified of the Apache, and because of the desperate situation the Apache were facing, the fear was justified. The prospect of Parnell and his band of killers escaping justice for want of a posse left her both saddened and infuriated. "The Jakes party will be leaving in the morning. They were overwhelmed by the killings."

"I understand," Rhine said. "Let them know we'll wire them a return of their funds."

"Do we tell them about Geronimo?" Portia asked.

Eddy seemed to think it over. "On the one hand they deserve to know, but on the other hand I don't want them scared witless with worry they'll be killed in their beds on their last night here."

Rhine made the decision. "We'll tell them. My worry is Regan. When she gets back from her mail run this afternoon I want her to stay close to home until we get word on Geronimo's whereabouts."

Portia agreed. More than likely the old war chief and his people were heading to the Mexican border to seek safety in the mountains they once called home, but as Rhine told the sheriff, they could be anywhere and she didn't want her sister accidentally crossing their path.

Eddy asked Rhine, "So what do we do about the posse?"

He shrugged. "I'll figure something out. Now that I don't have to ride for the sheriff, I'm going to go out to the ranch and see the damage. I want to find out if any arrangements have been made to transport the bodies to Tucson and if Kent's learned anything new about what happened."

Portia hoped he had. "Are you going to rebuild?"

"Yes, but after what happened today, we might want to rethink the dude ranch portion of what we offer our guests. I know the killings today probably wouldn't happen again, but word's going to get around and people might rethink visiting if they're afraid."

Eddy said, "Or reservations will climb from those hoping to witness that type of violence."

Portia knew they were both right and she was concerned. If guests stopped coming, not only would her family's life and income be affected but the lives and welfare of their employees would be impacted, too.

Rhine's voice brought her back to the conversation. "Whatever we decide, I will be holding on to that land. The more Tucson grows the more valuable it becomes. We could always lease out the ranch house after it's rebuilt."

Portia stood. "I'm going to get cleaned up and change my clothes. I told Phillip I'd have lunch sent to their rooms."

"I'll see to it," Eddy replied. "Make sure you get something to eat, too."

"I will."

Luz stood, too. "I need to get cleaned up and speak with my daughter."

Rhine nodded.

Eddy and Luz embraced. "Go get some rest," Eddy whispered. "I'm so glad you weren't harmed."

"So am I." Her eyes sad, she slipped out.

In her room, Portia wondered who her uncle might approach about being deputized. She also wondered how Kent was faring and how soon he'd return. She didn't want him accidentally encountering Geronimo either.

CHAPTER TEN

With the fires doused, there was nothing left for Kent and Matt to do. Both men had lost everything in the fires from razors to socks. The only personal items they still possessed were their saddles, horses, and the clothes on their backs.

"So now what?" the younger man asked.

"I want to take a look around and see if we can figure out which direction Parnell and the others might have taken. It could help us find them." The murders hadn't taken place that long ago but each passing minute put those responsible farther away from the scene.

"Then what?"

"We ride back to the hotel and see what Mr. Fontaine wants to do. If I know Rhine, he'll probably want to rebuild. You're welcome to hang on here until then."

"But I don't have a place to stay."

"Neither do I but he'll put us up."

"You sure?"

Kent nodded. He understood the younger man's worries. Being employed by Blanchard had given Matt a place to call home for the first time in years and he wouldn't be looking forward to being at loose ends again.

"What about pay?" Matt asked. "Mr. Fontaine won't pay us if we aren't working, will he?"

"I don't know what he'll decide, but if not I have some money saved up. Should be enough to keep us both above water until things are worked out."

"I can't ask you to do that."

"You didn't ask. I volunteered."

"But—"

"Look, we can sit here and argue or we can ride back to the hotel and get a bath and some food. How do you vote?"

Matt smiled. "I vote for the hotel."

"Thought you would. Hopefully Rhine will have some word on the posse by the time we return, so, let's go take that look around."

They were walking to their mounts when Rhine rode up. He dismounted and scanned what was left of the ranch house.

Kent told him. "They used kerosene. Burned both buildings right down to the foundations. Is the sheriff getting a posse?"

"No."

Kent stared. "Why not?"

"Geronimo escaped last night and the army wants all the lawmen in the area to help track the old chief down. O'Hara has no one he can spare." Rhine then explained why the sheriff couldn't deputize him or Kent.

The injustice of the illogical restrictions left

184

Kent tight-lipped. "So did he say we couldn't track Parnell down on our own?" Having to look over his shoulder for Apache while tracking down Parnell was a complication he hadn't planned on.

"No, but we'll have no legal status to arrest him."

Kent didn't care about that. He'd ridden in Wyoming's range wars and not everything done there had been legal either, but it had been right. "If we bring Parnell in, will they jail him or not?"

"I don't really know."

Kent was so frustrated he wanted to punch something.

Rhine asked Matt, "What can you tell me about Parnell?"

"Not much. He bragged a lot but you never knew how much of what he was saying was true."

"For example?"

"He claimed to have run guns to the Apache, that he'd ridden the Chisolm Trail with a Texas outfit, and that he had a Mexican wife. He also said he had a good friend in Tucson, which is how he wound up working for Mr. Blanchard."

"Did he say who the friend was?"

"Mrs. Landry's husband, Charlie."

Rhine paused. "I never knew that. I wonder if Charlie's back from—did Missy say Kansas City or St. Louis, Kent?"

Kent shrugged. He didn't remember but he did remember Mrs. Landry planned to disappear. He

185

wondered if Landry knew his wife had flown the coop on the wings of Rhine's bank draft. "If he is back, maybe he can tell us where Parnell's likely to be."

Kent then told Rhine about Howard Lane's help in putting down the fire. "He and his men rode over because they spotted the smoke. He had the bodies driven into Tucson. He's offering to help with the burial costs."

"Howard's a good man." Rhine studied Kent for a long silent moment. "There's not going to be much work for a foreman in the next few weeks but I will need help rebuilding. Are you moving on or staying?"

Kent smiled for the first time since the fire. "Too late for you to get rid of me now, old man. I'm here for keeps."

"What about you, Matt?" Rhine asked.

"I'd like to stay on, too, sir, if you'll have me."

"Good. Once things settle down, we'll talk about rebuilding and go from there. Kent you can have your old room back at the hotel. Matt, we'll put you up in one of the guest rooms."

"I'll be okay out in the stable, sir."

"Mrs. Fontaine is not going to let you live in the stable, son, and neither am I."

Matt dropped his head and smiled.

Although Kent and Matt had used the pond to wash up as best they could, their clothes were covered with soot and reeked of smoke. "We lost everything we owned in the fire," Kent told Rhine. "Do you have any clothes we can borrow until we get these washed up and can go into Tucson tomorrow to buy new?"

"I'm sure I can find something, and the hotel laundress will take care of what you're wearing now. Just set them in the hallway when we get back. Shouldn't take them long to dry on the line in this heat."

Kent was relieved.

"So were you on your way back to the hotel when I rode up?" Rhine asked.

"Yes, but I wanted to see if I could track Parnell first. With the ground being so rocky and churned up by all the horses and Lane's men, I doubt we'll find anything but you never know."

"Then let's see what we can find."

While they rode, Kent realized he hadn't asked Rhine how the hotel's guests were holding up. It wasn't every day city people had a personal encounter with murder. Had he not summoned the doctors to aid Buck, Ada Jakes and the widow might have been spared the grisly sight. Under normal circumstances he would've asked the women to stay back, but nothing about the incident qualified as such. He had no idea if Portia had ever witnessed something like that, but she seemed angrier with the taking of the men's lives than repulsed. First Blanchard and now Buck and Farley. It was a lot of death for a person to handle but she hadn't acted squeamish. Not that he'd expected her to. She was tough, that Portia. One of the many things that made her stand out and drew him in.

Arriving at the hotel, they turned their horses over to Cal. Kent asked him, "No trouble with the guests on the way back, Cal?"

The older man shook his head. "None. City folks leaving in the morning though."

Rhine nodded in agreement. "I forgot to tell you that."

Kent wasn't surprised by their decision. Life in the West could be cruel and harsh. It wasn't the game of pretend many of the dudes wanted it to be.

Leaving the stables, Rhine said, "The maids will bring you lunch and you can join us for dinner this evening. Matt, let's get you to your room. Kent, I'll see you later."

"Thanks, Rhine."

In his bedroom, a weary Kent stripped off his dirty clothes, set them in the hallway, and walked naked into the washroom to soak in the big clawfoot tub.

As Portia and her family mingled with the guests before dinner, she tried to convince herself she wasn't anxious to see Kent. She knew he'd returned earlier and was using the guest room he'd been given before. Logically she shouldn't need to know more than that, but being around him made her illogical and the parts of herself that were attuned to him missed his presence. Seated beside her was Ada Jakes, who seemed to have recovered from the day's ordeal. She was telling Portia about a women's convention being held in San Francisco and Portia realized it was the same gathering Eddy and her friends planned on attending. When she mentioned it to Ada, the woman asked, "Are you coming along, too?"

"Yes, and I'm very much looking forward to the speakers."

"Frances Harper will be giving the main address."

Portia was delighted. "I've always wanted to hear her speak."

"Then you shall have the opportunity. She'll be staying at my home. I'm having a dinner for her with a few select people the night before her talk. I'll make sure you and Mrs. Fontaine are sent invitations so you can be introduced."

Portia felt honored.

"In fact, why don't you and your aunt plan on staying with me and Winston?"

Portia smelled a trap but offered a smooth counter. "We usually stay with Uncle Rhine's brother, Andrew, and his wife when we visit the city."

"I see. Well, I will speak with her about the matter and see if I can't have you as my guests instead."

Portia didn't argue. As she discreetly glanced up to see if Kent had arrived, her eyes met Winston's across the room. He was speaking with Rhine, Phillip, and Matt. He smiled her way.

"You two would make an outstanding couple, you know."

Portia hadn't realized Ada was watching her so closely. "Maybe if I were looking to marry, but I'm not."

Ada patted her hand. "So you say, my dear. So you say."

Portia enjoyed Ada's company, but her attempts to play matchmaker were not endearing. Portia was glad when they were called to dinner a few moments later.

Everyone had just taken their seats when Kent walked into the dining room. "Sorry, I'm late. I fell asleep."

Portia thought it was a sin for a man to be so handsome. He had a slow easy way about him but beneath the exterior he crackled with a power that was raw, vital, and dangerous to a woman determined to keep her heart guarded and buttons done up. Her nipples tightened as if agreeing.

Eddy said, "No apologies needed. You had a long morning. There's an empty seat next to Portia."

Portia hoped her aunt wasn't playing matchmaker, too. She was beginning to feel like a pawn on a chessboard. *Not that you don't want him near.* She ignored that and hoped she didn't embarrass herself again by dropping her silverware. Winston was seated directly across from her. Regan was on his right and his mother on his left. As Kent made his way to the empty chair and sat down, irritation flashed across Ada's face but was gone just as quickly. It was as if the plainspoken woman somehow knew the heat of his nearness played havoc with her senses.

"I see you got back okay," he said quietly.

"I did."

"Sorry all the work you did on the roof went up in smoke."

"So am I."

Only then did he turn to the other guests. "Evening, everyone."

They nodded.

Portia warmed with the knowledge that he'd spoken to her first. Regan gave her a knowing grin.

Phillip Pratt, seated next to Matt on Portia's side of the table, cracked, "Mr. Randolph, my sister decided to eat in her room. Feel free to enjoy your dinner in peace."

Kent chuckled and saluted him with his wine. "Thanks."

The first course was a cold soup served in wineglasses.

Ada studied her glass with wondrous eyes.

"This is certainly a unique presentation. What is this?"

Eddy answered. "A cold cucumber and melon soup from Spain known as Melón Piel de Sapo."

Portia loved the sweet tangy soup. Its refreshing, creamy texture was garnished with diced red peppers and a thin slice of fried ham that rested vertically in the center.

Winston dipped his spoon and took a taste. "This is delicious. Perfect counter to the hot weather."

Eddy nodded. "Since you're leaving tomorrow, Rhine thought we should make this evening special, so thank him. The soup was his idea."

They voiced their thanks.

Ada glanced down at Eddy. "Mrs. Fontaine, Portia told me that you and your friends are coming to San Francisco for the convention."

"Yes we are."

"My women's group is one of the sponsors. She said you usually stay with relatives when you visit but Winston and I would love for you two to be our guests."

"Why thank you," Eddy replied. "Portia and I will discuss it and let you know."

"I may be speaking out of turn but I think she and my son would make a fine couple. Don't you?"

Eddy raised an eyebrow.

Winston cleared his throat and smiled. "My mother is a handful as you can see."

"I'm known for speaking my mind, and I'm not ashamed of that. She'd make you a fine wife and me a wonderful daughter-in-law. It's an idea that should be pursued."

Portia sensed Kent studying the Jakeses. "I'm flattered, Mrs. Jakes, but as I said—"

"I know, I know, but the right gentleman can change your mind. I never thought I'd marry either, but Gavin, my late husband, showed me the error of my ways. Being married doesn't mean you have to set aside your own desires, isn't that true, Mrs. Fontaine?"

"Well, yes, but—"

"See, Portia. Even your aunt agrees with me."

To his credit, Winston appeared embarrassed. "Let's change the subject, Mother, shall we?"

"If you insist, but I have one last point to make. Portia, I doubt you'll meet anyone around here who can match my son in intelligence and refinement." And she shot Kent a smug smile over her wineglass before turning to Regan and asking, "Tell me about this mail route of yours."

Portia's anger at the outrageous dig matched the glowing hostility in Eddy's eyes and the coldness reflected in Rhine's.

Kent, obviously not cowed, leaned over and whispered, "If you marry him, you'll shoot her dead within a week."

Portia snorted then did her best to regain her composure. Ada and Winston turned and eyed

193

her suspiciously but she pretended not to notice.

Ada Jakes's dig made Kent no never mind. Her son hadn't made Portia laugh just a moment ago, nor seen her eyes slide shut with passion. He added Ada to the list of folks who considered themselves superior, like the pompous Darian Day and Edward Salt. The list had ample room to add others should the need arise.

"Mr. Randolph, will you be escorting us to the train depot in the morning?"

He met Winston Jakes's gray eyes. "Yes."

"That will make me and mother feel safer with Geronimo running loose."

Kent wanted to say something sarcastic about being refined enough to protect their greenhorn asses but not enough to court Portia but kept that to himself. "The Apaches are probably south of the border by now. You shouldn't be in any danger."

"Good to know."

It occurred to Kent that the man might be trying to make amends for his harridan of a mother, so he decided to be pleasant and give him the benefit of the doubt.

Once the main course was served and they began eating, Winston addressed him again. "How long have you been employed by the Fontaines?"

"I worked for Rhine back in Virginia City."

Regan interjected. "He's known Portia and me since she was twelve and I was ten."

Jakes couldn't hide his surprise. "So long?"

"Yes. He's like family in a way," Portia explained, and the shy smile she sent Kent made his heart rear like a pleased stallion.

Regan said, "He calls her Duchess."

Ada blinked with shock. In response, Regan smiled innocently his way and proved to Kent once again why he found her such a joy. Ada seemed to be evaluating him from an entirely different place now. *Yes, you old biddy, I am a threat to your plans for your perfect son.*

She asked, "May I ask why?"

"No," Kent replied.

Rhine coughed to hide his laugh. Kent ignored the smoke pouring from Ada's ears and went back to his meal. She'd already labeled him unsuitable, so he might as well live up to it. She'd probably tumble out of her chair were he to boast of having attended Howard Medical School and that his father, like her son, was a doctor, but he wasn't ashamed of the path he'd chosen for his life, nor the man it had helped him become.

One of the maids came in and spoke quietly to Rhine, who nodded and stood. "Excuse me. Someone's here to speak with me. I'll be back shortly."

After his departure, the meal continued, but when shouting drifted in, Eddy shot Kent a look of concern. He stood and left the room.

He found Rhine and a big overweight man standing by the door that led out to the grounds. The man's face was red with anger and his eyes narrowed. His blue shirt was wet with sweat but whether it stemmed from the heat or his fury, Kent couldn't tell.

The stranger barked, "I will take you to court, Fontaine!"

Rhine always in control, shrugged. "Do whatever you feel necessary, but the deed was legally signed and recorded, and the bank draft deposited."

Kent guessed the man to be Missy Landry's husband. "Everything okay, Rhine?"

The man looked Kent up and down.

"Name's Randolph," he said by way of introduction.

Landry didn't respond.

"Mr. Landry is upset that his wife signed over the deed to her father's ranch."

"She had no right!"

Rhine pointed out, "The land was left to her in the will Blanchard drew up ten years ago, and she had a representative there to advise during our transaction."

"He said you bulldozed her."

"He's lying."

"I want that land back!"

"Does Missy claim I pressured her?"

Landry's jaw tightened even more before he admitted, "I don't know where she's at."

"Ah. If it's any help, she said she was going to join you in St. Louis, but according to my bank notice, the draft was deposited in a bank in Chicago."

"That bitch!"

Kent asked, "Have you heard about the murder of Farley and Buck?"

"I don't know nothing about it."

"So you have heard?"

He didn't answer.

Undeterred, Kent continued, "Before Buck died, he said Ty Parnell was the man who shot them. Do you know where he is?"

"No. Just got back yesterday."

"I hear you two are good friends."

"He didn't shoot nobody. Maybe if Fontaine hadn't pressured Missy to sell that land they'd still be alive."

Kent marveled at the man's response. "Are you saying the place was burned down and two men murdered because your wife sold Rhine that land?"

"I didn't have anything to do with it and neither did Ty."

Kent sensed Landry was lying through his teeth.

Rhine said, "I need to get back to my guests. If you want to pursue this legally, have your lawyer contact me. Good evening, Mr. Landry."

Kent said, "Nice meeting you. Hope you find your wife."

Landry looked like he wanted to explode a fist in Kent's face. Kent waited. Landry muttered an ugly slur and stormed out the door.

Rhine smiled. "You really need to stop taunting folks."

"Who me?"

"Although I did enjoy the way you set down Ada Jakes. Perfect couple indeed. Portia would end up setting that woman's hair on fire." Rhine then turned serious. "So, tell me truthfully where you stand with my niece."

"Noticed something have you?"

"Eddy and I may be aging but our eyes are still good." He waited.

Kent knew that after their decades of friendship, he was owed an honest reply. "Truthfully, I'd like to court her if she'll have me. Ada Jakes to the contrary, I think Portia and I would do well as man and wife."

Rhine studied him. "And if she chooses, say, Jakes?"

"Then I'll give them my best and step aside."

"Really?"

"Probably not. I'm more likely to shoot the bastard, throw her over my shoulder, and ride away."

Rhine roared with laughter. "Then you have my blessings."

"Thanks."

Now to convince Portia.

• • •

Portia was seated outside at the trestle table with Winston Jakes. He'd asked to speak with her after dinner. Although she was still upset with his heavy-handed mother, she decided to be polite and listen to what he had to say.

"Do you enjoy living here?" he asked.

"I do."

"I wouldn't be able to handle this heat on a daily basis."

He'd mentioned that before. She didn't point that out but played along in order to hear his real reason for seeking her out. "You become accustomed to it, and it can get quite cold during the winters."

When she finished silence fell between them until he said, "I want to apologize for my mother— again."

Portia hoped he didn't expect her to wave off the apology. "She deliberately insulted Kent. It was mean-spirited and uncalled for."

"In her defense, I think she senses he's competition. Is he?"

Portia studied him. "I've known Kent for a very long time. I met you and your mother yesterday."

"You haven't answered my question."

"I haven't known you long enough for an answer to be warranted, frankly."

He chuckled. "You are upset with her, aren't you?"

"I'm sure this isn't a first-time experience." Ada more than likely insulted people on a regular basis but couched it as being plainspoken.

He looked embarrassed. "It isn't, but our acquaintances tend to indulge her—let's say."

"Let's say, here, we don't indulge rudeness."

"Ouch."

"I admire your mother's views but not her manners."

"And me? What of me?"

"I really don't know you. Do you see her forwardness as something to emulate?"

"She's my mother. I have to be respectful, Portia."

"I understand that, but would she be so keen on my being her perfect daughter-in-law if she knew my mother was a whore?"

His eyes went wide as plates and he scanned her features as if searching for a visible sign of her parentage.

Temper climbing, Portia let him take a good long look.

"You're lying of course."

"No. In fact, Regan and I have no idea who our fathers are. We're not sure our mother does either."

He drew back as if she were a rattler poised to strike.

Her smile didn't reach her eyes. "You've failed the test, Winston. I'll see you in the morning for the ride to the train depot. Have a pleasant night."

Not protesting his dismissal, he left without so much as a backward glance.

A few minutes later, Kent walked up. When he peered down at her face, she didn't bother to wipe away the sheen of angry tears.

Voice filled with concern, he asked softly, "What's wrong?"

"I told the perfect son my mother was a whore."

He studied her for a moment. "And he ran off like his shoes were on fire, I'll bet." He took a seat and continued to view her with a gentle regard that touched her heart. "Want me to find him and put a few bullets in his hide?"

"No, I'd prefer to plug him myself, but Eddy would probably frown on me shooting a guest."

"I don't know, especially if you shoot his mother first."

Portia laughed. His ability to make her do so was a gift that burned away the lingering anger and resentment. She wiped her eyes. "Thank you."

"For what?"

"Making me feel better and proving that not all men are asses. You, my uncle, and Jim Dade are rare."

"I'll take the compliment. I know what will also make you feel better."

She viewed him skeptically. Surely he wasn't proposing his kisses as a cure-all.

"I'm talking about a ride to Carmichael Falls. What did you think I was going to say?"

She didn't respond.

"You thought I meant kisses, didn't you?"

"No.

"Fibber. Get your horse. Who knows, if you're a good girl, you might get kisses, too."

She punched him in the arm, hard. "Ow!"

"Your arm is like iron. Stop pretending to be a greenhorn."

"I may have to take your drawers for that."

Her mouth dropped open and she searched his face with wide eyes.

He howled with laughter. "Oh, Duchess. The look on your face. Go get your horse."

Portia wasn't sure what to do.

"Go. I'll be good. I promise."

"That's what scares me." She rose, gave him another look that made him firm his lips to keep from smiling. He failed miserably.

Certain she had no business going anywhere with him, she left to change clothes and saddle Arizona.

CHAPTER ELEVEN

With Kent's threat to take her drawers still fresh in her mind, Portia traded her skirt and blouse for a pair of denims and a shirt. She still didn't know if he'd been teasing, but she figured whatever his plan entailed, her undergarments would be harder to confiscate while inside the denims. A soft knock sounded on the door connecting her room to Regan's. "Come on in."

Regan took in her attire. "Where are you going?"

"For a ride."

"Please, not with Winston Jakes."

"No."

"He barreled by me a short while ago looking like he'd seen a ghost."

Portia brushed out her hair and repinned it. "I told him I was the daughter of a whore."

"Didn't take it well?"

She shook her head.

"Good. Maybe now he and the bullfrog will leave you be."

Portia knew she shouldn't be encouraging her sister, but the description of Ada Jakes was just so apt she chuckled.

Regan added, "You know she looks like one and with that gravelly voice, she even sounds like one."

Portia agreed again. "I didn't like what she said to Kent. Why do people do that to him?"

"Because he's the strongest, finest stallion in the herd and they're jealous."

Portia tied a bandana around her throat.

"I can ride with you if you want company."

"You're certainly welcome. Kent and I are going over to the falls."

Regan stopped. "You're riding with Kent?"

"Yes."

"Then I decline."

"Why?"

"He's not going to kiss you with your little sister looking on."

Heat burned her cheeks.

"And I'm not allowing you to use me to protect yourself from something we both know you want. You like his kisses, don't you?"

Portia tried not to smile but couldn't help it.

"There's hope for you yet, sister mine." Looking pleased, Regan retraced her steps to the door. "Enjoy yourself, Portia."

Once she was alone again, Portia eyed herself in the mirror of her vanity table. Would he kiss her? *Probably.* Did she want him to? She thought back on those few heated moments in Old Man Blanchard's house. *Definitely.* Feeling as shameless as she often accused Regan of being, Portia set out for the stables.

He was there and waiting. Seeing him holding

the reins of the already saddled Arizona, she said, "I can saddle my own horse."

"No one is saying you can't, Portia. I know how capable you are."

Chastened, she dropped her head for a moment. "Sorry. I suppose I should've just said thank you."

"Maybe, but you said what you thought needed saying. I don't have a problem with that."

Portia knew how prickly she could be at times and she appreciated his patience with that part of her. With that in mind, she whispered, "Thanks."

"You're welcome and just so you know, I'll probably do it again. My way of showing you kindness, Duchess. Nothing more. Ready?"

She mounted, but he remained on the ground by his horse. She got the impression that he was eyeing her behind.

He flashed one of those smiles. "Yes, I'm admiring the view. I may be one of those rare men, but I am a man, darlin'. I like you in denims."

"What am I going to do with you?"

"How about we find out when we get to the falls."

Shaking her head at his audaciousness she turned her horse. "Are you coming or not?"

"Now there's a question loaded with dynamite."

Having no idea what he meant, confusion filled her face.

"Never mind," he said, mounting up. "Lead the way."

Still stumped, she studied him and thought back on what she'd asked. Finally realizing the double entendre of her question, heat burned her cheeks. "I'm done talking to you." She rode away, trailed by the sound of his soft knowing laughter.

He caught up to her quickly and they reined their mounts to a nice easy pace. As it did most evenings, the heat had subsided a bit, but the mountains and the sky remained as vivid as ever. Their sure-footed horses had no trouble with the rocky trail or navigating the washes running with the last of the previous winter's snow melt. The landscape was quiet and serene.

"Ever thought about living someplace else?" he asked.

"When I was younger, I thought I might like to move to a big city like San Francisco. I've visited there many times, but after a few days I was always ready to come home." And she had. Even though Regan accused her of never leaving her office, she'd missed the quiet, the wide open spaces, the sunsets, and the peace the land seemed to hold. "How about you? You've lived a lot of different places, which would you like to call home?"

"Here, I think." He looked over at her. "Surprised?"

"Somewhat. You don't impress me as wanting to live in a big city either, but why here, of all places?"

"Not sure, but it calls to me, if that makes any sense. I took a ride the first evening after I arrived, saw the meadows and the mountains, took in the sky, and for whatever reasons, I felt like I'd finally come home. Made me think about buying a plot of my own and putting down roots—maybe finding a wife and starting a family."

Portia saw the honesty in his eyes and the impact of it pierced her so deeply, she had to look away. She readily admitted to not having had a lot of experience with men, but she'd never had one open himself up to her in this manner before and she was shaken by it, because for the first time in her life she considered what it might be like to be the wife of a man like him. Also for the first time, she didn't immediately discount the notion. Kent Randolph was slowly changing her and he made her want to embrace that change.

They rode silently for a time. She mined her thoughts, looking over every now and then to meet his steady gaze and wondering if he had been changed, too.

"Awful quiet over there, Duchess. Should I have kept that last part to myself?"

"No. I . . ." She wasn't sure whether to admit the truth or not. "I just never had a man share his dreams with me before."

"Most men I know have them, but the fear of being laughed at, or that it somehow diminishes a man, makes us keep quiet."

"But you shared them with me."

"Makes you special."

That, too, pierced her, and before she could further analyze her reaction, he asked, "And what are yours, if you don't mind me asking?"

"I'd like to have my own bookkeeping business."

"You have the skills, so when are you going to start?"

She thought on that. "I really don't know." She'd shared the idea with her uncle in the past and he'd pledged his support, but in spite of her outward confidence she'd been hesitant about approaching other businessmen because of the uncertainty of how she'd be received.

They reached the falls. Leaving their horses, they walked to the edge of the canyon. The sounds of the rushing water cascading over the lip of the rock face to the pool below filled the silence.

"Shall we sit?" he asked.

She nodded and led him to a log nearby. Of course the surroundings reminded her of the first time he kissed her, but she did her best to set that aside for the moment.

"So, what's inside you that's keeping you from starting your business?"

The question surprised her. "Why do you think it's something inside me?"

"Because on the outside you're tough enough to walk on water, so it must be something inside."

How does he know me so well? "You won't laugh?"

"Of course not."

"I'm afraid." She quickly glanced over to gauge his reaction but as always he met her eyes steadily.

"That's honest. What scares you?"

"That I won't be taken seriously because I can't write my name in the snow."

He stared and then laughed so loud he startled nearby birds into flight. "Where on earth did you learn that?" He thought back on all the snow-writing contests he'd participated in as boy.

"Old Man Blanchard, but don't tell Eddy. She'd be appalled."

"And well she should be. You're outrageous, woman."

"I'll take that as a compliment."

Their smiles met and unsaid words lingered and mingled. Portia thought he might kiss her, but he instead said, "I've known some pretty strong women and you rank right up there with the best. Fear is natural but you get on the bronc anyway, and if it throws you, you keep getting up and getting back on, okay?"

She nodded. She knew he was right because

it was something she'd been telling herself all along, but for some reason, hearing him voice it seemed to douse the doubts that had kept her from moving forward.

"Good girl. Now, come, let's find a place with a bit more cover so I can give you your reward." Taking her hand, he led her deeper into the trees.

The kiss that followed was gentle at first, an opening refrain of soft, sweet sweeps of his lips over hers that made the embers left from their last encounter flare to life. With each passing moment the intensity rose, heating her senses, making her lips part, urging her to get closer. He obliged and she wrapped her arms around him and thrilled to his groan of approval as their bodies met. He moved his lips to her throat above the bandana and tugged it free to give him access to the soft scented skin beneath. The distant sound of the waterfall matched the rush of her blood. Bold as ever he tugged her shirt free of her denims and slid his hands beneath. His warm palms worked over the band of silk binding her breasts and he whispered heatedly, "One day, soon, I'm going to have you naked except for this silk so I can show you exactly what it does to me."

The potent promise set off a shiver of excitement that radiated from the deep wanting between her thighs and spread like flame through her limbs. Her buttons were undone and when he brushed the halves open and took a silk-shrouded nipple gently between his teeth, she crooned aloud. His fingers played with the other while he fed and licked, and her breath stacked in her throat.

"Pull the silk down, Duchess. Show me what my loving has done to you. Let me see how tight and hard you are."

The raw request sent the flame soaring. Looking into his passion-hardened eyes, she unveiled herself and he stroked a slow circle around each aching bud. "Do you want me to make them harder, Duchess?"

Her back braced against a tree, Portia could barely stand due to the storm whirling inside. He leaned down and kissed her mouth possessively. "You have to say 'please,' darlin'."

Not wanting him to stop, she breathed, "Please . . ."

He treated her to a silent, wicked loving that left her gasping and arching into his masterful mouth. His palms slid up and down her bared sides, learning her, branding her, and slid behind to the skin above the waistline of her denims and down to cup her behind to bring her flush against the hard ridge that made him male. He raised his mouth to hers once more while that part of him moved wantonly against her. "Feel what you do to me, Duchess."

She did and, unable to resist the call, pressed herself closer, teased her tongue against the corners of his lips and moved her hips in sensual response. The contact gathered inside like thunderclouds and she lowered her hand to him. At her touch, he hissed a sharp intake of breath and covered her hand with his to show her what he wanted. Seeing and feeling what it did to him filled her with a surge of power, so she let him guide her for a few intense moments more only to have him abruptly pull away. Breathing harshly, passion glittering in his dark eyes, he turned his back and uttered a curse. "Close your blouse, Duchess."

"Did I do something wrong?"

He shook his head and whispered "Lord" hoarsely before saying, "No, baby. But you're an eyelash away from having your first time on a bunch of pine needles and tree roots. I respect you more than that."

"But—"

"Close your blouse."

Desire was still rampaging like a firestorm through her blood in tandem with an ache between her thighs. "And suppose I do want my first time—"

He shot her a quelling look that silenced her completely. "Fine," she snapped. Angry now, she forced her fingers to do up her buttons and stuffed her shirt tail back into her denims. "I'm ready to go back."

"I'm not. Give me a few minutes."

That snuffed her pique. Concern filled her. "Are you okay?"

"No, but I will be as soon as my body calms down enough to get in the saddle. It's a little worked up at the moment."

"Oh."

This time when he turned, he wore a smile and she met it with a shy one of her own. "I'm a little worked up myself. We need to be near a bed the next time we do this."

He laughed. "Are you trying to kill me? No. Besides, your first time should be on your wedding night with your husband."

"I'm not having either, so your point is moot."

"So you say."

"So I know." *He could be your husband.* She pushed that aside.

On the ride back to the hotel, although Kent's passion had subsided somewhat, just glancing over at her riding beside him made him want to find that bed she'd referenced and spend the rest of his life giving her pleasure. As it stood, he was going to have to do some self-pleasuring if he planned to get any sleep tonight because his body was still straining for release. He blew out a breath. He supposed were he to make another woman his wife, the memory of these private moments with Portia would fade with time, but more than likely he'd take the feel of her soft skin and the sounds she'd made in response to his loving to his grave. He wanted her like a man dying in the desert craved water. It was easy to see that she wanted him, too, but was it enough for her to let go of her stance on remaining unmarried? He needed an answer because she was the only woman he wanted as his wife.

Dusk was rolling in when they reached the hotel. After bedding down their mounts, they left the stable and made the walk to the doors. "Feeling better about Jakes?" he asked.

She nodded. "Much better. In fact, I haven't given him or his mother a moment's thought. Thank you for the novel cure."

"You're welcome." He didn't want her to leave him, and by the way she looked up at him, she appeared to be struggling, too. "You go on in. I want to check in with Matt. I'll see you in the morning."

"Good night, Kent."

"Night, Duchess."

Before going to her room, Portia searched out Eddy and found her in the kitchen taking inventory. "Do you ever rest?"

Eddy turned. "Pot. Kettle."

Knowing her aunt was referring to Portia's well-known work ethic, she dropped her eyes and grinned.

Eyes shining with amusement, Eddy asked,

"So, did you enjoy your ride? You certainly look as though you did."

Portia froze and wondered what had given her away, but was too embarrassed to ask.

"There's nothing to be ashamed of as long as you're careful. Do you know what I mean?"

Her eyes were very serious now, and Portia nodded. "Babies."

"Yes. As far as I know, this is your first time being swept away by someone and passion can override good sense very easily."

She thought back on telling Kent about maybe wanting her first time to be on a bed of pine needles and knew Eddy was right. She had been swept away and definitely hadn't been thinking clearly. It was good he was so honorable. She had a question for her aunt, but having never asked it before, more embarrassment burned her cheeks. "Um. Is there someplace in town where I can purchase—some precautions?" She was smart enough to know that if Kent didn't provide any, she needed to make sure she had her own.

"Talk to your sister."

Portia's jaw dropped.

Eddy chuckled softly. "She and I had the same conversation a few years ago. Regan's always blazed her own path, so when she asked, I told her what she needed to know rather than judge her, refuse, and send her out into the world unprotected. I realized it was safer that way."

215

Portia understood and was glad her aunt hadn't judged her either.

Eddy continued, "Kent has shown himself to be a good man. You could do a lot worse, Portia, and even though I can't wait to get Ada Jakes out of my house, what she said last night about not having to give up your dreams just because you give someone your heart is true. I know how set you've been on going through life alone. That doesn't have to change, but if you can find even a teaspoon of happiness with Kent, take it, because there are women in this world who'd sell all they own to have a man look at them the way he looks at you."

The advice was so heartfelt and overwhelming she didn't know how to respond. Eddy seemed to sense that. "No response is needed, sweetheart. You and I are a lot alike. We both live for our work and being swept away and out of control can be frightening."

Portia nodded knowingly.

"But sometimes being out of control can be freeing in ways that may surprise you. It certainly freed me. And no, I'm not sharing examples," she added with a laugh. "You'll have to gather your own."

"Thanks, Aunt Eddy."

"Come, give me a hug."

Portia walked into her embrace and hugged her tightly. "I love you so much," she whispered.

Her hope was that one day she, too, would be as wise, loving, and caring as this woman who'd saved her life.

"I feel the same way."

They drew back and studied each other for a long moment. Eddy placed a kiss on her forehead. "Now, go talk to Regan and get some rest. We'll celebrate the Jakeses' and that awful widow's leaving when you get back from the train."

Portia laughed and left her aunt to the inventory.

In her room, she knocked softly on Regan's door. Invited in, she stepped into the chaos and Regan looked up from her desk and put down the pen she'd been writing with. "How was your ride? Never mind, I can tell by your lips that you've been thoroughly and soundly kissed."

Amused, Portia peeked at herself in the vanity mirror and stilled. Her lips were swollen and full. Thoroughly kissed indeed. She now knew how Eddy and Regan had been able to tell. *Lord!* Uncomfortable and unsure of how to broach the subject she'd come in to discuss, she cleared her throat. "I need to talk to you about something and Eddy said, I—"

Regan smiled knowingly, "Do you need sponges, sister mine?"

Their eyes met and they both laughed like little girls caught being naughty.

Regan stood and gestured to a blue upholstered chair barely visible beneath the clothing piled atop it. "Have a seat. You've come to the right place."

Later, Portia lay in her bed in her darkened room. She wasn't sure what left her reeling more—her sensual encounter with Kent or the jaw-dropping conversation she'd had with her baby sister. Too exhausted to choose, she drifted off to sleep with a smile on her face.

CHAPTER TWELVE

Portia awakened at dawn. Later, she'd be ushering the Jakes party to the train depot but for the moment she had some thinking to do. Her previously planned-out life was transforming into one that was no longer staid and stern but filled with laughter, passion, and the excitement of new possibilities because of Kent. Did she want to cling to the old Portia who lived for work and little else or throw caution to the wind and open herself and head down a different path? Yesterday, he'd asked why she hadn't moved forward on her idea of starting her own bookkeeping business and for the first time she admitted how afraid she was of failing. She'd never voiced that before, not even to herself but she felt safe sharing her dreams and fears with him. Did that mean she was falling in love? Having never been in love, she didn't know. Eddy had mentioned grabbing a teaspoon of happiness and this new Portia wanted that and the only way to have it was to reach out and claim it. Her decision made, she left the bed to begin her day.

When Kent rode up with Matt to act as armed escort for the ride to Tucson, the sight of Portia standing outside with her charges filled his heart. She looked his way and smiled, but there was a glint of fire in her eyes he knew to be a sign of her temper. Wondering what was wrong, he dismounted and walked over just in time to hear Ada Jakes demand to know, "Did you put water inside so we won't die of thirst in this heat?"

"Yes," Portia responded with what sounded like forced politeness. The old bat shot her a dismissive glare and let herself be handed into the buggy by her son. Seeing Kent, Winston paused and raised his chin challengingly. Kent replied with a ghost of a cold smile. The man looked away and entered the buggy without a word or even acknowledging Portia's presence. Kent assumed the attitude stemmed from what Portia had revealed about her past and he guessed the Jakeses had added her name to his on their list of those they felt themselves superior to.

"Morning. How are you?"

"I'll be better once these greenhorns are on the train and I'm on my way back here."

He was about to reply when he heard the widow Gordon declare in a voice loud enough to be heard in Tucson, "I can't wait to leave this awful place." Clad again in her fancy brown traveling costume, she stormed over to Regan's buggy, adding, "And when I get home, I'll be sure to tell everyone I know what a terrible time I had."

"Please do," Regan tossed back, which seemed to throw the widow off her stride.

He saw Portia drop her head to hide her smile. Kent wanted to cheer.

After handing in his simmering sister, Phillip Pratt turned to Eddy and Rhine standing together watching the departure. "I want to thank you for a memorable experience. I will be returning."

Eddy said, "And *you* will be welcome."

He was the only one Kent heard offer any kind of thanks. Yes, they'd witnessed a murder but the service and the accommodations the hotel offered had been outstanding. Therefore, they had no reason to act as if they'd been raised by skunks. Seeing the Jakeses sitting in the buggy glaring straight ahead and holding themselves stiff as store mannequins, he asked Portia, "Are you ready to go?"

"Extremely."

"Then let's get moving."

As Rhine and Eddy stood watching, Portia gave them a wave and the small caravan set out for Tucson, escorted by the mounted and well-armed Kent and Matt. Cal and the trunks brought up the rear. Everyone in the area was on the alert for the escaped Geronimo and his band. According to the newspapers, Mexico had given the United States Army and its large contingent of Apache scouts permission to cross the border to hunt him down. There had been dozens of false sightings, horses stolen, cattle butchered for the meat, and yes, deaths.

Very aware of this Kent kept a sharp eye on the surroundings and was pleased when they arrived in Tucson without incident.

As he stood with Portia at the depot, waiting for the train to arrive, she was approached by Ada Jakes and informed in a cool voice, "Due to your unfortunate bloodline, Miss Carmichael, I won't be offering you an invitation to my soiree for Mrs. Harper. I do hope you understand."

Portia didn't bat an eye. "And I hope you understand that I'd rather not have an invitation from someone with your appalling lack of manners. Have a safe trip home, Mrs. Jakes."

Wanting to cheer again, Kent watched Winston lead his sputtering mother away.

On the short walk back to where Regan and the others stood waiting with the buggies, he said to the obviously furious Portia, "You handled that very well."

"I wanted to set her hair on fire."

Laughing at her warrior spirit, he walked her back to where her sister stood waiting with Matt and Cal.

"You look fit to be tied," Regan said. "Did the bullfrog offer a parting insult?"

"Yes." And Portia repeated the exchange.

Regan rolled her eyes. "As if someone wanted an invitation. She'll probably serve her esteemed guests flies."

Portia laughed. "I love you so much."

Kent thought that pretty much summed up how he felt about Portia. She moved him like no other woman had before and he was convinced his future would be bereft without her at his side.

"Before we head back, I'd like to check and see if there's any mail for us," Regan said.

"I have some errands to take care of as well," Kent said. Matt and Cal said the same.

"How about we meet back here in an hour?" Portia asked.

Everyone agreed.

Portia hadn't said anything about this, but with the start of her new business in mind, she set out to approach her first potential customer, Sadie Welch, owner of one of the city's most exclusive restaurants, an exclusiveness that banned members of Sadie's race. It wasn't an uncommon practice. Due to Jim Crow and the legions of Whites who refused to support enterprises that catered to a Colored clientele, many Colored business owners were forced to choose between profit and race. Some like Sadie Welch bridged the gap by offering a specific time or day of the week when their neighbors and family members were welcomed. For Sadie it was Sunday evenings.

The place was usually closed at the time of the day when Portia arrived, so she went around the back to the kitchen.

Julia Lane, her aunt Eddy's friend and wife of rancher Howard Lane, was one of the cooks. Seeing Portia, she called out, "Morning, Portia. How are you?" Julia was seated on a chair and plucking a chicken with such speed the feathers were flying.

"I'm well. Is Miss Sadie around?"

"Inside."

"Do you think she has time to speak with me for a few minutes?"

"Let me go and see. Be right back."

When Julia returned a few minutes later, she was accompanied by the tall, golden-skinned Sadie. In spite of her segregated business practices, Sadie was a member of the Tucson Good Works Society, an organization composed of local women of the race who did volunteer work to uplift and support people of color in the surrounding community. Portia and Regan were members as was her aunt and her friends.

"Hello, Portia. How can I help you?"

"I'd like to speak with you about a business proposal."

Sadie paused, her blue eyes taking her in for a silent moment. "Come in."

Portia was led to the book-lined office and offered a seat. From her chair behind the large mahogany desk, Sophie said, "So tell me about this proposal."

Portia did and when she finished, she said, "So,

I stopped in to see if I can be of any service to you and the restaurant."

She graced Portia with a kind smile. "I'm sorry, honey, but I already have someone doing my books. His father is also one of my investors. I can't change horses in the middle of the stream without suffering some serious repercussions."

Portia hid her disappointment. "I understand."

"However, I know how skilled you are, so I will ask around on your behalf."

The support brightened her mood. "Thank you so much."

"You're welcome. Good luck. I'll see you at the next meeting."

Portia left. Keeping an cyc on the time, she stopped in at the barbershop owned by Ephraim Forth. He, too, was kind enough to hear her out, but in the end he told her his nephew James Cordell handled his books. "And I don't have to pay him," he crowed.

Portia gave him a false smile and her thanks and left his small shop to the tinkle of the bell over the door. Refusing to be discouraged, she headed up the walk to speak to the owner of another barbershop and saw Darian Day, over-dressed as always leaning against the wall of his haberdashery. In spite of the climbing temperature, he was attired in a brown and black checkerboard suit, a buttoned-up shirt with a bow tie, and a black bowler sat on his head. Just looking at him made her perspire. She knew he wouldn't let her pass without speaking, so she tamped down her temper in advance.

"Well, well," he said, looking her up and down as if she were some type of dessert. "How are you, Miss Portia?"

"Hello, Mr. Day."

"When are you going to address me by my given name?"

When horses learn to knit. "It's a sign of respect."

"I see. What brings you to town? If you don't mind my asking."

Portia considered lying but there was always a ghost of a chance he might have information on a potential client, so she told him her plans.

"Women don't need to be in business" came his irritating reply. "You should just marry me. As your husband, I'd take care of all your— needs."

She wanted to sock him hard enough to send him flying into the street—fancy duds and all. "No thank you." As she continued on her way, he called out, "I'll be expecting a spot on your dance card next week." She didn't reply. He was referencing Howard and Julia Lane's annual two-day rodeo. The well-attended activities concluded with a big barn dance. She'd never danced with Darian Day before and she didn't see that changing.

Kent, Matt, and Cal were standing by the

buggies when Portia walked up. Kent looked at her face and frowned. "What's wrong?"

"I had the misfortune of speaking with Darian Day. He's enough to curdle anyone's day."

"Which is why Matt and I spent our money with Mr. Krause. Day will starve if he's depending on my patronage to put food on his table."

Cal agreed. "Not one of my favorite people either. He thinks the sun rises and sets because he tells it to."

Regan joined them on the heels of that and handed Kent a letter. "This came for you on today's train. I have a few for Eddy and Rhine, too."

He looked at the envelope. "It's from my father." He stuck it in his pocket.

Portia thought she saw a shadow cross his features but it was gone so quickly she assumed she'd imagined it. He and his father had been at odds when they all lived in Virginia City and she didn't know if they'd reconciled in the years since. As if sensing her regard, he raised his eyes to hers, but there was nothing in them that offered a hint at his thinking. "Are we ready to head back?" he asked.

Everyone agreed, so they started the journey home.

Upon returning, Cal drove the wagon to the stables, Regan and Portia did the same with the buggies while Kent and Matt unsaddled their stallions and turned them loose in the paddock. Leaving Cal with a wave, they were walking back to the hotel when Matt asked, "Do you think Mrs. Fontaine might have something I can do to help me earn my keep?"

Regan hooked her arm in his. "Let's go find out."

Their departure left Portia and Kent alone. "He's a nice young man," Portia noted.

"Yes, he is. Had a hard life growing up."

"So, what are your plans for the day?" she asked.

"Probably ride out to the Blanchard place after the sun drops a bit and take a look around. Howard Lane said he'd keep an eye out for the cows Parnell ran off. I'm hoping he's found them and brought them back. What about you?"

"Putting together the papers the banks will need to wire the Jakes party their refunds. After that I'm going to compose letters to send out to some of the area's businesses and mine owners to let them know I'm opening my business."

"Congratulations."

"Thanks. I had two people turn me down while we were in town today. It was disappointing but I'm riding the bronc and holding on just as you suggested."

"Good for you. I'm not sure how I can help but if I can let me know."

His support was endearing. "I will."

As they eyed each other, time seemed to lengthen, and her need rose to the surface, whispering his name. Since her morning talk with herself, she no longer wondered how or why she'd gone from being a no-nonsense woman devoted only to her work, to one who wished they were alone so they could pick up where they'd left off last evening. Staking her claim on that teaspoon of happiness, she wanted to feel his lips on her throat, savor his hands moving up and down her spine, and relish the searing sensations of his touch. She also wanted him to know that she and her sponges were ready for that first time. Who would've ever thought she'd look forward to being intimate with a man? The old Portia wanted to accuse her of being no better than her mother but she refused to take the bait. "I have a question for you."

"And it is?"

"Do you wish to put the sponge in for me, or should I do it myself beforehand?"

He looked confused. "Sponge?"

Enjoying his reaction, she started walking away and said over her shoulder, "Think about it and let me know. I'll see you later."

She took two more steps and heard him call out, "Stop. Right there."

Guessing he'd figured it out, she smiled and swung back around.

He beckoned with a finger. "Come here for a minute, please."

She complied and upon reaching him, looked up. "Yes?"

Arms folded, he scanned her face. "Are we talking about what I think we're talking about?"

"I'm pretty sure we are. Is that a problem?"

He chuckled softly, "Who are you and what have you done with the real Portia Carmichael?"

"I believe she's been transformed by a passion wielding cowboy."

He steepled his fingers against his lips and peered at her for a long moment. "Are you sure?"

"Do I impress you as being an indecisive woman?"

The heat now glittering in his eyes touched her like a hand. "You are going to be in so much trouble, Miss Bookkeeper."

He'd related the same mock warning the evening he'd kissed her for the first time, but now she had a clearer understanding of just what that meant. As a result, the pulse between her thighs sprang to life.

He added, "I want you to wear a skirt the next time I get you alone. No denims."

"Why?"

"Because I'll be taking your drawers as punishment for how hard I'm going to be for the rest of the day thinking about you and your sponge. You really are trying to kill me."

Thrilled by his words, she didn't agree to the order but gave him a serene smile instead. As she walked away, she was trailed by his laughter.

Kent hadn't been kidding about his arousal. Watching her exit, he was as hard as he'd ever been for a woman and it had occurred instantly. He didn't know where she'd gotten the sponges, but he had to smile because he'd just purchased rubbers while in Tucson earlier. He couldn't wait to get her alone. Once she was out of sight, it took him a few moments to will his body back into a calm state and for his mind to remember what he'd planned to do before being nearly knocked to his knees by her and her talk of sponges, but once he had everything back in order, he went inside to find Rhine.

His knock on the frame of the opened door made Rhine glance up from his seat behind his desk. "Come on in. Regan said the trip to Tucson went well."

Kent settled into one of the brown leather chairs. "It did. No Apaches or outlaws."

"Good. Glad we got that group out of our hair."

Kent was, too. "I'd like to talk to you about something if I can."

Rhine sat back. "Sure. What's on your mind?"

"You mentioned the possibility of maybe leasing the Blanchard property."

"I did."

"Would you consider letting me lease it with

an option to buy it outright at some point in the future? I have some money saved up."

The famous Fontaine poker face descended over Rhine's features. After a few long minutes of silence, he asked, "What about future income? Where would it come from?"

"Horses. If I make one trip a year and bring back a reasonable amount to sell, I think I could make a business and be able to pay you and any hands I'd need to hire."

"Thought you were too old for horse wrangling."

"Was when I thought I'd be working for you. Working for myself is a different matter." And if he could convince Portia to be his wife, he needed a way to provide for her and any children they might have.

Rhine asked, "Can you give me some time to think about it?"

"Sure." He hadn't expected Rhine to agree to the proposal without giving it some thought.

"I also may have to deal with Landry and his bogus claim."

"Understood."

"Okay. I'll let you know soon."

"Thanks. In the meantime, I'm going to grab something to eat. I want to ride over there after dinner and make sure nothing else has happened. I take it you haven't heard anything from the sheriff about the posse?"

"No and it angers me."

"Same here."

"The Ranchers Association meets tomorrow. I'll ask if anyone has any ideas. You should probably attend, too."

"Sure."

Rhine said, "I don't have anything pressing later on. How about we ride over to the Blanchard place together?"

"Fine with me. Let me know when you're ready."

Rhine nodded. Kent rose to his feet and left him to his work.

With his mind on the many ways he planned to pay Portia back for his constant state of arousal, Kent sat on the bench outside his bedroom and took out the letter he'd received from his father, Oliver. In a way he was pleased the old man had taken the time to write, and as he read further, Kent found himself equally pleased that not only were his father and stepmother, Sylvia, doing well, but they were planning to visit him and the Fontaines. What gave him pause however was the part in the letter referencing Sylvia's great-niece, Ruth, who was traveling with them and who would, his always meddling father wrote, *make you an ideal wife.*

Kent tossed the letter aside and put his head in his hands. "Dammit!"

CHAPTER THIRTEEN

Three days before the rodeo, Portia was working in her office when her uncle Rhine stopped by. "How are the letters coming along?" he asked. "Do you need my help?"

"No. I'm almost done." She was sending out letters to all the guests scheduled for the rest of the spring and summer to let them know that due to circumstances beyond the hotel's control, the dude ranch was closed and their deposits would be refunded. "I received a few cancellations even before I sent out the letters from people who'd read about Geronimo's escape in the newspapers. Many of the wedding parties from back East have already cancelled as well."

"Not something I like hearing but it's understandable."

"On a happier note, I'm also sending out letters on my own behalf."

He looked confused. "Concerning what?"

"I've decided to open my bookkeeping business, so I'm alerting some of the other businesses to the services I plan to offer."

A smile spread over his features. "That's wonderful, Portia. You and I talked about this a few years back but I thought you'd given up on the idea."

"No. I was just afraid I'd fail," she admitted.

He stilled and studied her for a moment. "Takes a strong person to admit something like that."

She nodded and thought about Kent's support. "I plan to keep doing the books here though, if that's okay with you."

"Of course, but you may become so successful I'll have to increase your salary to keep you on."

"You don't have to worry. I'm not going anywhere and what you pay me now is just fine." He'd given her her start. She'd always be grateful for his faith in her abilities, no matter what the future held. "Any advice for me?"

He thought for a moment. "Yes. Don't listen to naysayers about what you can't do, and get up every day and do your absolute best."

"Thank you, Uncle Rhine."

"You're welcome. Proud of you, Portia."

She was proud of herself. That she might fail still loomed inside but it wasn't consuming her anymore. "So what's happening with the search for Parnell? Are you going to be discussing a posse at the Ranchers Association meeting this evening?"

He looked frustrated. "No. The meeting's been cancelled because none of the White members wanted to leave their homes because of Geronimo."

She was frustrated by that news as well. Were Farley and Buck ever going to get the justice they deserved?

Rhine did have a bit of comforting news. "The sheriff dropped off one of the Wanted flyers earlier today." He removed the folded bulletin from the inner pocket of his suit coat and passed it to her.

"This is a very good likeness," Portia said, looking at Parnell's unshaven thin face.

"The sheriff's daughter drew it. He said she'll be going back East to one of the art schools in the fall. He had enough of them printed to put up in town and to pass out around the territory to other lawmen."

"Let's hope it helps," she said.

"I agree."

Portia passed the paper back to him.

"I'm going to let you get back to work, but again, I'm real proud of you, Portia. If I can be of any assistance let me know."

"I will, Uncle Rhine. Promise."

He nodded and left her alone.

Smiling, she went back to work only to have Regan stick her head in the door a few minutes later. "Are you coming to the meeting? Everyone's here. We're waiting on you."

For a moment, Portia had no idea what her sister was talking about, but then she remembered the Tucson Good Works Society was meeting that afternoon. She jumped to feet. "Oh shoot. I'm sorry. Let me get my report. I'll be right there."

"You really need a keeper," her sister said with a shake of her head as she left.

Portia stuck out her tongue at the empty space and searched out the papers she needed.

The tradition of women of the race forming groups to assist and uplift their communities could be traced back as far as 1793 when the lady parishioners of Philadelphia's Episcopal Church of St. Thomas, the first Black Episcopal church in the nation, formed the Female Benevolent Society of St. Thomas. In the years since, women of color nationwide built on that tradition by coming together to support everything from abolition to literacy to the caring of the sick, elderly, and the destitute in their neighborhoods, and since the passage of the Fifteenth Amendment, female suffrage.

The Tucson Good Works Society was founded ten years ago. It was a small group but, like others, dedicated to caring for their community. Portia was the secretary. Her aunt Eddy served as the current president and opened the meeting. The first order of business was to formally approve the plan to attend the convention in San Francisco. In spite of the ill-mannered Ada Jakes, Portia continued to look forward to the event. Regan headed up the group's volunteering efforts and reported on the campaign to help provide supplies for the small school run by Mamie Cordell out of her home. "There was enough money left over from our last fund-raiser to purchase more readers and enough paper and pencils to last the rest of the school year." Although there were only five children enrolled, every educated child was an asset to the race.

The meeting continued with a discussion of ways they might help alleviate the suffering caused by the appalling conditions at the San Carlos reservation. Although a hundred women and their children escaped with Geronimo, many more stayed behind.

"We've contributed clothing in the past—maybe we can increase our donations," restaurant owner Sadie Welch suggested.

Portia added another idea. "What if we send letters to some of the large churches back East like Mother Bethel and St. Thomas in Philadelphia to ask for their help? I know the Apache aren't our race but if people knew about the deplorable conditions, maybe they'd be moved enough to lend them aid."

The women thought that to be a wonderful idea and after a lengthy discussion decided to implement both suggestions.

When the meeting ended, Eddy thanked everyone for coming. She, Portia, and Regan walked outside to see the ladies off. After their departure, Eddy left for the kitchen to supervise the food that would be going to the upcoming Lane rodeo, and because she didn't need their help, Portia and Regan sat outside at one of the tables beneath the oaks.

"I always feel good after one of our meetings," Portia said.

"I do, too. Helping people should make you feel good, don't you think?"

Portia agreed.

"Speaking of feeling good, I'm being nosey but have you had the chance to use your sponges yet?"

"You are being nosey. But the answer is no. We haven't had any time alone. He's been over at the ranch house digging up all the charred wood from the fire and hauling it away. By the time he gets back here, he's so exhausted from working in the heat, he's been going straight to bed after dinner."

"You should sneak him into your room some night soon or sneak into his."

"With Rhine and Eddy just up the hall, I think not."

"I forgot about that."

"Good thing one of us is still thinking clearly." Portia shook her head with amusement. She loved her sister and hoped life never parted them. She wouldn't know what to do if it did. "Now, my turn to be nosey. What was it like—that first time and why didn't you tell me about it?"

Regan hesitated. "I didn't tell you because I didn't think you'd approve."

Portia looked into her sister's serious eyes. "Sadly, you're probably right." Portia didn't know if other sisters shared such secrets but thought maybe not due to how personal it was.

Regan added, "And the first time was terrible. Neither one of us had any experience so we didn't know what we were doing. It was kind of painful, too, but—"

Portia went still. "But?"

"The next time. Oh my word. I wanted to shout, 'Hallelujah.'"

Portia laughed. "You know society says women shouldn't be having conversations like this."

"Society also thinks we're not smart enough to vote, you shouldn't love numbers, and I shouldn't deliver the mail. Society can kiss my mare's behind."

Portia agreed, but Regan's description of her first time was troubling. "Was it really painful?"

"It was, but you're at an advantage."

"Why?"

"Kent was a cat house king. He'll know what he's doing, which means you'll be just fine."

The next day, Kent rode with Rhine and Eddy to Tucson to meet his father, who was coming in on the evening train from Chicago. Kent wasn't sure how the visit would go or how long his father would be staying, but he promised himself he'd keep an open mind with the hope everything would go well.

When the train arrived, Oliver Randolph, leaning on a cane, stepped off the train with his wife, Sylvia, and her great-niece, Ruth. Eddy and Sylvia, upon seeing each other, let loose squeals of joy and immediately embraced like the long-time friends they were. Kent, followed by Rhine, embraced Oliver as well, and Kent had to admit it was great to see him.

"You look good, son," Oliver said, assessing him.

"You do, too," Kent replied. Truthfully his father looked frail and seemed to be moving much slower than the last time they'd seen each other a few years ago. The cane was new, too, but he chalked that up to Oliver getting up in years. "How was the trip?"

"Long," Sylvia said, giving Kent a hug and a peck on his cheek. "You're as handsome as ever."

He smiled around his embarrassment.

She then said, "Everyone, this is my great-niece, Ruth Adams."

The young woman accepted their greetings shyly. She appeared to be in her early twenties, had a pretty heart-shaped face and warm brown skin, and her frame was tall and thin. She shot hesitant glances Kent's way, making him wonder just what his father had told her and what her expectations of him might be. He figured he'd find out soon enough. Once their trunks were gathered and placed in the boot of the Fontaines' buggy, Oliver's party piled in. Kent mounted Blue and they struck out for home.

Portia and Regan, along with a small army of female volunteers spent the day over at the Lane ranch helping Julia with the setup for the rodeo. There were tables to wash down, lanterns to hang from the trees, chickens to pluck, and decorations to put in the barn for the dance. By the time they rode for home that evening, they were exhausted and ready for dinner. Portia knew that Kent and her aunt and uncle had ridden to Tucson to meet the train, so when she and Regan returned, seeing Oliver, and his wife, Sylvia, wasn't a surprise.

However, the visitors were surprised. Sylvia said, "Oh my goodness. Look at how you two have grown up!"

Portia and Regan had been in their teens the last time the Randolphs visited the Fontaines.

Oliver added, "Beauties, too. Just like your aunt."

Portia was pleased to see the smile on Kent's face. She hoped it meant he and his father were enjoying each other's company so far.

They were then introduced to Sylvie's great-niece, Ruth. Portia thought she seemed pleasant enough. She was a teacher, which Portia always considered an honorable and valued profession until meeting the pompous Edward Salt. She realized she hadn't seen him or his parents in some time. She hoped that meant they'd given up their quest to squirm their way into Rhine's good graces and had left Tucson.

At dinner the conversation flowed around the table about the upcoming rodeo, how old friends were faring back in Virginia City, Geronimo's escape, and more. Portia noticed that Ruth kept looking at Kent. The observations were discreet and short but he was definitely her main focus. He was so engrossed in the lively conversation that if he noticed Ruth's interest he didn't let on, and Portia had to wonder what it all meant. Had the woman developed an instant attraction to him in the way Elvenna Green had? And why did Portia feel the urge to shake her and demand that she stop looking at him? *Lord, I'm jealous!* That admission might have surprised her if she hadn't suffered similar feelings with Elvenna. Previous to her, Portia had never had a reason to be jealous because she'd never been taken with a man before, nor had she ever had to compete with another female for her place at a man's side. This was all new territory, so rather than behaving in a manner that would embarrass herself and everyone else at the table, she turned away from Ruth and concentrated on the meal and the conversation.

Kent was indeed aware of Ruth's interest. Every time he glanced up, their gazes met and hers would go racing away. He planned to get his father alone as soon as possible to find out what he'd told the young woman. He was also keenly aware of the muted fire in Portia's eyes. He'd caught her shooting daggers at Ruth when she thought no one was looking. Had she noticed the young woman watching him and become jealous as a result? He'd chalked it up to his imagination, but as his father told Rhine about Virginia City's annual baseball game between the Black and White members of the area's Republican party, he saw a very distinct chill in her gaze. Portia jealous? *Interesting.*

His father's question brought him back to the present, "So, where are you living, son?"

"Here, temporarily." And he explained the circumstances that led to him living with the Fontaines.

Oliver turned to Ruth. "Now, had he gone ahead and finished his medical studies, he'd be in an established practice by now and not having to depend on the kindness of his friends."

You could hear a pin drop. Kent picked up his wineglass and gave his father a salute. "I see nothing has changed with you."

Sylvia said coolly, "Oliver, you promised me you wouldn't badger him. He's chosen his life, and you've chosen yours. Let him live his the way he wants, for God's sake. He's not a child."

Kent saluted Sylvie, drained his glass, and got up and walked out.

Ruth made a move to go after him, but Portia,

already on her feet, shot her a raised eyebrow. The young woman cleared her throat, settled back into her seat, and focused her gaze on her lap. Only then did Portia say "Excuse me" to the others and leave the table, much to Sylvia and Oliver's surprise.

Outside, she found him seated at one of the tables. His features were tense and there was anger and muted pain in his eyes. "Thought you could use some company." She didn't like seeing him unhappy.

"Promised myself I'd not let him get to me, but I did."

She sat. "He was rude, but now that he's gotten that off his chest maybe the rest of the visit will be tolerable."

"And Blue will learn to spell my name."

She smiled.

He turned her way. "Apparently Ruth will make me a perfect wife."

"What?"

He told her about the letter.

"Is that why she's been watching you all evening?"

"Noticed that, did you?"

"She made it impossible not to."

"Was that why you were looking at her the way you were?"

Portia played dumb. "What do you mean?"

"Like you wanted to throttle her."

"No."

"Fibbing again?"

She raised her chin and remained silent. Once again he'd been able to read her correctly.

"Just so you know, if a man spent all his time focused on you that way, I'd want to throttle him, too."

Portia never dreamed she'd be moved by a man's protective declaration. "Good to know."

The silence that followed left them studying each other and feeling the attraction that neither could deny.

"Been a few days since we've had a chance to talk. How are you?" he whispered. The slow finger he ran down her cheek burned so sweetly her eyes slid closed. "I've missed you."

"I've missed you, too."

Wanting more than just that faint caress, she told him about the letters, the meeting, and what she and Regan had done earlier that day at the Lanes but left out the conversation she and Regan had shared on the ride home.

"I want to kiss you, but if I do, I won't be able to stop, so tell me about the rodeo. Is it a big deal?"

And she wanted to be kissed, endlessly. "The biggest."

"Prize money?"

"Quite a bit."

"Might like to help myself to some of it."

Her attention was focused on his lips and the smile that curved them as he watched her. Who knew wanting a man could make a woman hunger? "You've participated in rodeos before?"

"A few. Bull and bronc riding are my favorites."

She was impressed and looked up to see him viewing her so seriously she went still.

"I've asked Rhine to let me lease the Blanchard place with hopes of buying it outright at some point in the future."

She was both surprised and pleased. "This is about putting down those roots you spoke of."

"It is. If he says yes, I'll be starting a horse wrangling business so I can pay my bills and put food on the table."

Once again, she wondered what a life with him would be like.

"Do you think a wife would mind if I'm gone say, two months out of the year in order to provide for her?"

Drowning in his eyes and the tone of his voice, Portia felt her heart pounding so loud, she was sure people could hear it inside. "Not if that wife shared her husband's dreams and could spend his time away chasing her own."

Portia felt like she'd stepped out on a precipice and knew without a doubt that if he asked her to be that wife, she would say yes. As a husband, he'd walk beside her through life, not make her trail behind just because society deemed he should, and he'd be one of those rare men like her uncle Rhine who took pride in their wife's ambitions.

"How's your dream going?"

She forced herself back to the present. "Still waiting to hear back from the letters I told you I sent out."

"Keep riding the bronc."

She nodded. "I will."

They were still studying each other silently when Regan came out. "Eddy sent me to tell you you're about to miss dessert."

They reluctantly severed the contact and Kent said, "Can't have that. We're coming."

Regan went back inside.

He stood and held out his hand. "You ready?"

"Yes." She placed her hand in his and let him draw her to her feet as if it was the most natural thing in the world.

He kissed her fingers, causing a quiet warmth to ripple over her. "Thanks for helping me calm down."

"You're welcome."

Inside, Portia still on his mind, Kent piled his plate high with Eddy's signature peach cobbler, then mounded ice cream on top. He pointedly ignored his father who seemed to get the message and kept his distance. But when Kent finished his dessert, Oliver walked to his side. "Can I speak with you privately for a few moments?"

"Why, so you can upbraid me again?"

He dropped his eyes as if embarrassed. "No. Rhine said we could use his office. Do you know where that is?"

Kent didn't bother hiding his irritation. "Follow me."

Upon entering the quiet space, Oliver sat but Kent remained standing.

"First of all, let me apologize for what I said. It served no purpose other than to anger you and make me look like an old fool."

Kent agreed and wanted to ask if he was seeking forgiveness because Sylvia had demanded he do so, but he didn't ask.

His father sighed. "I'm dying, Kenton."

Kent froze.

"The doctors have given me six months to a year tops to get my affairs in order."

Kent ran frantic eyes over him and for the first time really focused on him. And what he saw scared him: the sparse gray hair, the tired eyes, slumped shoulders, and sallow skin. He was also incredibly thin. Kent had chalked up his appearance to his being old. Oliver was in his late seventies, but now he realized that there was more at play. "Does Sylvia know?"

"Yes. She and I have spent the past six months going from doctor to doctor hoping to get a different diagnosis, but they all told us the same thing."

"Are you in pain?"

"Constantly."

Kent didn't know what to say. Yes, he and his father butted heads like bighorn sheep but this was too awful to think about. "Is there anything I can do?"

"Other than taking me as I am and not fighting me over the money I plan to leave you, no."

Kent replied in a voice softened by emotion. "Oliver, I don't need your money."

"I know how proud you are, Kenton, but you will need it for the family you and Portia may make together."

Kent couldn't help the wry smile that curved his lips. "You picked up on that, did you?"

"You should've seen the look she shot Ruth when Ruth tried to go after you. I think everyone in the room knew which way the wind was blowing after that. My apologies for thinking I could control who you'd choose to love, too."

And because his father was dying and the knowledge was heartbreaking, he replied sincerely, "Apology accepted."

Later as Kent lay in bed surrounded by the darkness, his heart still ached. For all their differences and years of conflict, the knowledge that Oliver would spend the last months of his life wracked by pain from disease was not something he'd ever envisioned. He wiped away the tears dampening his cheeks. *Why couldn't he simply die of old age while he slept?* he wanted to shout, but he knew fate didn't care. Having never known his mother, Kent hadn't grieved her, even though he'd desperately wanted a mother like other children while he was growing up. But Oliver had always been there, even when he hadn't wanted him to be, and Kent could already feel the hole his death would leave in his life. They'd discussed the money he would inherit and it was a surprisingly large sum. Oliver had come to Virginia City in the early sixties at the beginning of the silver boom, and like many of the city's residents, his accumulated investments had left him a wealthy man. If Rhine approved Kent's request to purchase the Blanchard property, he'd have no problem meeting the price, and there'd be more than enough left over to found the beginnings of a good life for himself and Portia. Oliver's impending demise made Kent want to go knock on her door right then and there, and ask her to be his wife because each passing day brought them both closer to their own deaths, and he wanted to spend every second of his remaining time on earth by her side.

Because the members of the Fontaine household, including Matt and Kent had agreed to help out the Lanes, Portia had been left with the task of getting Ruth and the Randolphs to the rodeo. But when she went to their suite to see if they were ready, Sylvia said, "Honey, Oliver isn't feeling well this morning. Would it be okay if we stayed behind?"

He looked listless and tired. "Certainly," she replied. "Is there anything I can do for you to make you more comfortable, Mr. Randolph?"

He gave her a weary smile. "No. I just need to rest up. The train ride took more out of me than I expected."

"I understand. Sarah and the maids will be here, so if you need anything just ask. They'll bring you meals, too."

Sylvia said, "Thank you. Ruth still wants to go though. Can she ride over with you?"

Portia took in the girl's face and reminded herself to be kind. "Do you need a mount or would you prefer we take the buggy?"

"I don't ride."

Portia kept her disappointment hidden. She preferred to travel by horseback. "Then we'll take the buggy."

Leaving the Randolphs behind, Portia and Ruth set out on the hour ride to the Lanes' ranch. It would have been a much shorter journey riding Arizona, but Portia swallowed her pique and kept the horses at an even pace. "Where are you from originally, Ruth?"

"Chicago so I'm not accustomed to all this heat."

"Definitely different than what you're used to."

"It really is. Can I say something?"

Portia looked over. "Sure."

"I want to apologize for last night. Mr. Randolph gave me the impression that his son would be receptive to me as a potential intended but obviously hadn't talked to his son beforehand."

"No apologies needed."

"Thank you for being so kind. Can we start over—you and I?"

Portia decided she liked Ruth Adams after all. "Certainly."

"Good," she said, sounding relieved. "Kent wouldn't happen to have a brother, would he?"

Portia saw the humor twinkling in Ruth's eyes. They laughed, and Portia looked forward to the rest of the day.

The Lanes' reputation of putting on a great event was so well earned, travelers came from as far away as California, Texas, and the northernmost provinces of Mexico to compete, eat, and have a good time. As a result, the closer Portia and Ruth drew to the ranch, the more congested the road became with buggies, wagons, and riders. Portia waved at the people she knew and when they called out greetings, she responded in kind.

"I wasn't expecting all 'this," Ruth exclaimed, taking in all the traffic and riders.

"We'll probably have to park a good distance away. Hope you don't mind walking."

"I don't. This is exciting. I'll bet a girl could find a husband here."

Portia grinned. "Are you truly looking for one?"

"I am. I have a good job and a wonderful life back in Chicago, but I'm ready to get married and have some babies before I'm too old."

"Then how about I introduce you around?"

"I'd like that."

And Portia knew exactly who she wanted Ruth to meet. They found a place to park the buggy and joined the crowd for the walk to the event. Entering the main area was like stepping into an outdoor fair. There were large rings set up for the various horse races, a corral for the bull and bronco riders, and everywhere you looked were legions of people of all races and ages. Making their way through the crowd, they heard conversations in both English and Spanish along with laughter and music. In the air were the mouthwatering smells of roasting pigs and beef. Women were frying tortillas and grilling chilies next to fragrant pots of beans.

"This is amazing," Ruth said happily. "I've read about rodeos a few times in the Chicago papers but seeing it with my own eyes takes my breath away."

Portia was glad she was enjoying herself. "It's come down to us from Mexico, and celebrations like this one are held all over this part of the country."

"What do we do first?"

Truthfully, Portia was hoping to spot Kent but knew finding him in the large crowd was going to be difficult. But the fates were with her. "I see Kent and Matt. Let's find out if they've signed up for any of the contests."

"Lead the way."

It took a few minutes to make their way through the crowd to his side but when he saw her, his smile brought out her own.

"Good morning. Was hoping to find you," he said.

"Same here. Morning, Matt."

"Morning, Miss Portia. Morning, Miss Adams."

Portia asked, "Have you two signed up for any of the competitions?"

Kent replied, "I'm on my way to the registration table now. Matt's decided he's not entering."

"I've been at these things enough times to know that I'd only be laughed at. Think I'll spend my time eating and looking at pretty girls."

Portia saw him staring longingly at Bonnie Neal, a pretty young brunette holding a frilly green parasol to protect her from the sun. She was speaking with an older woman and when the woman moved on, she turned and looked over at Matt.

Kent seemed to have noticed his young ranch hand's interest, too, because he asked, "Do you know her?"

Matt nodded. "Her daddy is one of the big ranchers. Her name's Bonnie Neal, but she doesn't even know I'm alive."

Portia asked, "Then who's she smiling at?"

Matt went still.

Even with the thick crowd passing in front of her like a river current, it was easy to see that Matt had her attention. "You should go over and say hello," Kent said.

Looking terrified, Matt shook his head.

"Go say hello, Matt."

"You think so?"

Kent pushed him gently. "Go. We'll see you later."

Portia watched him approach Bonnie and his shyness reminded her of James Cordell.

Kent said, "I probably shouldn't yell at him to stop staring down at his boots and look her in the face, should I?"

Portia and Ruth grinned, and Portia said, "No. You'll only embarrass him."

"Then I need to stop watching." Fitting actions to his words, he turned his back and Portia doubted she'd ever get over how silly he could be at times. "Did Oliver and Sylvia come with you?" he asked.

She shook her head. "He isn't feeling well. The train ride took a lot more out of him than he thought. Sarah and the staff will take good care of him though."

He nodded.

She thought she saw a shadow cross his face and it made her wonder if the father and son were still at odds.

"Are you enjoying yourself, Ruth?" he asked.

"I am but I want to apologize for last night."

"Not necessary."

Portia put in, "I told her not to worry about it."

"Portia's right. Oliver misled you."

"Apparently he did, so thank you for not holding it against me."

"You're welcome."

Portia was pleased with his refusal to lay the blame at Ruth's door. The young woman looked uncomfortable enough.

Kent eyed them and asked, "So, are either of you going to sign up for any of the contests? Steer tying? Bull riding maybe?"

Portia laughed, "No. Although growing up, Regan and I used to enter the youth events."

"Really?"

"Yes. Target shooting and the horse racing relays. Three years running, we won both. The boys hated us."

"Good for you!" Ruth crowed.

Portia explained to Kent why they were there. "I'm waiting to introduce Ruth to James Cordell."

He raised an eyebrow. "Are you playing matchmaker, Miss Carmichael?"

"You did with Matt. I'm trying to keep up."

Portia saw the humor in his eyes and when the contact lengthened, the desire. For her.

Ruth cleared her throat. "The woman trying to be matched up is waiting. Shall we go? I'd like to keep up as well."

Her comical plea dragged them back to the present. Wading into the moving sea of people, they set out.

James was among the three men seated at the registration table writing down the names of the contestants and placing their entrance fees in the strongboxes at their feet.

"Which one is he?" Ruth asked from where she and Portia were standing.

Kent had left them to study the roster of events posted on a sign nearby.

Portia pointed him out. "James is a book-keeper," she added in case Ruth was curious about what he did for a living.

Ruth's face gave nothing away, but she didn't turn on her heel and walk off either, which gave Portia hope.

A few minutes later after discreetly observing James and his interactions with the men in line, Ruth said, "I'll look forward to the introduction."

And the introduction did go well. Portia told James that Ruth was a family friend visiting from Chicago. "I know you're probably very busy here, James, but I was hoping you could show her around when you have the chance. I can't because I'm supposed to be helping your mother and the other ladies, but I don't want Ruth to miss all the fun."

Seemingly mesmerized by the tall willowy Ruth, James nodded horselike. "I—I'd . . . Sure. I'll be ending my shift in just a few minutes."

"Thank you, James. Will you see that she gets something to eat as well, and maybe escort her to some of the competitions? She's never been to a rodeo before."

"I'd be honored."

True to his word, he quickly finished the registration of the next man in line, said something in parting to the ticket taker in the next chair and came around the table to where Ruth and Portia stood waiting. Ever the gentleman, he extended his arm to Ruth. "Shall we?"

The pleased Ruth accepted and shot Portia a smile before they melted into the crowd.

Kent walked over to her. "Do you think they'll hit it off?"

Portia shrugged. "It's worth a try." She liked James. He didn't have a chance with her but he might with Ruth. "Did you decide what you're going to enter? I like the fancy lariat event."

"I do, too, but I'm not good enough with a rope for that. Saw an old vaquero at a rodeo who could use his rope to spell out the letters of his name."

"I don't think anyone here is that good."

"I know I'm not, so I'm going to stick to the

steer tying and the bull riding. Blue and I do pretty good with the racing so I might try one of those, too."

Portia removed the red bandana from around her neck and tied it around his upper arm. "For luck."

"Why thank you. I'd kiss you if I didn't think it would start tongues wagging."

She saw smiles on the faces of some of the people standing nearby who'd watched her tie on the bandana. "I think the wagging has begun, but I'll take my kisses privately for now if you don't mind."

"No, I don't, but do you think we'll find time to be alone before the snow falls? I'm almost at the point of throwing you over my shoulder and riding for the border."

She laughed. "I'm going to go find Regan. She's heading up some of the children's races. I'll be cheering for you at your events."

He nodded and she left him in line.

The rodeo events were usually set up the same way every year, so Portia knew where Regan would be. She was happy that James and Ruth seemed to hit it off. As she'd told Kent, she was looking forward to cheering for him and couldn't wait to see how he'd do.

Regan was in charge of the children's target shooting contest and as she stood at the fence watching, Edward Salt appeared suddenly at Portia's side as if by magic.

"Good afternoon, Miss Carmichael."

"Mr. Salt." Her disdain for him masked, she kept her eyes trained on the event and clapped along with the crowd when a little girl using a bow placed her arrow in the target's bull's-eye.

"I've been thinking about you."

Not in the mood for whatever he had in mind, she asked, "What do you want?"

"You."

She sighed. "I'm not available."

"I hear you're in line to inherit your uncle's wealth. That makes you quite the heiress. Not many Colored women can claim that."

She stared at him coldly.

"A man would have to be insane not to want all that you are."

"Surely you don't believe I'd have anything to do with you knowing what you're really after."

"Oh, I want what's between your legs, too. Don't get me wrong."

Portia walked away, only to have him grab her by the arm. "Little bitch. Don't you dare walk away when I'm talking to you."

"Release me," she snarled. She saw some of the men she'd known most of her life, including host Howard Lane, making their way to her side. Glad for their concern but certain she could handle Salt on her own, she gave the odious snake a smile that didn't reach her eyes and said softly, "You know, I do like a forceful man."

Under the praise his grip lessened. She cupped his face and while he grinned, she drove her knee so forcefully into his groin, he screamed. Eyes bulging, he grabbed his privates, fell to his knees, and writhed on the ground, mouth and eyes wide with shock and pain. Those who'd been watching cheered. She curtsied.

Mr. Lane arrived and glanced down at the curled-up moaning Salt. "Came to help, but doesn't look like you need it."

"Best I could do without a gun." She thought back on the times her mother had emerged in the morning with her eyes blackened by a customer's fist. Portia had vowed never to be similarly victimized. Had she been armed, Salt would be nursing more than bruised privates.

Howard said to the men who'd come with him, "Get him out of here."

They dragged him to his feet and he croaked, "You'll pay for this, bitch!"

Howard hit him with a right cross that knocked him out cold. More cheers went up. Lane snapped, "When he wakes up, remind him that we don't take kindly to varmints threatening our women."

His toes trailed on the ground as they hauled him off.

Howard asked, "Are you okay, Portia?"

She nodded. She was admittedly shaken when he initially grabbed her, but having defended herself and having enjoyed watching Howard put the final nail in Salt's coffin, she felt much better.

"Then go get you some ice cream. As I remember that always used to cheer you up."

Giving him a kiss on his cheek, she set off to do just that.

Later, Portia had plenty to cheer about. Kent made it through the qualifying rounds of the bull riding and would ride for the prize money on the rodeo's final day. He won second place in the steer-roping contest, and he and Blue came in third in the can race. The event called for riders to pick up tin cans from the ground while their horses ran at full speed. Each ride was timed. Riders were sometimes injured when they lost their balance and tumbled out of their saddles from leaning over too far. From the way he and Blue worked together, it was obvious they'd been in similar contests before. Even though they didn't place first, both Kent and his mount finished the competition unscathed, and that was a first-place win as far as she was concerned.

After the competitions, she and Kent got food and carried their plates to join her family, along with Matt, Ruth, and James Cordell, on blankets spread out on the grass to enjoy their meals. They caught up on each other's days and listened to the lively music rolling across the crowded meadow on the wings of the evening breeze.

Kent was worried about his father. Although

Oliver hadn't indicated that his death was imminent, that he hadn't been up to enjoying the day's festivities had been on his mind all day. He planned to check on him as soon as they returned to the hotel. In spite of Oliver being in his thoughts he'd managed to enjoyed the Lane rodeo. He hadn't won any first-place money but by taking second and third place he'd beat out a lot of the others and none of them had sported Portia's bandana. Seeing it still in place made the day even more special.

They were listening to Regan's hilarious telling of a goat tangling with a pony during one of the children's races when a man Kent didn't know walked up. He did recognize the little lady with him, Matt's Bonnie Neal. Matt kept his head down as if he was afraid the man had come to shoot him for talking to his daughter.

"How are you, Rhine?" he asked.

"I'm well, David. How was the trip back East?"

"Fine. I just got home a few days ago. Sorry to have missed Blanchard's funeral. The old man was one of a kind."

Rhine nodded.

"I just found out that Farley and Buck were killed. Sorry, ladies, don't mean to disturb you with talk of their deaths."

No one seemed offended so he continued, "Sheriff O'Hara said you wanted to put together a posse?"

"I did, but he said my race would be a problem."

"Told me about that." He shook his head as if he found that asinine. "Farley and Buck were good men. They helped me out last summer when I broke my leg. I never would've got my cows to market had it not been for them. I know a lot of folks are scared because of Geronimo and all, but I had O'Hara deputize me anyway. If you'd like the help out, I'd be honored to have you and anyone else you know by my side. Parnell's probably in Mexico by now but I still want to take a look around."

"When do you want to start?"

"Let's wait until the rodeo's over tomorrow. As I said, Parnell's probably gone so another day probably won't matter. We'll meet up at Blanchard's place at sunrise. That fine with you?"

Rhine indicated that it was.

"See you then." He touched his hat to the ladies. As he walked way, his daughter shot Matt a smile that turned him beet red before she hurried after her father.

Rhine looked over at Kent. "I guess we have a posse."

"Looks like we do."

"Neal's a good man."

Judging by what he'd just witnessed, Kent had to agree.

After dinner, there were poker games, music, and dancing. By the time dusk rolled in, many people were gathering their families and preparing to head home. Eddy and Rhine were among them.

"We'll see you young people in the morning," Eddy said. Hand in hand she and Rhine went to retrieve their buggy.

Regan planned to spend the night with the Lanes to help with the next day's preparations. After saying her good-byes, she strolled off. James offered to see Ruth home, which made her smile. Matt had drifted off after dinner and was on the grounds somewhere enjoying himself, so that left Kent and Portia on their own.

"Did you drive or ride?" he asked.

"Drove the buggy."

"Are you ready to head back?"

"I am."

"Lead the way."

CHAPTER FOURTEEN

With Blue tied by his reins to the back of the buggy, Kent drove. At his side, Portia savored the evening and his presence.

"You could sit a mite closer, Miss Carmichael."

She scooted over until she was cushioned against his side.

"Better."

Filled with peaceful contentment, she said, "I hope your father is feeling better."

"Me too. I'm not sure he's said anything to Rhine and Eddy, but he's dying."

She drew back. She now knew the reason for the shadow that crossed his face earlier. In spite of the good time he'd had today, she'd sensed something not quite right beneath the surface. "I was wondering if something was bothering you."

"Doctors have given him a year—maybe less."

"Kent, I'm so sorry."

"So am I."

They rode through the deepening darkness with the moon overhead. "I wanted him to stand up with me at our wedding."

She stilled and studied his face. "We're having a wedding?"

"I hope we are. What do you think?"

She snuggled closer. "I think I'd like that."

"Really?"

"Yes." And instead of second-guessing the decision or tensing up and waging an inner debate, her peace and contentment deepened. The choice felt right.

"Hallelujah!" he shouted.

She laughed.

"Do you want something big and fancy?" he asked.

"No, but Eddy might, and if she does, I'll probably agree because she means the world to me after all she and Rhine have done for me and my sister. I will insist it be as soon as possible though."

"Good."

She was glad he didn't want to wait either. Now that she'd aligned her mind with her heart's lead, she was impatient to begin their life together and explore all marriage to such a special man had to offer, not the least being endless kisses. She was convinced their marriage bed would be special as well, in spite of the small worries she harbored about the pain her sister had described.

He stopped the buggy.

"What's wrong?"

"Nothing. Just need to take care of something I've been wanting to do all day."

And when he leaned over, she knew what would follow because she'd had the same thoughts all day, too. He traced a slow finger over her bottom lip before pressing his lips to hers fully. A warmth spread along with a rising desire for more. Unlike previous times, he didn't wait to move his hands over her body, sliding his hands over her breasts to awaken and tease. Still plying her mouth, their tongues dancing sinuously, he cupped her breast before dropping his head to awaken her completely. She moaned. Buttons were undone, and because she'd begun the day thinking she'd be riding Arizona to the rodeo, she was encased in the black silk that he found so arousing. He ran kisses over the tops of her breasts and without his asking, she brazenly moved the fabric aside so he could play as he wished. She was rewarded so magnificently her hips rose in rhythm. She ran her hand over the strong muscles of his neck, glorying in the texture of his skin and hair, all the while easing him closer because she wanted him to have all she could give. She arched, sighed, and moaned in response to his loving and felt the storm only he could set in her blood begin to gather. He returned to her mouth, leaving her breasts damp to the night air while his hands slowly moved down her bared sides to her hips and along the length of her thighs. She'd worn a skirt and his caress singed through the fabric to the flesh beneath. "Open for me, Duchess."

She parted her legs and her skirt rose. His palm was hot as it journeyed. The sensations sent her hands beneath his shirt to explore the hard yet soft flesh of his chest and back. She wanted to touch him everywhere, wanted to learn his shape, map his ribs, and lick at the hollow of his throat. Putting her desire into action, she dragged her tongue over the spot and heard him groan. He paid her back by moving his hands between her waiting thighs, and when he touched her, she sucked in a breath and lifted her hips on a groan for more.

"You're very wet, Duchess. Makes me want to do this . . ."

She gasped.

"And this . . ."

She whimpered passionately.

"And now, this . . ."

He slid a finger inside and worked her with such expert wickedness, she shattered on a strangled cry and spiraled to the moon. Pulsing and moaning, she heard him whisper against her ear, "I'll be spending the rest of our lives making you fly apart, woman . . . so get ready."

And when he finally headed the buggy for home, the overwhelmed, soon to be Mrs. Kenton Randolph knew that, yes, their marriage bed was going to be fine indeed.

Upon their return they made the announcement. The overcome Eddy cried. Kent's father, who looked to have regained his strength, offered his congratulations as did Sylvia and Ruth.

"Will you stand up with me?" Kent asked him.

Oliver froze and stared. "Wouldn't you rather have Rhine take that role?"

Portia said, "He'll be too busy giving away the bride. If that's okay with him?"

Standing with Eddy, Rhine responded in a voice thick with emotion, "I'd be honored, Portia."

Kent turned back to his father. "So, what do you say, Oliver?"

Tears in his eyes, he nodded. "Yes."

Sylvia wiped at her own tears, and laughed, "Eddy, as much as you hate it, you're going to need a new gown."

With love in her voice and her gaze on Portia, Eddy shook her head. "I won't mind this time. Not at all." She raised her coffee cup. "To the happy couple, and to love."

"Hear! Hear!"

As Portia and Kent accepted hugs of congratulations, Portia was sad that Regan wasn't there but knew she'd be happy, too, and say yes when Portia asked her to be her maid of honor.

It was the second day of the rodeo and Kent stood looking into the pen holding the bull he'd be riding in less than an hour. The animal was an enormous doe-brown, longhorn named Bushwhacker.

"Weighs over a thousand pounds," said a cowboy eyeing the brute, too. His name was Cody and like Kent he'd qualified the day before to ride in the finals. "It killed a man at a rodeo up in Wyoming last year." Upon leaving Kent with that, he walked away.

Kent didn't know if the tale was true or not. Cowboys were known for lying, especially during a contest. Putting a scare in your competition could increase your chances of claiming the prize money, which in this case was fifty dollars, not a small sum. However, Cody's estimation of the bull's weight looked to be right and tip to tip the width of the horns had to be a good five feet or more. A bull of that size could very easily kill a man.

Standing beside Kent, Rhine asked, "Are you sure you want to do this?"

Kent was admittedly having second thoughts. He'd no idea the animal would be so massive. "My name's on the list. I back out now, people might think I'm scared."

"As opposed to thinking you have good sense?"

Still focused on the bull, Kent shrugged. "It's the cowboy life. This is how it works."

"I'll put that on your headstone."

"Thanks."

Once Kent got his fill of seeing what he might be in for, he and Rhine went back to the main gathering. "Do you know where our ladies are?" His father and Sylvia were with Regan. Ruth was with James.

"I always look for Eddy around the food," Rhine

said. "No idea where Portia might be though."

"Let's find Eddy—maybe she knows."

The crowd was even larger than the day before and trying to move through all the people took some time. The spicy aromas of the food tempted him mightily but Kent knew better than to eat before a ride. He'd get something after the competition, if he survived.

They found both women setting out cakes on one of the long tables. Rhine went over to speak to his wife.

Portia was arranging the desserts at the other end of the table. When she looked up and saw him approaching, her welcoming smile made him momentarily forget about Bushwhacker until she asked, "Did you see the bull?"

"Yes and Rhine thinks I should take my name off the entry sheet."

She stopped. "Why?"

"The bull's one of the biggest I've ever seen."

"Do you think you can ride it?"

"I do." And that was the truth. He just wasn't sure if he could for the eight seconds required.

"No one will think less of you if you back out," Portia pointed out gently.

"But I'll think less of myself." Male pride was driving him, and be it brainless or not, he wanted to win. That pride also made him want to show off for the woman he loved. "Are these cakes for sale?"

"No, for auction. Our Good Works Society does this every year as a fund-raiser. Do you have a sweet tooth?"

"I do."

"What's your favorite?"

"Portia's."

She laughed and he nodded polite greetings to the other women adding cakes to the line. While they worked they kept taking peeks at him, making him wonder if they knew he and Portia were getting married.

"Matt won the pie eating contest a little while ago," she told him.

"Really?" he replied with a laugh.

"Who knew that rail-thin body could hold so much. Of course he was pretty sick afterwards, but he gets bragging rights for the year."

Kent was sorry he missed it. "Do you know where he is now?"

"He was with Doc Finney. She has a tent over on the other side of the bunkhouse."

"He wanted to help out during the competition, but I think I'll just let him nurse his pie hang-over."

"That might be best."

Cal Grissom walked up. "You ready, Kent?"

Cal volunteered to help out, too. He'd done a bit of bull riding in his younger days.

"Ready as I'll ever be."

Portia came out from behind the table. "I don't

have a bandana for you to wear, so this will have to do." She gave him a slow sweet kiss more potent than a hundred bandanas. "Good luck, cowboy."

Sitting on the top rung of the corral waiting for his turn, Kent watched Bushwhacker shed the first two riders as if they weighed no more than roosters. None of them lasted three seconds, let alone the required eight. A raucous crowd filled the risers fanned out around the oval. He spotted Portia seated with her family and his. Her kiss had been a pleasant surprise. He had no idea why she'd suddenly dropped her no kissing in public rule but he was glad she had. He'd be needing all the luck he could find.

Cody, the cowboy who'd spoken to him earlier, was up next. The previous contestant had been bucked off in less than a second, leaving the crowd so disappointed they couldn't decide whether to laugh or rain down cat calls, so they did both.

Kent hadn't seen Cody's qualifying rides but now, watching him, Kent noted confidence and expertise in the way he sat the bull and wrapped the braided rope around his gloved hand.

"He's ridden a bull or two," Kent said to Cal.

"Or five or ten."

Kent grinned.

And that experience showed when the bull

shot out of the chute and went to work. Cody rode him well. The rules prohibited the rider from touching the bull with anything other than the hand cinched to the animal's back, so the free hand was kept high in the air. As the bull did its best to unseat the cowboy, Kent focused on both man and bull, committing to memory how low the animal dropped its thick neck and head when it bucked and how high the hind legs rose when it kicked and spun. For such a big animal Bushwhacker was nimble and agile. The crowd chanted a countdown of the seconds. When it reached eight, Cody was still in control. Grudgingly impressed, Kent wondered how much longer he'd stay on. The bull must have been asking itself the same question because it executed a move that seemed to throw its body in every direction at once. The crowd roared. Cody lost his grip and hit the ground. Scrambling, he ran like hell to the fence and cleared it two steps ahead of the charging bull.

Kent was next.

Seated on the broad back of the restless bull, Kent carefully cinched his gloved hand to the connecting rope and concentrated on pulling in deep calming breaths.

"Let's hope he's tired," Cal cracked.

The bull's owner, an old rancher from Texas, grinned. "This bull can do eight—nine runs a day. He's probably more mad than anything else."

That wasn't what Kent wanted to hear.

"Are you ready?" Cal asked.

Kent nodded.

The owner crowed, "Then get ready for the ride of your life! Good luck!"

The bull cleared the fence and Kent was thrown up and down. He felt the jolt in his ribs, spine, and the bones in his legs. Keeping his free hand high and hoping his head didn't fly off, he let the bull do its best to put him on the ground. He had a vague sense of the screaming crowd but didn't dare let his concentration slip. The bull was tricky and strong. At past events, he'd always been able to count off the number of seconds in his head. Not this time. Between trying to stay upright and make it look effortless for the style points the judges added to the scores, he had no idea how long he'd been riding. Kent felt the animal gathering its strength and knew he was in for the move that had unseated Cody. Sure enough the powerful contortion made him lose his grip. He hit the ground, hastily found his feet, and ran for the fence. With the bull right behind him, he scrambled over the top rung, then leaned forward to catch his breath. Every bone in his body ached. Dropping to his knees, he decided, win or lose, his bull riding career was over. Next he knew, he was surrounded by his giddy family and friends.

"Fifteen seconds!" Cal yelled, joyously slapping

him repeatedly on his throbbing spine. "You won!"

All Kent wanted to do was go home and lie in his big soft bed but Portia was kissing his cheek, Regan was hugging him and squealing, and his father was grinning from ear to ear, which made all the pain worth it.

That evening, Kent was still sore, but getting gussied up to escort Portia to the dance had overridden the aches and pains. They'd just come off the dance floor after a lively reel, and the happiness on her face filled his heart.

Suddenly, Rhine and Eddy were in the center of floor. Kent and Portia along with everyone else stared curiously.

Rhine's voice rang out. "May I have your attention please?"

The musicians stopped playing.

"My wife, Eddy, and I would like to announce that our niece Portia Carmichael has agreed to become the wife of our long-time friend and champion bull rider Kenton Randolph."

After a moment of shocked silence, the barn exploded with cheers and applause. Rhine beckoned Kent and Portia to join him, and Portia said under her breath, "If I didn't need him to give me away, I would shoot him for this." Kent knew she didn't like being the center of attention, but she was smiling. An amused Kent took her hand and they walked out to stand with Eddy and Rhine. They were welcomed with another avalanche of applause.

Rhine said, "The wedding will be in ten days and you're all invited. How about something special from the musicians?"

Portia looked like she really wanted to shoot Rhine then, but when the musicians began to play a slow Mexican waltz and Kent led her slowly and expertly around the floor, the love shining in her eyes was for him alone.

After the dance, the crowd lined up to offer personal congratulations. Some even teased Portia for being so sure she'd never marry, but she took the gentle ribbing with the good spirit in which it was given.

But when Darian Day, overdressed in the same black long-tailed evening coat he'd worn to Rhine and Eddy's anniversary dinner, stepped in front of them, she had trouble hiding her dislike.

"So," he said. "I suppose I won't be getting that spot on your dance card you promised me."

"I don't recall promising you anything."

His eyes swung to Kent. "You're a lucky man."

"I know."

"Too bad she married so far down." He sniffed.

Portia replied, "Not as far down as I am speaking with you now."

His face twisted with anger.

"Move along," Kent said. "You're holding up the line."

He stalked away and Portia said, "I really should be allowed to shoot him, you know."

"I know, darlin'. Maybe next time."

On the ride home, she was cuddled into his side. "Tell me something about yourself I don't know."

He paused and thought. "I was in a Mexican prison for three years."

She stiffened and looked up. "What? Why?"

"I was caught in bed with a don's wife."

"Really?" There was such a marked inflection in the word, he began to worry if maybe he should've offered up something simpler like how strawberries gave him hives.

"You knew she was married?"

"I did." Anxious to know what she was thinking, he waited for her to say more, all the while hoping she wouldn't demand he stop the buggy and tell him the wedding was off. Granted, he probably should have said something about it earlier, but it never came up.

"Are you going to be unfaithful to me at some point, Kent?"

There was such seriousness in her tone it broke his heart. He felt like he'd failed her in a deep and profound way even though he hadn't known he'd be in love with her someday. "No, Duchess. Never. I was young and stupid back then. Did all my thinking below the waist instead of above my shoulders. I love you too much to hurt you that way."

As if attempting to discern the truth she studied him for a bit longer. When she finally resettled herself against him he let out an unconsciously held breath.

"I guess I should be thankful you were truthful and that her husband didn't shoot you dead."

"I certainly am."

"What happened to the wife?"

He shrugged. "I don't know." Rumor had it that the don purchased her a new carriage and enough jewelry to outfit a queen as a way of atoning for neglecting her while he spent his nights with his various mistresses, but Kent didn't know if it was true or not. "Now, your turn. Tell me something I don't know about you."

"Had I a gun yesterday, I would've shot Edward Salt dead."

Concern flared and he pulled back on the reins to stop the horses. "Explain."

So she did, and when she was done, parts of him smiled at her humorous description of Salt rolling on the ground in misery, but others, the parts that loved her and needed to protect her wanted to find the bastard and kick his ass into next month. "If he even looks at you again, he'll have me to answer to."

"And if I ever catch you in bed with another woman you'll have *me* to answer to."

Keeping his smile hidden he replied, "Yes, ma'am."

• • •

Kent, Rhine, and Matt set out at dawn to meet up with David Neal and the other members of the newly formed posse at the Blanchard place. As they rode, Rhine told Kent his lawyers had successful squashed Charlie Landry's bogus claim of ownership. "So if you still want the land, it's yours."

"I do. Oliver tells me I have an inheritance coming so hopefully it will be enough to meet your price."

"There won't be a price."

"What do you mean?"

"Eddy and I have decided to give the land to you and Portia as our wedding gift."

Kent stopped his horse. "Why?"

"Because we can."

Kent met Rhine's eyes and tried to make sense of the startling offer. "But what about your wanting to own that land?"

"I'd rather give it to you and Portia."

"But—"

"Do you want the damn land or not, Kent?"

"I do."

"Then say, 'Thank you, Fontaine.'"

Kent dropped his head. When he raised it again, he complied. "Thank you, Fontaine."

"Good, now let's get moving before Neal thinks we're not coming."

When they reached the Blanchard place, the

blackened stone foundations of the ranch house and the bunkhouse were all that remained. Waiting with David Neal were six riders. Kent knew Howard Lane, but not the others. Neal made the introductions. A few had been at the rodeo's barn dance and congratulated Kent on his upcoming marriage, but because the posse was there for a grim purpose, not much time was spent on small talk. It was agreed that since they were sure Parnell wasn't holed up in town, they'd spend the day searching some of the abandoned shacks close by. If that proved fruitless they'd discuss other options. It wasn't much of a plan, Kent decided, but it beat doing nothing.

So they set out, and the search gave Kent a broader look at the place he'd chosen to be his home. Once again he marveled at the magnificence of the countryside with its mountains, washes, and waterfalls. The landscape varied, too. One moment they were riding through desert and saguaro and the next through stands of thick pines and carpets of wildflowers. At one point they were so high in the mountain range he had a remarkable view of Tucson and the valley spread out below. By the time they stopped to rest themselves and their mounts beside a fast-running stream, they'd searched many of the abandoned homesteads but were no closer to finding signs of Parnell and his cohorts then they were at dawn.

Rhine asked Neal, "Isn't the old Silverfish Mine nearby?"

"Yes. About five or six miles east. Do you want to ride over and take a look around before we head back?"

The men agreed and so they remounted and rode east.

They found a body just inside the mine's shaft. The corpse had been preyed upon by carnivores, most likely big cats or bears, but what remained bore the signs of badly burned flesh and remnants of a scorched black leather vest with silver buckles.

"That's Parnell's vest," Matt said with authority. "Or what's left of it."

The stench of the corpse forced them back outside into the sunlight where they drew in breaths of fresh air.

Kent told the others, "When Matt and I first got to the fire that day there was a strong smell of kerosene in the air."

Neal shook his head. "Dumb bastard must've accidentally splashed some on his clothing as he was pouring it around the buildings. When he lit the fire, he went up in flames, too."

Kent thought that was probably a pretty good guess. There was no way of knowing if Parnell had been badly burned and still clinging to life or already dead when his companions left him at the mine, but it no longer mattered. Justice, in a warped and twisted way, had been served. Buck and Farley could rest in peace.

"I'll let Sheriff O'Hara know what we found," David Neal added. "He can decide if he wants to continue the search for the men who were with Parnell or not, but I don't see how he can."

Kent didn't either. Buck had only identified Parnell.

Leaving what was left of the body to the mountain, the posse set out for home.

Portia spent the day discussing the initial details of her wedding with Regan, Eddy, Sylvie, and Ruth and wondering how Kent and her uncle were faring in the search for Parnell. She hoped they'd find some evidence the sheriff could use to bring justice to the two men whose lives had been taken so ruthlessly.

"I will be making the cake," Eddy stated firmly. "None of this, 'sit back and enjoy the day' business."

Portia chuckled. "Yes, ma'am." Although Portia had managed to wrest control from Eddy for the anniversary celebration, she knew she'd never win this battle so she didn't even try.

Regan asked, "Do you want to get married at the church or here at home?"

"Here, please, I don't want to spend the day traveling back and forth. The guests probably won't either."

From there they talked about her gown which Luz Salinas one of the best seamstresses in the territory would be making. They'd be calling upon friends to help supply all the food that would be needed to feed the multitude of people expected to attend.

Eddy said, "And Portia, since you're the bride, your sister, the ladies, and I will take over the planning."

Portia opened her mouth to protest only to have Eddy wag a finger. "Now, now. If I survived that anniversary party, you can survive this."

"But this is my wedding. I should have some say."

"You'll have plenty of say, honey, but you won't be doing any of the work, so just sit back and enjoy your day."

Amused, Portia asked, "Why does that sound familiar?"

Eddy replied, "I think I may have heard that phrase before, too, somewhere."

Portia sighed and smiled, "Okay. What's good for the goose is good for the gander, I suppose."

"Exactly."

Sylvie weighed in. "Oliver and I want to pay for your honeymoon. Do you and Kent have a place in mind?"

"We haven't talked about it, but the women's convention is in San Francisco during the week after the wedding, so I'm hoping he'll agree to have it there. If he prefers not to, we'll pick someplace else after the convention and let you know." Although, in Portia's mind, the choice made good sense. The convention encompassed only one day, and they could stay over a bit longer and take in the sights.

Eddy added, "Oh, and, Portia, Rhine and I want to give you and Kent the Blanchard property as a wedding gift."

Portia's eyes went wide.

"So until you get a house built, we're offering you the bridal cottage out back."

Portia's brain was still stuck on the first offer. "I thought Uncle Rhine had other uses in mind for that property."

"He did, but now the use will be up to you and Kent to decide."

Still stunned, Portia glanced at Regan who smiled.

Portia was silent for so long, Eddy prodded her, "Well, do you want the use of the cottage after the wedding or not?"

"Yes." Newly married guests sometimes used the hotel as a honeymoon destination and were given the well-furnished one-bedroom cottage on the outer edge of the property. Not only was it furnished but it offered beautiful mountain views and complete privacy. She couldn't see Kent turning down the offer. For sure, neither of them wanted to use their assigned bedrooms in the family wing as their chief domicile, not even temporarily. Deciding she'd sort it all out later, she said, "Thank you so much, Aunt Eddy, and thank you especially for the land."

"You're welcome. Rhine and I will do whatever is needed to get you and Kent into your new place as soon as possible."

Portia hugged her tightly. Ideally, the role Eddy was playing belonged to her mother, Corinne, but since she'd abandoned her claim, Eddy was all she needed. "Thank you." She'd told Eddy at least a thousand times how grateful she was for the way she saved her life, and she felt as if, even if she said it a thousand times a day for as long as she lived, it would never be enough.

"You're welcome."

When Kent and Rhine returned, they shared what they'd found.

Eddy said, "How ironic that he may have died from the same fire."

Portia agreed. She didn't have it in her heart to mourn Parnell's passing, but she was glad he wouldn't be around to hurt anyone else.

Once the conversation was over, Kent wanted to get cleaned up, so Portia walked with him. He asked her, "Did you know Rhine was going to give us the Blanchard land?"

She hooked her arm in his. "No, Eddy surprised me with the news earlier. I think it's wonderful. We'll have our own place."

"Have to have a house built first."

"I know, but in the meantime, she says we can live in the honeymoon cottage out back."

"There's a honeymoon cottage?"

"Yes. We can see it after you're done. Also, Sylvia and your father want to pay for our honeymoon."

"That's nice of them. Do you know where you'd like to go?"

"San Francisco." And she explained about the convention.

"If that's what you want to do on the honeymoon, it's fine with me, as long as you don't get so worked up at the convention you decide you don't want to be married anymore."

They were now standing in the shadowy hallway of the family wing.

She laughed, "You're stuck with me now, cowboy."

"Good."

As Portia had been hoping, he eased her close and kissed her so thoroughly she was left spinning.

"Been looking forward to that since we rode out at sunup," he said afterwards. "Once we're married it'll be nice to be able to kiss you every morning to start the day."

She agreed.

"Be nice to do other things every morning, too," he added, waggling his eyebrows.

"I'm looking forward to that, too."

He gave her another short kiss. "I'll see you soon as I'm done."

She returned to the living area where Rhine was still talking with Eddy and the others, so she asked him, "Can I speak with you in your office for just a moment?"

"Sure."

He kissed Eddy on her forehead, which Portia found endearing, and they left.

Inside he said, "Take a seat. What can I do for you?"

She sat and, thinking about his generosity, emotion welled up inside her with such potency she felt the sting of tears. "I just want to say thank you, for the land, for raising me and Regan—for all you've done for us these past fifteen years— for everything."

He looked at her with wonder. "Portia, are you crying?"

She dashed away her tears and chuckled. "No."

He stood and came around to where she was sitting and opened his arms. She stepped into the embrace and as they hugged each other tightly, she savored how much he meant to her, too. Just like she'd done with Eddy, she whispered, "Thank you, Uncle Rhine. Thank you so much."

He finally leaned back and held her eyes. "Eddy and I were never blessed with children so I always considered you and your sister as mine. Whatever I can do to make you happy makes me happy as well."

When she first arrived in Virginia City, their initial relationship had been rocky but once she learned to trust him, she'd given him her heart.

"And I'll be letting Kent know that if he puts even one minute of sadness in your life, I'll be taking a bullwhip to him."

He handed her his handkerchief and she blew her nose through her smile. "I love him very much."

"Good to know. He's the younger brother I never had, and he's grown into quite a man."

"He told me about the Mexican prison."

"He was filled with hubris back then."

"He called it stupidity."

"That too." Rhine pulled her close again and kissed her brow. "I'm so glad you found someone worthy enough to give your heart to."

"I am, too."

They spent a few more minutes talking about Rhine getting together with her and Kent to draw up plans for their new house and where they might find a carpentry crew to get it built. "We can talk about it all after the wedding," he said.

"I'd like that. I'll let you get back to Aunt Eddy. Thank you again, Uncle."

"You're welcome."

At dinner that evening, Ruth announced that she would be taking the train home in the morning. Everyone voiced their disappointment. "I'm due back at school soon even though my students would probably love for me to stay away longer."

"Someone here can take you to the station," Eddy pointed out. "Just let us know when you'd like to leave."

"Thanks, but I've already made arrangements. James has offered to take me."

"Well, now," Regan teased in a knowing voice, and Ruth dropped her eyes and smiled.

"Portia, I want to thank you for introducing us. We're going to be writing. His father is coming to Chicago later in the year for a church convention and James will be accompanying him. He's a very nice man."

"I was hoping you'd like each other."

"We do. Quite a bit."

Portia was pleased.

"I'm sorry I'll miss the wedding though."

Sylvia said, "Who knows, maybe there's a wedding in your future."

Ruth didn't respond but she did smile.

Eddy asked Sylvia, "What about you and Oliver? You two aren't leaving right after the wedding are you?"

"We'll see how Oliver feels," she said.

Portia wondered if the Randolphs had shared Oliver's prognosis. It wasn't her place to ask, so she didn't.

Oliver said, "I definitely want to stand up with my son."

Kent looked pleased and raised his wineglass in his father's direction.

"Portia's going to be good for you, Kenton."

Kent glanced over at Portia and the love in his eyes was reflected in his reply. "I know."

After the dinner cleanup, Portia and Kent slipped away to see the cottage. When they walked in Kent took a look around. "It's much larger than I imagined."

The front parlor was lavishly furnished with a sofa and a few comfortable-looking upholstered chairs. There was artwork on the walls and a fireplace served as the focal point. There were fine rugs scattered about that pulled on the colors in the drapes on the two French doors that led outside. There was a small kitchen off the parlor. The lone bedroom with its adjoining washroom was at the back of the house. The four-poster brass bed was large and covered with fine linens.

"Now this is a bed," Kent said, pressing his hand into the mattress to test its give. There was a large armoire, a chest of drawers, and a vanity table with an attached mirror. She waited while he stepped into the washroom. "I think this tub will fit two."

She laughed, "I believe that is why my aunt and uncle purchased it."

He walked back out and looked around again and said suggestively, "The things I'm going to do to you in here. Good thing we're not near the hotel. I don't want Rhine running in with his gun drawn when he hears you screaming."

The heat in his eyes seared her, setting off a familiar tightening that made her want to move into the space and share the big bed with him as soon as possible. She also wanted to ask him to teach her how to please him, but she wasn't sure she had the courage to broach the subject, at least not yet.

He walked to her and gently lifted her chin so their eyes would meet. "Penny for your thoughts."

"I want to learn to make you scream, too." There, she'd said it.

He traced her lips in the silence. "Do you?"

She nodded.

He kissed her gently. "Then we'll put that on the list."

"Thank you."

CHAPTER FIFTEEN

The next morning, they all said good-bye to Ruth. She and James drove off in his buggy, accompanied by a small contingent of armed riders that included his father and some of the men from the church. Geronimo and his followers were still at large, and although the army and the hastily cobbled-together posses were frantically crisscrossing the territory, he managed to elude them. Numerous sightings both real and imagined continued, and to have the newspapers tell it, he and his band were often seen in various places at once. People did their best to go about their normal lives but they kept their weapons close and remained vigilant.

After Ruth's departure, Kent and Portia, accompanied by Rhine, Matt, and Cal, rode out to the Blanchard place to get a feel for where they might want to build the new house and how large or small it and the outbuildings would be.

"I think I'd like the house built a bit more to the west," Kent said. "That way the horse paddock can be larger and give us better access to the pond."

Portia agreed. It would also allow the house to be on higher ground and less likely to be affected by flash flooding from the rains. They were discussing the placement of the barn when Matt said quietly, "We got company."

Everyone looked up and froze. Apaches. The five riders approached almost silently, moving like specters in the shimmering heat. As they neared, Portia saw the lined brown face of a short man who could only be Geronimo. She'd seen his likeness in the newspapers. Beside him rode a woman in men's clothing. Lozen. The sister of the great Apache chief Victorio. She was one of her people's fiercest warriors. Her feats and exploits were the stuff of legends and she was a shaman so powerful, she could supposedly sense the location of the enemy. Her gift of prophecy was said to be one of the reasons Geronimo managed to avoid capture. Her presence sent chills up Portia's spine.

For a long moment, the two groups assessed each other silently. Finally, Lozen spoke. "Where's the old man?"

Rhine nodded at Portia and she knew he wanted her to respond. Keeping her voice calm, she replied, "He died of old age, but his friends were murdered and his house was burned to the ground."

The band murmured angrily and Lozen studied her closely. "Were the killers caught?"

"No, but the leader is dead."

Beside her, Geronimo nodded as if the answer was a satisfying one.

"He was a friend," Lozen stated.

"Mine too."

"We came for beef. Our people are hungry. The old man was always generous."

Portia thought about the women and children who'd escaped with them and wished she could help. "The murderers ran off the cattle and they haven't been found. All we can offer is water for your horses."

There was no doubt in Portia's mind that the woman possessed an unearthly power because it emanated from her like charged air before a storm.

Lozen's eyes touched the faces of Rhine, Kent, and Matt before focusing again on Portia. She gave Portia a terse nod. The Apache band reined their horses around and walked them to the pond. While the horses drank, Geronimo and the others did, too. They filled their canteens, remounted, and without a backward glance rode off slowly the way they'd come. Only after they were out of sight did Portia realize she'd been holding her breath.

Cal cracked, "I don't know about anyone else but I think that's more than enough excitement for one day."

Still focused on the area where Lozen and her band had disappeared, Portia agreed.

Matt asked, "Do you think they'll be back?"

"Probably not," Portia told him. With Mr.

Blanchard gone, she doubted they'd have a reason, and with the army searching for them they couldn't afford to spend long periods of time anywhere for fear of capture. When she and Regan were young Mr. Blanchard often told them tales about his early days in the territory and how helpful the Apache had been in showing him the best places to hunt and fish. Portia supposed by secretly providing them with beef, he'd been returning the favor.

A few days before the wedding, a man from Flagstaff stopped in. His name was Frazier Nogales. "I'm here to see Mr. Fontaine," he told Portia, who'd answered the bell. "David Neal said he's looking for a good carpenter to build a house?"

"Yes. Come in, Mr. Nogales. Let me get him."

So Rhine, Portia, and Kent met with the man in Rhine's office and were impressed with his credentials and experience. "Been building houses all my life," he said. "My brothers and I learned the trade from our father and uncles, who learned from our grandfather and great uncles in Sonora when this territory was still part of Mexico."

When told that the house and land would be a wedding present to Portia and Kent, he nodded approvingly. "My daughter was married last year. I built her and her husband a home up near

Oracle. I'll be a grandfather in September," he added proudly.

Portia liked him.

He brought out some plans for them to look at and they talked about the size, shape, and orientation. He asked to see the land and a trip was arranged. Kent said, "Whatever we decide, the house will need an office on the back with a separate entrance for my wife's business."

Portia went still.

Mr. Nogales eyed her. "What kind of business?"

"Bookkeeping."

He studied her for a moment then asked about her experience. When she told him she'd attended Oberlin, handled the books for the hotel, and had apprenticed at a bank in San Francisco, he appeared impressed. "My wife keeps my books, but she doesn't like it and never has. She's been begging me to find someone to replace her, and now with the new baby on the way, she's putting her foot down. She doesn't want to be doing figures when she could be up in Oracle spoiling the grandchild. Are you looking for new customers?"

Portia held on to her excitement. "I am."

"Then let's get your build under way and we'll talk about your replacing my Luisa and how much it will cost me. Agreed?"

"Agreed." She decided then and there that because Kent Randolph always seemed to have her best interests at heart, she'd just become the happiest woman on earth. As they went back to discussing the house plans, she reached over and gave his hand a grateful squeeze and he shot her a wink.

Later that evening they were sitting outside enjoy the evening breeze and the beautiful sunset.

"Thank you," Portia said to him.

"For what?"

"For requesting an office be built into the plans. Because you did, I may have my very first client."

He eased her closer into his side and placed a soft kiss on her forehead. "You're welcome, but you would've thought of the office eventually and found your first client."

"But now, I don't have to wait for eventually."

"Have you picked out a name for your business?"

"Yes. Carmichael Bookkeeping," she replied proudly.

"Simple and to the point."

"Sort of like me."

"Nothing simple about you, Duchess. You're smart, tough, focused, kind."

She drew back to look into his face. "When have I been kind?"

"You introduced Ruth to James."

She settled back against him. "I suppose you're right, but it was also to point him at another woman, so maybe not so kind." She heard his chuckle rumble in his chest.

"And you're honest, I like that, too."

"They say love is blind."

"Love is also patient," he added quietly. "Love is kind. It bears all things, believes all things, hopes all things, and endures all things. Love never ends."

Portia was so moved by his words, her voice came out as a whisper. "Did you make that up yourself? That's beautiful Kent."

"No. It's from the Bible. First Corinthians. Chapter thirteen verses four to eight."

"The Bible?"

"Yes. It was the only thing we were allowed to read when I was in prison. It didn't make me a preacher but after three years I knew it pretty well."

"I'm marrying a Bible-quoting cowboy. What else is hidden inside you, Kenton Randolph?"

He kissed her. "You'll have the rest of our lives to find out."

The next day, true to his word, Mr. Nogales returned and to Portia's surprise he brought his wife. She was a petite woman with long dark hair and a ready smile. While he and Kent went out to tour the ranch property, Portia and Luisa sat in Portia's office to talk over the transfer of their ledgers. "How long has your husband had the business?" Portia asked taking notes.

"Ten successful years and I've been doing the ledgers. It's now time for someone to take them off my hands."

"Your husband told us about the baby your daughter is expecting. Congratulations."

Her face lit up. "Yes. I'm going to be an *abuela*."

"Is this your first?"

"Yes."

Then they got down to business. For the next hour Portia asked questions about payroll, suppliers, the operating structure, and how they handled their banking. Luisa answered each question succinctly and expanded the explanations when it was warranted. By the time the men returned, Portia had a good handle on all she needed to know. With Mr. Nogales in the room, they then discussed rates. Portia envisioned having to negotiate what she felt would be fair compensation but she was surprised when they offered a figure that exceeded her expectations.

Mrs. Nogales explained why. "Because of bigotry it's sometimes difficult for us to find someone we trust to provide us the service you're offering. The reason I've handled our ledgers all these years is because those we hired in the past either treated us with contempt or thought we were too ignorant to know they were bent on cheating us."

Her husband added, "If you do as good a job as I think you will, Miss Carmichael, you'll be worth every dollar we pay you and we will spread the word, not only to the people we know but to the Chinese businessmen and women facing the same prejudices. Don't be surprised when they come courting, too."

Touched by that, Portia said, "I'll do my best to honor the faith you're putting in me. Thank you very much."

"You're welcome," Luisa said. "And congratulations on your wedding."

"Thank you for that, too."

The couple stood. In parting, Mr. Nogales said, "I'm looking forward to building the house for you and your husband. I'll see you soon."

After their departure Portia sat at her desk and thought about the conversation. Would she be embraced because she was a person of color? Truth be told, she'd never envisioned filling such a niche, but thinking about it, she supposed it made sense considering the times and mood of the country. It meant her business could be all she imagined, and maybe more.

Kent and Portia had a late afternoon appointment in Tucson with Reverend Cordell to receive wedding counseling, a service he offered to all couples as a condition of his conducting the ceremony. In the buggy on the way there, Kent looked over from his seat behind the reins and noted Portia's quietness "Penny for your thoughts, Duchess."

"The reverend is not the most progressive thinker so I'm trying to prepare myself."

He laughed.

"I'm serious, Kent. I can only imagine what kind of advice a man like him will give us. He's given sermons denouncing female suffrage as a tool of the devil, for heaven's sake. If Eddy didn't have her heart so set on having a wedding with all the pomp and circumstance, I would've been content having Sheriff O'Hara marry us in his office."

"There you go being kind again."

"I suppose."

He tried to reassure her. "It'll be fine. We'll grit our teeth, smile, and head home. It won't be that painful."

He was wrong. This being Kent's first dealing with the corpulent Reverend Bertram Cordell, he now understood why James rarely had much to say. His father spoke nonstop. For over an hour he detailed Portia's duties to her husband from a list that included everything from always being obedient and cleaning house to nightly foot rubs. Kent covered his snort of laughter with a cough. His duchess was not pleased. Dressed in a black suit and vest with a gold pocket watch chained to it, he looked for all the world like a politician. He certainly pontificated like one.

When he told Portia to always defer to her husband no matter how much she disagreed because the male mind was far superior to the female mind, Kent saw her jaws lock so tightly he thought her teeth might shatter.

Three-quarters of the way through yet another long-winded soliloquy, this time on a woman's duties to her children, Portia asked him, "So, Reverend, what are Kent's duties?"

So far he hadn't mentioned anything specific.

"Why to be the head and mind of the household, Portia. Haven't you been listening?" He turned to Kent and said, "See? This is why females need our guidance. I don't think they hear a word we say sometimes."

Finally, after ninety long minutes of rambling sentences, cock-eyed opinions, and questionable Bible verses, they were allowed to leave.

Outside, Portia climbed into the buggy and folded her arms in a huff.

Kent got in on his side and said, "Obviously I was wrong."

"Thank you for loving me, Kent, because if I was married to him, I would have killed him so many years ago, I'd be paroled by now."

Howling with laughter, he slapped down the reins and drove them home.

After dinner, the women left for the guest suite Rhine had dubbed Wedding Headquarters to handle whatever details still needed their attention and Rhine retired to his office to do business. That left Oliver and Kent alone, so he asked, "Would you like to ride over and see the property where Portia and I are having our house built?"

"Sure."

Kent brought the buggy around and the shadow crossed his heart again as he watched his father slowly make his way onto the seat. Oliver winced a few times in response to what must have been sharp flares of pain but he didn't ask for help and Kent didn't offer so as to allow him his dignity.

On the drive over Kent kept the horses to a slow but steady pace so as to not jostle his passenger too much and they talked about the beauty of the surroundings. "Pretty country here," Oliver noted. "I expected there'd be more desert like Virginia City. All these trees are surprising."

"The trees took me by surprise, too, but there is desert not that far away."

They shared a silence for a short while before Oliver said, "So tell me what you been doing since the last time we were together. What's it been, three—four years?"

"About that." Kent filled him in on the jobs he'd worked, their locations, and how long he'd stayed at each.

"You always were restless."

Kent smiled.

"Even as a child you had trouble sitting still. I think that's something a mother teaches. I didn't have time. Too busy seeing to folks' ills so I could keep a roof over our heads and food on the table."

"And I appreciated it, even if I didn't act as if I did."

"We're too much alike. Proud. Stubborn."

"What was she like?"

"Your mother?"

"Yes."

"The softness I needed to balance my hardness. A much better woman than I deserved, frankly, which could be why God took her from me when he did. Even after marrying her I was still pining for Sylvie."

His father had been in love with Sylvia for decades before they finally became man and wife fifteen years ago. Only when Kent was older did he learn the two had engaged in an affair while Sylvia was married to her first husband. "Be faithful to Portia, Kent."

"I plan to."

They'd never had a discussion like this before and Kent wondered if Oliver wanted to get all this off his chest because he knew he was dying.

When they reached the property Kent set the brake and started to step out, but Oliver said, "I'm not going to get out, son. I'm in too much pain to walk around. I just want to look. Point and show me where the house will be built."

Swallowing his guilt for subjecting his father to the ride, Kent complied, then answered his father's questions about how soon the construction would begin and when the house would be ready to move into. They spent a few more minutes talking about the horse wrangling business he wanted to start and the office that would be built on the back of the house for Portia's business.

"Those are grand plans, Kenton. Good plans."

Kent enjoyed the praise.

"We should probably get going, and don't feel guilty for bringing me out here. I needed to see it because I might not be around when it's time for you to move in."

"Okay," he whispered.

Driving back, Kent was glad they'd spent the time together, even if it had been brief. A question that had been plaguing him for some time came to mind. He turned to ask Oliver if he knew whether his mother had any family, but he was asleep.

When they reached the hotel, rather than awaken him, Kent gently picked him up and carried him inside. The country doctor who'd been so hale and hearty now weighed no more than a child. The realization brought such strong emotions, tears stung his eyes.

Sylvia was waiting for them inside as if knowing she'd be needed. Kent followed her to their room and laid him softly on the bed.

"Thanks, Kent," she whispered.

Kent left her and, because cowboys weren't supposed to cry, he went to his room and closed himself in so no one would know.

CHAPTER SIXTEEN

It was so hot the morning of her wedding, Portia almost dreaded having to put on the beautiful gown made by Luz Salinas. She was clothed in all the layers a woman traditionally wore, and adding the gown on top would only increase her discomfort. She prayed she didn't faint from heat stroke. Regan, already dressed and looking beautiful in her pale blue gown, entered to help her with her hair.

"I'm jealous," Regan said, plying the hot hair iron.

"Why?"

"Because later today, you'll be Mrs. Kent Randolph and I'll still be *Miss* Regan Carmichael."

"Haven't found your mail-order husband yet?" Portia teased.

Regan went so still, Portia turned around so she could see her face. "Regan?"

She didn't respond, but the guilt on her face let Portia know instantly that something was very wrong. "Tell me or I swear I'll go and get Aunt Eddy."

"I was going to wait and tell you in a few days."

"Tell me now, please."

"I've found him. He's a doctor in Wyoming. We've been corresponding for a few weeks now."

Portia stared.

"He sounds perfect, Portia. He's a widower. Only eight years older, and he has a young daughter. And before you say anything else, I have agreed to marry him."

Filled with panic, Portia shouted, "What! You really are going to be a mail-order bride? But why?"

"One, because there's no one here I want to marry and, two, for the adventure of it."

"Sweetheart, this is marriage you're talking about. This isn't an adventure like delivering mail. Suppose he isn't who he claims to be? What if he turns out to be someone who harms you? What if everything he's written is a lie?"

"What if it isn't?"

Portia had no response for that, but she worried that the man might be taking advantage of her sister's quest for love. "Does Eddy know?"

"No, and I'm still trying to decide how to approach her and Uncle Rhine with the news."

"Lord, Regan."

"This is why I didn't want to tell you. You're not supposed to spend your wedding day wondering if I've lost my mind."

"Have you?"

"No. From his letters, he needs me, Portia, and so does his daughter."

Portia's love for Regan and the need to keep her safe competed with her desire for Regan to find her own version of the happiness she'd found with Kent. Portia reminded herself that Regan was a grown woman and in many ways more experienced in life than she was, but still, to go all the way to Wyoming to be the bride of a man she'd only corresponded with for a few weeks?

"Can you try and be happy for me?"

"Oh, honey, you know I am, but are you sure this is wise?"

"I am."

Portia wanted to shout that she couldn't go but knew she didn't have that right. Nor did she want Regan to sneak off in the middle of the night without so much as a good-bye. The girl had always been headstrong. "Okay. I'm not going to fuss. If you have your mind made up, then I'll support you if Aunt Eddy and Uncle Rhine go through the roof."

Regan smiled and hugged her. "Thanks, Portia."

Portia held her tight and wanted to weep. They'd been together their entire lives. It had been them against a world that had initially offered nothing but poverty and heartache. What would life be without her? She was already feeling the loss. Easing away, she looked Regan in the eyes. "But if this man turns out to be a monster, I expect you to pack up and come home."

"I will. Promise."

Regan went back to doing Portia's hair but Portia couldn't rid of herself of her worry. As if reading her thoughts, Regan said gently, "Stop worrying, Portia. Everything will be fine, you'll see."

Portia nodded but the worry remained. Eventually as they talked about all the day had in store, Regan's plans no longer plagued Portia like a sore tooth. She knew the worry would return eventually but she let the prospect of becoming Mrs. Kenton Randolph rise to the fore again. With that in mind, she got dressed.

The gown was a lovely cream color with a lace inset between the neck and bodice. It had a flowing skirt, small capped sleeves that left her arms bare and was easily the most beautiful gown she'd ever seen. Her new shoes were cream colored and accented with soft gold bows. Her stockings and garters were the same color as her gown. Looking at herself in the full-length mirror, she almost didn't recognize herself.

"You look so gorgeous, Kent's going to want to eat you with a spoon."

A soft knock interrupted them. It was Eddy. She was dressed in a resplendent mauve gown that she wore as if she were royalty. When she looked at Portia tears welled in her eyes. "Oh my. Look how beautiful you are."

Regan wiped at her own tears. "Aunt Eddy, stop. You'll have us all weeping in a minute."

"But look at her," she said again.

Tears stung Portia's eyes. "You look beautiful, too."

"Thank you. I just came in to tell you the guests have arrived and your uncle Rhine's waiting out in the hallway. When you're ready, just come out."

Eddy kissed Portia's cheek. "I love you."

"I love you, too."

She kissed Regan's cheek, too. "I love you, too, and you can't get married for at least twenty more years. I won't know what to do if I lose both of my girls."

Eddy left wearing a watery smile and when the sisters were alone again, they shared a guilty look. Regan said, "I'll wait for you outside."

"Thanks for your help."

Regan gave her a wink and was gone.

Refusing to let her worry about Regan rise again, Portia drew in a deep breath, picked up her bouquet of wildflowers, and stepped out into the hallway.

Her uncle Rhine, clad in formal black and white attire, said, "You look very beautiful, Portia."

Butterflies were taking flight in her stomach. "Thank you."

"Are you ready to get married?"

"Yes."

He gallantly offered his arm and escorted her away.

• • •

When Portia appeared on Rhine's arm, she was so beautiful it made Kent ache. He'd never experienced such a sensation before. He wanted to hand out blindfolds to every man in attendance and demand they be tied on so he'd be the only who could see her. Her hair was up, and she wore a light application of face paint that made her cat-eyed features even more alluring. Beside him, his father Oliver whispered, "You have a gorgeous bride, Kenton."

Kent thought the word didn't even come close to describing his duchess.

Rhine walked her to Kent's side and after placing a kiss on her brow, stepped aside to stand with the teary-eyed Eddy. Kent took her hand in his. He looked down, met her shining eyes, and he was so happy inside he wanted to kick up his heels and yell "Hot damn!" With the sober-faced Reverend Cordell standing before them, Bible in hand, he decided that was probably inappropriate, so he calmed himself and prepared to recite the vows.

The vows were recited, the marriage sealed and blessed, and Reverend Cordell said to Kent, "You may now kiss your bride."

Their kiss was met with much hooting and hollering and applause from the large crowd. When he finally turned her loose and they faced the people who'd gathered, he said in a voice only she could hear, "Now, everybody go the hell home so I can make love to my wife."

She giggled, elbowed him gently and said, "Behave."

The reception took place in the ballroom and the Fontaine Hotel and its staff did the newlyweds proud. There was enough food to feed the entire territory and the champagne flowed like waterfalls. There was music, dancing, and many toasts. Matt got so drunk off two flutes of champagne, Regan found him asleep outside beneath one of the tables. Kent remarked that his assistant foreman couldn't hold his pie or his liquor. As evening arrived and the sun went down, Portia was glad she and Kent were married, but after all the celebrating her feet were hurting, she was hot and tired, and all she wanted to do was take off her gown and crawl into bed. Eddy walked over. "You look exhausted. It's okay if you and Kent want to leave."

"We can?"

"Yes."

"Oh, thank you."

A multitude of raucous guests escorted Portia and Ken to the cottage. After opening the door, he scooped her up in his arms to carry her over the threshold and they roared their approval. Grinning, he turned to them and said, "Thank you and good night."

He carried her inside and kicked the door closed. On their way to the bedroom, the cheering outside could still be heard, but as they entered it, only silence remained. She looked up into the eyes of her husband and said, "Finally we're alone."

"Finally." And he gently set her on her feet.

"A few minutes ago my feet were hurting, I was hot and tired, and all I wanted was to take off this dress and crawl into bed."

"And now?"

"I still want to take off this dress and crawl into bed, but with you."

"Perfect answer—partially."

She was confused. "What do you mean?"

"I get to take off your dress."

She laughed. "Will you always be this outrageous?"

"As long as we're both breathing." He ran a slow thumb down her cheek. "Thank you for marrying me."

Her heart swelled with all the love she had for her outrageous cowboy. "You're welcome."

Their wedding night began with a series of lazy lingering kisses that were as familiar as they were welcome. In spite of the day's heat and the discomfort, they'd both been waiting for this moment for a long time. After tonight, she'd be a woman in every sense of the word.

He whispered, "Turn for me, love."

She complied. He undid the line of small covered buttons that ran down her spine and when he finished, helped her ease her arms free of the delicate capped sleeves to expose the cream-colored silk shift that covered her corset. He brushed adoring lips over the flesh bared by the garments, the back of her neck, and the crowns of her shoulders while his hands moved up and over the breasts mounded by the veiled corset. "You have on too many clothes, Mrs. Randolph. How about you step out of your dress?"

She did and he placed it on the chair nearby.

Her shift was disposed of next, which left her dressed in her corset, gartered stockings, drawers, and fancy shoes. He liked the sensual vision she presented and ran a finger over the tops of her breasts. "I'm surprised you didn't drop from the heat with all these things on, but I like this corset."

"Do you?"

"Very much."

Edged in lace and adorned with tiny seed pearls, it was made for a man's adoring eyes, but it was soon rucked down so he could feast wantonly, and all she could do was moan and stand on legs that shook in response to each passionate circling of his enticing tongue and draw of his expert mouth. His hands found the dampness between her thighs and by the time he removed her drawers and they moved to the bed, she was rising and twisting on the edge of orgasm. "Let yourself go, darling," he whispered encouragingly. "I have plenty more for you."

He slid in one finger and then two and slowly used them to mimic the way he planned to love her later. The heat in the room climbed and her legs widened. He increased the pace and savored how wet she was and the sight of her nudity framed by the opened corset, as she rose and fell to the decadent rhythm. He captured her lips. "Come for me, Duchess. I know you're ready."

And a breath later she did, bucking wildly and calling his name.

Kent smiled the smile of a pleased male and eased his fingers free. He was on the verge of orgasm, too, but she was his and he was greedy, so he teased the stiff little bud at the apex of her thighs and dropped his head.

When his tongue found her she cried out. "What—"

"I just want a small taste, darlin'."

He raised his head and, seeing the wonder in her eyes, he chuckled. "No?"

She fell back as if outdone and he laughed. "Oh, baby, we're going to have so much fun, you and I."

And Portia had to admit, it was fun until he slid himself inside and the size of him stretched her so painfully.

"Just relax, love. I won't move until you've caught your breath."

Regan was right. It did hurt and she was left bereft because she wanted to enjoy this part of the marriage bed, but she wouldn't if it hurt this way. He was holding himself above her and there was genuine concern on his face.

"It'll only hurt this one time. Promise. You ready?"

Biting her lip, she nodded and tensed when he began to move again. After a few minutes her body accepted him, the pain lessened, and she began answering his slow strokes. The flame caught again, this time more intensely. Feeling the familiar storm begin to gather, she smiled up. "Oh, Kent."

"Liking it now?"

She wanted to reply but her body was responding so feverishly no words were needed. Caught up in the whirlwind as he increased his pace, she hooked her heels over his thrusting hips, ran her hands up and down his strong arms, and knew she'd died and gone to heaven.

"Welcome to the marriage bed, Mrs. Randolph."

His thrusts were harder, stronger, and he reached down and raised her hips without missing a beat. He threw back his head, "God, you're so tight. I could do you all night, woman."

And then, as his orgasm broke, he roared and stroked harder, rougher, and she didn't care because she was coming again, too, this time with a scream, and she didn't care if they heard her in Tucson.

In the silent aftermath, he kissed her and she ran her fingers up the sweat on his back and down his spine. He was heavy but she didn't mind. He finally broke the seal of their bodies and rolled off and lay beside her breathing harshly. "I don't think I'm ever letting you out of this room."

She chuckled softly.

He studied her and she did the same to him. He asked, "Are you okay? I probably should've been gentler."

"I'm fine and so were you. When can we do it again?"

He laughed, dragged her atop and they did again, and again. When the sun came up, they finally fell asleep in each other's arms.

For the next three days, they made love, many times, ate food delivered to the door by the hotel staff, and talked about everything from the silly to the serious.

One evening while outside watching the sunset, she said, "Who would have ever thought we'd end up married to each other?"

"I know. When I first met you, you were a skinny little thing with big eyes who didn't smile."

"That's because I was so terrified of you and Rhine and Jim. All men really."

"I know."

"You did?"

"Yes. When any of us came into a room you'd

leave or stand with a piece of furniture between you and whichever man it was."

"I thought I was prey."

"Rhine and Eddy talked with us about you and Regan."

Portia thought back. "I remember the day we arrived in Virginia City. It was right after Aunt Eddy was shot. When she recovered, Regan and I asked her a hundred questions. We didn't know what marriage was and I remember to this day how appalled she looked when I asked if we were going to have to have relations with Uncle Rhine. She said no of course, but it took me a long time to actually believe her. My mother's customers were mostly brutes, so I thought all men were that way."

"We're not."

"I know," she whispered. "When my mother sent us away, my insides felt like pieces of a broken glass and I didn't know how I was supposed to go back together." The memory tore open the bandage she always wore over that hurt and tears sprang to her eyes. She dashed them away. "You'd think I'd be over that by now."

"I don't know if you ever get over something like that."

"You're good for me, cowboy. I'm glad you love me."

He hugged her tight and whispered, "Always."

CHAPTER SEVENTEEN

After the newlyweds rejoined the world, Mr. Nogales and his men began building the house. He told them it was too early to estimate when they'd be able to move in due to all the work needed to level the site and set the foundation, but the Randolphs didn't care that there was no date. They were happy enough knowing the work had begun. Mr. Nogales's sister, Angelica, owned a brick making operation in Flagstaff and she hired Portia to do her books, too. Carmichael Bookkeeping now had three clients. Mr. Nogales, his sister, and the Fontaine Hotel. Portia was delighted.

"I've decided to name the ranch the Duchess Randolph in your honor," Kent said one morning, walking into her office at the hotel.

"You're pulling my leg."

"No and here's proof." He showed her a piece of paper that had drawn on it a stylized *D* over an upside down *R*. "It'll be the brand for our cattle. I'll get it registered the next time I go into Tucson."

Portia was touched by the tribute. "Can I reward you with kisses?"

"Only if I can get more than kisses later."

"You have a deal."

They were in the middle of the kiss when Regan's voice interrupted them. "Lord. You two are as bad as Uncle Rhine and Aunt Eddy."

Kent turned Portia loose and headed to the door where Regan stood. He gave his sister-in-law a peck on the cheek. "We love you, too."

And he left to ride out to the ranch.

Smiling at her husband's exit, Portia asked, "What can I do for you, Regan?"

"I'm ready to talk to Aunt Eddy and Uncle Rhine. Can you come with me?"

Regan nodded tightly.

To their credit, their aunt and uncle took the news rather calmly, Portia thought, but it didn't mean they liked it. As Portia had done on her wedding day, they pointed out all the things that could go wrong.

"How do you know this man isn't lying to you?" Rhine asked.

"I don't."

Eddy sighed. "Regan, I love you dearly and you are old enough to make your own decisions but are you sure you want to travel all that way for what might turn out to be fool's gold?"

"If it is, I promise to come home."

Rhine said, "I'd feel better about this if he came down to meet us and then escorted you back."

"I would, too," Eddy admitted.

"He's the only doctor in his part of the territory and he doesn't want to leave his patients alone for the length of time it would take him to get here and go back. Which I understand. That says to me how seriously he takes his profession."

Or he could be lying, Portia thought to herself.

They spent a few more minutes discussing all the things that might go wrong, but Regan had her mind made up and so stuck to her guns.

Rhine looked upset but there was pain in his eyes, too. Like Portia he was already missing Regan. "When is he expecting you?"

"In a few weeks."

Eddy looked stricken. "So soon?"

Regan nodded.

"Then let your uncle and me know what we need to do to help you get ready."

"I will and thank you for not making this harder to tell you. I've been worried."

"You just transferred that worry to us," Eddy said with a sad smile.

"I'm sorry."

"No apology needed. As I said, you are old enough to direct your own life. I just have to accept that. I don't love you any less."

The two embraced and Regan whispered, "Thank you."

A few days later, tickets in hand, Eddy, her lady friends, and Portia and Kent boarded the train bound for San Francisco and the women's conference. Regan stayed home to continue seeing to her move to Wyoming. Portia and Kent were set to stay a few days longer and she planned to be extra sweet to him for agreeing to come along.

Upon arrival, they took cabs to their hotel and rested up for their dinner that evening with Rhine's half brother Andrew, his wife Freda and their son Little Drew.

The conference the next day turned out to be an exciting affair. Women from all over the West converged on the grove behind the local Baptist church to hear speeches, plot strategies for advancing suffrage, and reaffirm their commitments to uplifting the race. Portia had never seen such a gathering of determined, forceful, and articulate women, and it filled her with pride. She saw Ada Jakes at a table selling pamphlets. The woman looked her off. Portia didn't care. She saw Winston, too, with a dark-skinned woman on his arm. His eyes widened at the sight of Portia but he didn't approach her and she didn't approach him either.

The highlight of the day was hearing the words of famed speaker Frances Watkins Harper, a force of nature for both the race and women since the days of abolition. She was in her winter years, her hair graying but her voice was still strong, her message fiery, and when she finished, an inspired Portia and everyone else leapt to their feet to applaud.

Portia and Kent had dinner that evening at a small restaurant and she filled him in on the day.

"Sounds like you had a good time."

"Oh, I did. Mrs. Harper's talk was so moving it made me want to grab a placard and start marching."

"But you want to stay married?" he teased.

"Of course."

They finished their meal, and after paying the check, they left the eatery and took a slow stroll back to the hotel. The route took them past many shops and businesses and even at that time of the evening, the walks were crowded with people. Her excitement for the day notwithstanding, Portia glanced up at her handsome husband and decided she loved being married. Waking up in the morning with him by her side filled her with more happiness than she ever thought imaginable. She knew no marriage was perfect, and that there would be times they'd disagree, argue profusely, or be so annoyed they'd want to be alone for a period of time, but for now she was content.

"Penny for your thoughts, Mrs. Randolph."

"Just happy."

"Good. No new bride should be unhappy."

She was about to say more when she noticed a woman about her aunt's age walking towards them dressed in the height of fashion. Her ensemble was the color of emeralds and was as beautiful as it was costly. She was next to a distinguished-looking older gentleman attired in a nice brown suit. From the way her gloved hand rested so lovingly in the crook of his arm, they gave the impression of being married, too. As the couple neared, the woman's brown eyes locked with Portia's and they both stared at each other in shock. The woman quickly looked away and she and the man passed by without a further glance, but Portia's heart was pounding so riotously, she stopped.

Kent asked with concern, "Are you all right? You look like you've seen a ghost."

"I have. My mother just walked by us."

He swiftly turned around. Portia eventually turned, too, but the couple was no longer in sight. She didn't know if they'd been swallowed by the crowd or stepped into one of the shops. What she did know was that Corinne Carmichael, the woman who'd mailed her daughters to Eddy and disappeared from their lives, was alive and well.

Later as she talked to Eddy about it at the hotel, Eddy asked, "Are you sure it was Corinne?"

"Positive. And from the shock on her face, she recognized me as well."

Eddy sighed. "I'd like to find her but I can't imagine how we'd go about that."

"Frankly, the way she averted her eyes, I don't think she'll want us to find her."

"You're probably right, but I wonder what she's been doing all this time and why she never sent us so much as a word in the fifteen years since she gave you girls to me. Women don't normally get up one morning and decide to abandon their children. You and your sister deserve at least an explanation."

Portia agreed. Watching Corinne look away when they passed each other felt like being stabbed in the heart with a red-hot poker, bringing back the painful memories of all the nights she'd cried in the dark after arriving in Virginia City and how unloved she'd been made to feel.

Eddy was pacing and looking genuinely upset. "I want to find her and shake her until her teeth rattle."

Portia understood her aunt's anger and the desire for answers. Corinne's short two-line letter to Eddy simply stated that the new man in her life didn't want to provide for two children that weren't his own. That her mother had agreed to such an outrageous directive only added to the hurt. Was the gentleman with Corinne the same unfeeling man, or someone different who had no inkling of her past? It was yet another question needing an answer.

Eddy stopped pacing and from the tense set of her lips, Portia knew she'd come to a decision. "Whether Corinne wants to be found or not, she owes you girls an explanation, and if I have to hire an army of Pinkertons to bring that about, that's what I'll do."

"But, Aunt Eddy—

"No, Portia. What good is being married to a wealthy man if you don't use that wealth? We'll hear from my sister, and it will be soon. Count on it."

Later, as she lay in bed in Kent's arms, she tried to tell herself she was all right but knew it was a lie. "Eddy's going to hire the Pinkertons to find my mother."

"Is that good or bad?"

She rose up to look into his face. "I'm not sure. On one hand, she made it perfectly clear on the street today that she doesn't want any contact from me, but on the other hand, I keep wondering what would make a woman abandon her children the way she did. I know she said it was the new man in her life, but there has to be more, don't you think?"

"I don't know, darling, but I do know I don't like seeing you in pain this way."

She settled back into his embrace. "If we have children, I'll never do that."

He kissed the top of her head. "I know."

Portia thought back on her mother's plan to sell her virginity, and the horror of who she might have become as a result made her eyes sting with tears. She almost told Kent about it but decided to keep it to herself; she was horrified enough for them both.

"While you and the other women were plotting to take over the world, I got you something."

Corinne was momentarily forgotten. "What?"

"Hold out your hand and close your eyes."

She did so and heard a small rustling and then felt him lightly take her outstretched hand. What felt like a ring was gently pushed onto her finger and excitement grabbed her.

"Open your eyes, please."

When she complied, the thin gold band on her finger sparkled in the light of the lamp. "This is beautiful, Kent."

"Do you like it?"

She turned her hand this way and that. "I do." Wedding rings were becoming more and more popular with married couples. "But I don't have one for you."

"You can fix that when Carmichael Bookkeeping makes its first million dollars."

She laughed and threw her arms around him. "I love you so much."

"I love you so much, too."

When they arrived home, they were met at the door by a solemn Sylvie, and Kent sensed bad news. "How is he?" he asked.

"Almost gone but I think he's been holding on until he can see you."

Inside his father's quiet room, Kent slowly approached the bed. Oliver was lying so still that

331

for a moment Kent thought Sylvie was wrong and that he'd already slipped away, but his eyes slowly opened and a small smile followed. "Hello, Kenton." His voice was a whisper. "How was San Francisco?"

"It was fine."

"Good to see you."

Heart tight, Kent replied, "Good to see you, too."

"I'm getting ready to leave here. Glad you won't be alone, now that you have your duchess. Glad we settled our differences, too."

Kent knelt by the bed. "So am I."

"You'll take care of my Sylvie?"

"Of course."

The eyes drifted closed and Kent panicked, but when the eyes fluttered open again, he let out a pent-up breath. "I saw your mother a bit ago. She's still beautiful," Oliver said.

Tears wet Kent's cheeks.

"Hoping St. Peter will let me in the gates so she and I can talk."

"I hope so, too," Kent whispered.

His father studied his face. "You shedding tears for your old man?"

Kent nodded.

"I love you, too, son. More than I ever let on. Don't make that same mistake with your own son. Let him know."

"I will."

"I knew you'd make it back for me to talk with you one last time."

Kent was pleased that he had.

"Will you get Sylvie for me? I need to say good-bye."

Kent stood.

"Good-bye, Kenton."

"Good-bye, father."

Dr. Oliver Randolph left the world a short while later. He wanted to be cremated, a relatively new movement touted by Queen Victoria's surgeon, Sir Henry Thompson, so a grieving Sylvie, Kent, and Portia accompanied the casket by train to a crematorium in Lancaster, Pennsylvania, only the second such facility in the nation. At the end of the cremation process, Kent was presented with a small wooden box.

"What is this?" Kent asked.

"Your father's remains. Some families like to spread the ashes in their loved one's favorite place or disperse them into the wind."

Kent didn't know whether to be moved or repulsed. He passed the box to Sylvia. "You can decide."

Kent was solemn for the rest of the way home. Sylvia returned to the territory with them, saying that with Oliver gone, she had no one to return to in Virginia City and would figure out what she wanted to do with her life once the sharpness of her grief softened. Kent wasn't sure when or if his would ever soften. For a man whom he'd battled seemingly his entire life, Oliver's death broke his heart.

Portia would remember the month of June 1885 as a time of loss. Her heart ached for her grieving husband, her still unfound mother, and for Regan. Standing with Regan and the family at the train station as she prepared to travel to her new life in Wyoming, Portia didn't want her to go.

"Please don't cry," Regan said, holding Portia tight as the tears ran freely down both their cheeks.

Eddy, crying, too, stood beside a stoic Rhine. They'd resigned themselves to the choice Regan had made but were still saddened by it. Portia was, too, but knew it was necessary to let her go.

As the train pulled into the station, Eddy hugged her niece one last time. "Make sure you wire us just as soon as you arrive."

"I will."

Rhine held her next. "I love you, little girl. Take care of yourself. If Kent and I need to ride up and shoot this man, let us know."

"You have my word."

When the time came to board, she turned her ungodly amount of luggage over to the conductor, threw the family a kiss, and disappeared inside.

Grieving for her sister, Portia took solace in watching her and Kent's house rise like a phoenix from the ashes of the old Blanchard homestead. She visited every day and savored each day's progress no matter how big or small.

A week after receiving the wire that Regan had indeed arrived in Wyoming, Portia was working in her office at the hotel when Eddy knocked on the opened door.

"Hey, Eddy. What can I do for you?"

"This came today."

She handed Portia an envelope. "It's from Corinne. The Pinkerton detective I hired found her."

Portia beat down her trembling. "Do I want to read it?"

"No, but you should."

Filled with dread, Portia slipped the single sheet of vellum from the envelope and read. *E. Do not contact me again. Have a good life now. No desire for the old. Make this clear to Portia and Regan. I repeat. Do not contact me again. C.*

"I guess that's that," Portia said softly.

"I'm sorry, honey."

Portia nodded. "Thank you, Eddy. I'll move on with my life."

"As will we all."

After her aunt's departure, Portia walked over and closed the door. With her back against it, she surrendered to the emotion and silently wept.

CHAPTER EIGHTEEN

While June would be remembered for its sadness, July brought joy. Mr. Nogales finished the house and she and Kent moved in on the first day of the month.

As they marveled at how beautiful and spacious the new house was, Kent said, "I think we should christen the place by making love in every room."

She laughed.

"I'm serious, and once the rooms are marked we start with all the flat surfaces. I think I'd like to have you laid out on the kitchen counter wearing nothing but your garters while I lap you up."

Having gone to paradise and back with him so many times, she thought she'd lost the ability to blush, but she hadn't.

"So . . ." He walked over to her and loosely laced his arms around her waist. He brushed his lips over her neck. "Where shall we start?"

They started right there in the parlor where they were standing. Her clothes were slowly removed, piece by piece, and in the end he laid her down on his shirt and took her in the center of the room on the newly installed and polished pine floor.

"This is a two-for-one romp," he said, pulling her atop him. "We're in the parlor and on a flat surface."

She looked down into his face. "Whatever am I going to do with you?"

"Not sure," he said, "but how about you start by riding this?" She complied, and as he slipped inside, she rode him until he roared.

Over the next few days, they'd christened nearly every room in the house and topped it off in the washroom, where he took her first against the wall and then in the large claw-foot tub. He'd loved her so thoroughly she vaguely remembered being dried off and carried to the bed, but nothing more.

Portia had never been treated to breakfast in bed—she'd always been too busy making sure the hotel's guests were the ones to enjoy that treat. So when she was awakened by his entering the bedroom, tray in hand, she was delighted. On the tray was an omelet spiced with peppers along with bacon, grits, and toast. "I think I may keep you," she said, showing him a smile.

"After all the lovemaking we've been doing, I *know* I'm keeping you. Though I still have to have you in the kitchen and in your office."

"We're not making love in my office."

He laughed. "I ordered that desk for you to work at and for me to bend you over, so expect to be ambushed when you least expect it. We'll call it The Bookkeeper and the Naughty Cowboy Husband."

She dropped her head. He was unbelievable, and yes, all hers.

He kissed her softly. "You agreed to be my wife. This is part of the benefits. I'm going to see to the horses."

"Good-bye."

He tossed her a wink, put on his hat, and left.

Alone, she chuckled softly and began eating. The image of herself bent over the desk with him behind her crept into her mind. As it continued, her senses flared, and she decided she might enjoy being ambushed by the naughty cowboy husband.

And she did. Two days later, reaching for the Nogaleses' ledger, she accidentally knocked over the tin cup holding her pencils. It slid off the front edge of the desk spilling the pencils all over the floor. Momentarily irritated by her clumsiness, and because she had to get out of the chair to retrieve them, she walked around, picked up the cup, filled it with the pencils again and set it back in its spot. Standing in front of the desk, she was about to walk back to her chair when she spotted a lone pencil that had not made it to the floor. As she reached over to grab it, she heard, "Good afternoon, Miss Bookkeeper, and don't you dare move."

She dropped her head and laughed softly. *Ambushed.*

He came up behind her and whispered, "Perfect timing."

While Kent vividly described all the naughty things the cowboy planned to do, her skirt was slowly raised and her drawers slowly lowered and taken. Then his hands began a slow dance of arousal. He reached around and undid the buttons on her blouse and soon her breasts came out to play. "I should visit you in here every day."

Portia whimpered with pleasure.

He filled her, coaxed her into the age-old rhythm, and as the pace increased she bent forward to grab the edges of the desk. "Yes, just like that," he rasped.

Soon pencils spilled to the floor along with ledgers and books, and she didn't care as long as he didn't stop. Her pleasure climbed, his strokes became stronger, and the sounds of mutual desire grew louder. Portia lost track of time, her name, and everything else that seemed to matter before he'd entered a few moments ago. Her naughty cowboy was so very wicked, she shattered on a scream and he followed her off the edge of the world with a roar.

When she could see again, she turned and looked at him over her shoulder. He asked, "Ever taken a bath in the middle of the day with a naughty cowboy?"

She laughed, "No."

He picked her up. "Then you're in for a treat."

As he carried her out, Portia looked back, saw the mess they'd made of her desk, and didn't care.

It was now the end of July. They'd settled into the house, her business was going well, and Kent was in contract negotiations with the army to supply them with horses starting after the New Year.

Portia decided to surprise Kent by making breakfast. He'd done all of the cooking since they'd moved in and she thought it time she share the load. She grabbed eggs from the hens, took some bacon out of the cold box, sliced bread, and began.

In the bedroom, a tired and sleepy Kent awakened to the smell of something burning. At first he thought it might be a dream but when it persisted he sat up and noted that, one, Portia wasn't in bed and, two, yes, something was definitely burning.

Hurrying out of the room, he saw tendrils of smoke curling out of the kitchen. Inside he found his wife using a small towel to bat at flames rising from what had once been toast. Swallowing his smile, he cleared his throat, "Good morning, Mrs. Randolph."

She shot him a peeved look. "I wanted to surprise you with breakfast, but thought I'd try to burn the house down instead."

The kitchen looked like a cyclone had visited. There were eggs shells and little puddles of spilled milk on the floor, pieces of what appeared to be a broken plate and a saucer on the counter, and something black and foul-smelling stuck to the surface of the cast-iron skillet on the stove.

"I'm a woman," she said angrily. "I'm supposed to be able to cook. If something happens to you, I'll starve to death."

Knowing she'd probably gut him if he laughed, he instead held out his arms. "Come here."

She walked to him and he eased her close. Above her head he grinned widely, which prompted her to say, "I know you're secretly laughing, Kent Randolph."

"Laughing with you, Duchess, not at you."

She made the sound women make when they know their men are lying.

He kissed her hair. "Tell you what, if you want to learn to cook, I'll teach you." He leaned back so he could see her face. She was still mad. "You have talents a lot of other women don't have. I married you for your fierceness, your toughness, and that bear-trap mind of yours. Your lack of skill in the kitchen doesn't make me love you any less."

"I don't like doing things I can't do well."

"I understand, so let me help you, okay?"

Lips tight, she nodded.

He eased her back against his chest. "I love you so much."

"Thanks for putting up with me."

"It's my pleasure."

So for the next month, in between his dealing with the horses and her going back and forth between her clients in Flagstaff and in Oracle, Kent taught his wife the basics of cooking: how to fry eggs and make omelets, how to fry bacon so it remained recognizable. Her first attempts at biscuits were hard enough for the biblical David to have used in his slingshot against Goliath, but Kent slathered them with butter.

Seated at the table, she looked his way. "They aren't very good, are they?"

Determined not to hurt her feelings, he bit into one, prayed he didn't break a tooth, and mumbled, "They're not that bad."

"You truly do love me, don't you?"

He nodded and hoped eating just the one was enough to prove it.

"I'll try again."

"Keep riding the bronc. You'll get better."

CHAPTER NINETEEN

Kent glanced up at the clock. By all rights, Portia should've been home an hour ago. He didn't want to start worrying just in case she'd stopped by to visit Rhine before coming home. Thirty minutes later and still no Portia, so he saddled up Blue and rode over to the hotel.

Rhine and Eddy were eating dinner.

"Evening, Kent," Eddy said. "What brings you by?"

"Was hoping Portia was here."

Rhine shook his head. "No,"

Kent swallowed his worry. "She was taking the last train from Flagstaff. I wonder if it got held up for some reason?"

"That line is pretty dependable."

Eddy asked, "Do you think she and Arizona ran into trouble?"

"I don't know but something's not right. I can feel it. I'm going to ride into Tucson and see if the train came in or not. Maybe I'll run into her on the way."

Rhine asked, "Do you want me to go with you?"

"No—"

The bell rang and Kent sighed with relief. "Maybe that's her now."

But it was Sheriff O'Hara. "Oh good, Kent, you're here. This was delivered to my office earlier this evening."

Kent was confused.

"You need to read it."

And what he read filled him with equal parts anguish and rage.

Rhine asked, "What's it say?"

"Someone has Portia. They want ten thousand dollars in the next thirty-six hours or they'll kill her."

"Where's the money supposed to be taken?" Rhine asked.

"Wired to the account of a John Brown in Boston." Kent looked up at the sheriff. "You said it was delivered? By who?"

"I don't know. I have a mailbox out in front of my office for mail and wires from the telegraph office, and it was in there. Checked it last around four this afternoon and there was nothing inside. Left the office to take care of some things, had dinner with my wife, and when I returned I checked again and that was in there. It was addressed to you, which I thought odd, so I opened it."

Kent was glad he had. "Do you know if the train from Flagstaff got in on time?"

"Haven't heard that it didn't. Why?"

"She was due back on it this evening."

"The conductor lives in town. How about you

ride back with me and see if he remembers her or saw anything."

"Good idea. I also want to check with the livery to see if she picked up her horse."

"I'll go with you," Rhine said. "Eddy will you be okay here?"

"Yes. Go on. Find her please."

Kent's fear hadn't lessened, but his rising fury was keeping him from being consumed by it. How dare someone do this to her? But he would find her even if he had to ride into hell to do so, and when he got her back, someone was going to die.

Portia felt pretty good about herself when she stepped off the train. She'd gone up to Flagstaff to meet a new client and the prospect looked good. Because there had been a cow on the tracks, the train from Flagstaff to Tucson had been late arriving and the sun was almost down. If she hurried to the livery, she and Arizona could make it home before full dark. There were very few people on the walks as she made her way. The livery was accessed off an alley and, as she entered, Edward Salt stepped out of the shadows. She would've swept by him had he not had a gun pointed at her, so she swallowed her fear and faced him bravely. "What do you want?"

"Not so high and mighty now, are you?"

"A gun will give any coward courage."

The words were barely out of her mouth before pain exploded in the back of her head and everything went black.

When she came to she was lying in the dark. Groggy and disoriented, her head aching, she closed her eyes again until everything stopped spinning and forced herself to sit up. She was seated on a dirt floor. It took another few minutes for the cobwebs to clear and for her to remember how she'd gotten there. *Edward Salt.* The scene replayed in her mind. He'd had an accomplice who'd hit her over the head with something that must have knocked her out. Touching the tender spot caused her to wince. How long had she been here? And where was here? Looking around she saw only darkness. What was Salt up to? She didn't know, but she did know that when she didn't come home, Kent and her family were going to move heaven and earth to find her. That gave her hope and helped her manage her fear. In the meantime, she needed her raging headache to subside so she could think more clearly and find a way to free herself on her own, if she could. She thought she might be in a cellar. It was too dark to be sure, but her main focus was finding a way out and getting home to Kent because she knew he was probably sick with worry.

She heard a creaking sound above her head and tensed. A door opened, bringing with it the light of a lantern and a shadowy figure. She could now see her surroundings. There were earthen shelves in the walls, verifying that she was indeed in a cellar of some kind. The figure backed down the wooden staircase and she once again faced Edward Salt. But a second figure joined him, and she was surprised to see Mr. Blanchard's son-in-law, Charlie Landry. She wondered if he was the one who'd struck her in the alley.

Salt sneered, "How far the haughty have fallen. I told you you'd pay for making me a laughing-stock at the rodeo."

Landry added, "Now your husband and that cheating uncle of yours will pay."

She looked between the two of them. "What do you mean?"

Charlie said angrily, "You and Randolph are on land that should be mine. If Fontaine hadn't cheated me out of it, none of this would be necessary."

"So you're holding me for ransom?" she asked.

"Yes. Ten thousand dollars. I'd hoped having Parnell burn the place down would make Fontaine change his mind about buying the place, but it didn't."

"Why did Parnell kill Buck and Farley?"

"We didn't want to leave any witnesses. We thought they'd be gone."

"So you were with Parnell that day?"

His eyes widened when he realized he'd implicated himself, and he didn't reply. She also wanted to know how he and Salt came to be in this plot together, and if Salt's parents were involved, but she didn't ask. Instead she said, "You do realize that no matter how this pans out, my husband's going to kill you both." She doubted Kent would go that far, but they didn't know that, and the fear that flashed momentarily in their eyes proved it. She was pleased. "So what are you getting out of this, Salt?"

Forecasting his death had apparently spooked him. Looking a bit less confident than he had when the visit began, he said, "Let's go, Landry."

He climbed the stairs, Landry followed, and they left her alone in the dark.

In Tucson the conductor verified that the train had been about an hour late. There'd been a couple of steers standing on the tracks. He also remembered seeing Portia. "She's been riding with me pretty regularly the past few months."

"Did you see which way she went when she got off?" the sheriff asked.

He hadn't. "What this about? She in some kind of trouble?"

Kent said, "My wife is missing."

The old man's eyes widened. "If you need volunteers for a search party, let me know. She's a nice little lady. Be glad to help."

They thanked him and rode to the livery. The owner, Cassius Digsby, lived up above the establishment. While the sheriff knocked on his door, Kent and Rhine walked to the stable. Arizona was there. Kent hugged her neck, needing the connection to his wife, and left her in her stall for the time being. He'd return for her once all the leads were exhausted. *Where is my Duchess?* He tried not to think about Portia being injured or tied up. He knew wherever she was, she was no doubt furious. He also knew she was tough and resourceful, two things in her favor. But he needed to find her before he lost his mind.

Sheriff O'Hara came down with the livery owner, Digsby. He'd known Rhine since they moved to the territory. "I'm sorry to hear about Portia being missing. I was just about to send somebody out to the hotel. It's not like her to leave Arizona. I thought something might be wrong."

"There is," Rhine said. "Sometime between her getting off the train and walking here, she was taken."

Digsby said, "I didn't see or hear anything. It could've happened in the alley though. It can be pretty shadowy there once the sun goes down. Easy place for someone to hide. Talk to Raoul. Maybe he saw something."

Kent didn't know the man.

The sheriff said, "He has a small eating place that opens into the alley. We passed it coming in."

They went immediately to the business and to Kent's relief it was still open. Inside there was no one seated at the three small tables.

A tall Mexican man walked out from the back. "I'm supposed to be closing but the stove's still hot, Sheriff."

The sheriff nodded, introduced Kent and Rhine, and explained why they'd come. "Sorry to hear about your wife, Mr. Randolph, but she didn't come in here. I would've remembered because that was right around the time I was arguing with Edward Salt and Charlie Landry."

Kent froze. "Over what?"

"Them trying to weasel out of paying the bill. Salt's done that to me twice now. Told him to never come back."

Kent and Rhine shared a look, and O'Hara asked, "Do you think they may be the ones who have her?"

Kent nodded and explained why. The sheriff said, "Let's go visit Landry first."

The sheriff knocked. Kent and Rhine stood in the shadows flanking the door. Landry answered the bell. "Sheriff O'Hara. What can I do for you?"

"Want to talk to you about something, Charlie. Shouldn't take but a few minutes. Can I come in?"

He hesitated for a moment, but pushed open the screen door to let him in. Only then did

Kent and Rhine step into view. Charlie cried out, turned, and ran. Kent raised the lever action shotgun and blew out a wall. Charlie screamed. Kent fired again, took out the ceiling, and plaster and wood rained down. Charlie dropped to the floor, hands over his head, screaming, "Don't kill me!"

Kent walked over determinedly, dragged Landry up by his hair, and stuck the Winchester between his eyes. "One chance. Where's my wife?"

Charlie jumped like a landed fish. "She's in the cellar. Outside! I—I . . . This was all Salt's idea. Please!"

Kent slammed his face into the floor, breaking his nose. Without a word to Rhine or the staring O'Hara, he walked past them and outside.

In the cellar, both Portia and Salt looked up at what sounded like muffled thunder. Placing the lantern on the cellar floor, Salt hurried to the stairs and was halfway to the door when it opened and the working end of a long gun showed itself. "Back up," she heard her husband growl.

Salt froze.

"You okay down there, Duchess?"

"I am," she called happily, and tears of joy sprang to her eyes. The joy was quickly replaced by anger at Salt for putting her and her family through this ordeal, so she marched over to where he stood still frozen on the stairs, and without warning, grabbed the hems of his trousers and yanked. His feet flew off the stairs, his knees hit the wood followed by his chin, and he issued a high-pitched cry of surprise as he tumbled and bumped down the stairs. He was out cold when he landed in the dirt at her feet. Pleased, she stepped over him and began to climb. Now, she could go home.

A few days later, the sheriff stopped by to let them know that Landry and Salt were jailed, charged with abduction and extortion. According to them the abduction hadn't been planned. Salt saw Portia coming and only intended to scare her with the gun. Landry was the one who bashed her over the head with his revolver and decided to hold her for ransom as a way to get back at the family for his wife's sale of the land. Interestingly enough, there was a bevy of Wanted notices for the Salts from St. Louis to Boston for forgery, false impersonation, and other con artist activity. The parents weren't in on the Salt and Landry scheme though. After being unable to fleece Rhine, they'd moved on, but the law was hot on their trail.

That evening, after the sheriff departed, Portia sat on her porch and watched the sun go down. Last year at this time she'd been a hard-working, no-nonsense woman with her mind made up on how she would live out the rest of her life. Now she was married to an incredible man, had her own home and her own successful business, and in the spring, she'd be having her own baby. Eddy said she was the walking embodiment of that old saw: We plan—God laughs. She would probably miss her mother for the rest of her life, but Corinne's actions would undoubtedly make her a better mother, if only in the sense of knowing what not to do. She knew Kent would be a wonderful father, and if the baby was a boy they'd agreed to name him Kenton Oliver Randolph the Second. If it was a girl she'd be named Eddy Regan after the two most important women in her life. Portia missed Regan terribly. Her letters were few and far between, but she hoped her sister was happy. Watching Kent walking up the path to the house, she was so grateful for him and his love. Her naughty cowboy husband was one of a kind and she was glad he was hers.

EPILOGUE

After fifteen hours of labor and screaming that she'd never let Kent Randolph near her again, Portia gave birth to a healthy, beautiful, eight-and-a-half-pound baby boy. As planned, he was named for his father and grandfather: Kenton Oliver Randolph. Sylvia, who'd been a nurse during the war and was a midwife, aided the delivery. After making sure Portia was well and asleep, she carried the baby out to the parlor to meet his father. "Here's your son, Kent."

Taking the precious bundle from his step-mother, Kent's heart swelled at the sight of the miracle he and Portia had made, then stared up at Sylvia in surprise. "His eyes are open. He's looking straight at me."

"I know. As the old people used to say: this one's been here before." She went back into the bedroom and Kent sat down in the rocker and held his son. "How are you, little fella?" he asked softly. Kent couldn't get over how perfect he was. "You know, you had your mama cursing my name in there, but it's okay. I still love her, and I love you, too. Promised your grandfather, who you're named after, that I'd tell you that, and I plan to keep my promise."

He thought about Oliver and how proud he'd

be to have a grandson. The baby was looking up into his face as if understanding every word, and it tickled him so much he laughed softly, "I think you're going to give me and your mama fits."

Kent sat and rocked his son for a long time. He told him about all the horses they were going to ride and the hunting they'd do. Promised to teach him how to cook and how much he was going to love his great-aunt Eddy and great-uncle Rhine. Kent wanted to sit with the baby forever, but he knew his son needed his mama so, gently cradling the baby against his chest, he went into the bedroom to set him in his cradle and to tell the sleeping Portia how much he loved her. Kenton Randolph the First, former bartender, cat house king, and Mexican prisoner, was now a husband and a father, and the last two descriptions made him the happiest man on earth.

Dear Readers,

This concludes the second book in the Rhine Trilogy and I do hope you enjoyed it. With all the issues and heartache Portia carried inside, I knew it would be difficult for her to give her heart to someone, but Kent Randolph proved to be the man for the job, even if I didn't know he would be her hero when the story began. Hope you enjoyed seeing Rhine and Eddy from *Forbidden* and, yes, they are still very much in love.

The Fontaine Hotel is loosely based on the Mountain View Hotel founded in Oracle, Arizona, in 1895 by Annie Box Neal and her husband William "Curly" Neal, who were both of African-American and Native-American descent. The Mountain View was a combination hotel and spa and catered not only to European royalty but to wealthy visitors from places like Russia, Australia, and China, too. Look them up.

The great Apache chief Geronimo surrendered on September 4, 1886, and was promptly declared a prisoner of war. He and his people eventually wound up in Florida along with the Apache scouts the army employed to hunt him down. He died at Fort Sill, Oklahoma, in 1909.

The Apache warrior Lozen, also captured in 1886, was sent to the barracks at Mount Vernon,

Alabama, where she died of tuberculosis in 1887. Although her name has faded from America's memory, her bravery and fearlessness remains legendary with her people.

I only touched briefly on African-American women and the fight for suffrage but hope to get back to it in depth sometime in the future. Until then, if you'd like to do some research on your own, here are two excellent sources:

African American Women and the Vote: 1837–1965 by Cynthia Neverdon-Morton, et al.

African American Women in the Struggle for the Vote: 1850–1920 by Rosalyn Terborg-Penn

The final book in the trilogy will belong to Portia's sister, Regan. Will the man she's agreed to marry sight unseen actually be who he claims to be? We'll find out.

Thanks again for the support and love. Thanks also for spreading the word about my books to everyone you know. It's much appreciated.

Until next time, happy reading.

B.

Books are produced
in the United States
using U.S.-based
materials

Books are printed
using a revolutionary
new process called
THINKtech™ that
lowers energy usage
by 70% and increases
overall quality

Books are durable
and flexible because
of smythe-sewing

Paper is sourced
using environmentally
responsible foresting
methods and the
paper is acid-free

Center Point Large Print
600 Brooks Road / PO Box 1
Thorndike, ME 04986-0001 USA

(207) 568-3717

US & Canada:
1 800 929-9108
www.centerpointlargeprint.com

LARGE PRINT
Jenkins, Beverly, 1951-
Breathless

JUL   2017